Books by Liz Crowe

Brewing Passion

Tapped
Lightstruck
Conditioned

Lightstruck

ISBN # 978-1-78686-163-4

©Copyright Liz Crowe 2017

Cover Art by Posh Gosh ©Copyright 2017

Interior text design by Claire Siemaszkiewicz

Totally Bound Publishing

Published in 2017 by Totally Bound Publishing, Think Tank, Ruston Way, Lincoln, LN6 7FL, United Kingdom.

Totally Bound Publishing is a subsidiary of Totally Entwined Group Limited.

Brewing Passion

LIGHTSTRUCK

LIZ CROWE

Dedication

To my intrepid editor, Sue.
And many thanks to my German slang helper, Jasper (a.k.a. my friend's German exchange student who was, I'm sure, thoroughly embarrassed by my word requests!). *Lightstruck* is a brewing term that means an 'off flavor' that occurs when finished beer is exposed to either sunlight or artificial light. Brown bottles are used to protect the beer from interactions with light sources, as green and clear bottles will allow the chemical change to occur resulting in the off flavor. It is interesting to note that some beer brands have accepted this flavor as part of their profile and it is seen as a positive attribute. — Beer Advocate Magazine

Prologue

On her wedding day, Evelyn spent the requisite number of hours primping and sweating the details. One detail in particular.

"Are you sure… I mean, this is kind of…shit."

"Relax. It's all good."

She glanced at Melody. Evelyn had never had a ton of women friends. In fact, she'd always claimed she preferred men to women when it came to socializing. Easier, less fraught, minimal drama.

Once again, Evelyn congratulated herself for hiring Melody to be in charge of the formerly floundering Fitz Pub. The woman oozed confidence and the sort of inner peace Evelyn thought the stuff of cheesy Internet memes. She was unafraid of her own inner emotional life and that balanced Evelyn in a way she never realized she needed.

And now, she really needed all of that. And some more. Considering she was about to walk down the aisle with a man she'd spent so much energy rejecting as a legitimate possibility for herself, it felt more than a little surreal. Not to mention the rather alarming surprise she had planned for him.

She smiled at the memory of him—of her Austin—and how joyously they'd reunited.

He was already house hunting for a bigger place, where Ross could have his own space, even though Ross had protested that it wouldn't look right. She'd half-agreed with him, until a few mornings ago, when Ross had come up from behind her as she studied her changing body in a full-length mirror, turning side to side, front to back. With a smile, he'd put both of his hands under the slight curve of her belly before sliding them up, inevitably, to her boobs, which were also changing, growing heavier, her nipples darkening. She'd sensed his erection pressing against her ass and had been about to turn and accommodate him when she'd sensed something wet hit her shoulder.

Knowing that any sort of emotional acknowledgement was harder than pulling his own teeth, she'd smiled and let Ross cradle the baby — their baby — growing inside her in his hands, as tears had rolled down his cheeks in silence. She hadn't said anything. There'd been no need.

As she regarded herself now in the mirror, her smile faded and she put a hand on the shelf of her stomach, wondering just how much this little wrinkle would alter their dynamic. Austin claimed not to care at all that Ross had fathered the child. If anything, he thought it the most ideal beginning to their lives as a family.

But still…the two men — her two men — were straight-up alpha males and many times she wondered how it could possibly work. How could she love them both? And if she did, what in the world was she doing marrying one of them?

For the thousandth time, Evelyn thanked God for his mercy in returning Austin to her, and for letting her keep Ross in the process. Such an excess of riches might've scared some women but Evelyn was determined not to let superstitious nonsense color her future.

"Sweet *Jesu*, woman. Relax." Melody sipped from her glass of dark porter. The smell tempted, but Evelyn waved it away. She'd moved past the mild nausea stage pretty quickly and had tipped over into something new and different and very, very sexy. It was as if she were ripe, full of promise and hornier than a sailor on shore leave. "You're gonna mess up your makeup, *chica*. Cut the waterworks already."

But Melody's own gaze was watery as she patted Evelyn's cheekbones with a tissue.

"Honestly I don't even understand why you have any right to feel upset about a damn thing. Marrying one. Getting two? Fuck me six ways to Sunday… Oh, right, you already do that, you silly cow."

"Shut up, *puta*. You're not helping." Evelyn grinned at her friend.

Melody rolled her eyes and muttered a long string of Spanish words she couldn't make out.

"Oh, hell." She stared at herself in the big mirror in the bride's room of the church. "He's gonna kill me."

"Very possibly, yes," Melody said.

Evelyn turned away from the mirror. The tone of Melody's voice was odd. Strained in a way she'd never heard.

Melody had not required an abortion after all. She'd had a messy, scary miscarriage that had landed her in the hospital for a week. A week that Trent had spent lurking around, trying to get her to see him only to be rejected over and over — loudly, usually accompanied by thrown objects. Evelyn had stayed with her around the clock, knowing Melody would have done the same for her. She'd tried hard to convince her friend to at least talk to Trent. The poor man had been out of his ever-loving mind with panicked worry over her. But Melody wouldn't even allow her to speak his name after a while.

A knock on the door interrupted her train of thought.

"Hey, ladies, can I…?" A newly familiar face appeared in the doorway. Evelyn sucked in a breath. Melody took several steps back. "Sorry," Brock said, retreating as if sensing the stress his appearance had caused.

"No, no, I'm sorry," Evelyn said, motioning for him to step inside. "Come on in."

Brock Fitzgerald entered the room, filling it with the force of his personality and extreme good looks. He had his twin's bone structure, but his take on the Fitzgerald genes manifested into a more model-like arrangement of his features, slightly fairer of skin and hair, more chiseled of facial features, with eyes the oddest shade of hazel she'd ever seen. Since the moment she'd seen his email, she'd spent some time getting to know him—or at least as much as he would allow.

She'd agreed to hire him after he'd reappeared, reaching out to her, asking for help, but she'd wanted to surprise Austin. When she'd agreed to marry him, and had set a date, she'd also decided on her own that Brock would escort her down the aisle.

Ross had been more than a little dubious but went along with it, once he met Austin's long-missing twin and had found him worthy—if on probation for causing Austin so much unnecessary grief.

"Dear God, you are exquisite," Brock said, putting his hands on her shoulders and smiling at her into the mirror. "My brother is one lucky son of a bitch." He took her hands and gave them a squeeze.

Evelyn sucked in a breath and tried to convince herself that this—any of this—was a good idea.

Tried, and failed.

"Knock knock."

Evelyn jerked her hands out of Brock's grip.

"Hey, hon, I need to talk to you about something," Austin said through the door.

"Don't let him in here," she whispered to Melody. "I mean it."

Brock stood, tucking his hands in his tuxedo pockets, squaring his shoulders and facing the door. "Let him in, Evie," he said.

She glared at him, as panic ran up and down her spine. Melody stood, arms crossed over her chest, her eyes on the half open door.

"Evie?" Austin said as he stuck his head into the room. "Who the hell calls you tha—oh."

"Austin," Brock said with a wide smile. "I wanted to surprise you."

Evelyn clutched the skirt of her wedding dress, anxiety at foisting this on him twanging all her nerve endings.

Austin stepped into the bride's room, his face slack, his eyes dark with something resembling anger. He had an envelope gripped in one hand with handwriting on it. "Brock…you're…here? Now?"

"Austin, I…" Evelyn said, moving toward him.

He held up a hand, keeping his gaze on his long-lost brother. When he spoke, his voice was flat, devoid of emotion, and terrifying. "I'm sorry, but it was my understanding that you were, I don't know, dead or something like it. Which would explain your non-communication with me, your fucking twin brother, for the last, what, six years?" Austin's face flamed an alarming shade of red.

When Evelyn tried to move closer to him, Melody grabbed her arm.

Brock seemed to deflate at his brother's words. Then he squared his shoulders and lifted his chin in the face of Austin's fury. "Yeah, well…I'm not dead. I was gone for a while, but I guess, I needed space."

"Space," Austin repeated, his jaw clenched. "You needed space. You needed…fucking…" He blew out a breath. "Does our mother know you've decided to pull a Lazarus? What about Caroline? You sneaking back into that poor girl's life again?"

"Yeah, Mom knows." The two men glared at each other across the room. "And what I do or don't do with Caroline is none of your fucking b—"

"Excuse me? This is *my* day, gentlemen," Evelyn interrupted, stamping her foot, her heart pounding so hard it deafened her. "Cut the crap. You"—she pointed at Austin—"get out of here and back into the chapel. Unless you've changed your mind, of course." She rested a shaking hand on her stomach. The baby inside her—a girl, she already knew but had told neither Ross or Austin—gave a quick flutter, a new trick this week, as if sensing her mother's stress and reminding her to be aware of her blood pressure.

Austin seemed to snap out of a trance and turned to

face her, blinking fast. It broke her heart, how undone he looked. She steeled herself and motioned over his shoulder, indicating the direction he should go. He sucked in a long breath and held out the envelope with a shaking hand.

"He's gone," he said.

Evelyn stumbled backward. Melody caught her by the elbow and shot a barrage of Spanish curse words in Austin's direction before helping her down into a chair. She pulled out the note, read the sparse lines and closed her eyes.

"What is it?" Melody demanded, trying to pry the paper out of Evelyn's cold fingers.

Austin crouched by Evelyn's chair and put his hand on her leg. "Ross left."

"Left?" Melody spat out. "*Jesu,* you three are worse than the worst *Telenovela.*" She kept muttering as she handed Evelyn a cool glass of water.

"Are you going to be okay?" Austin's soft query made tears fill her eyes again. She nodded, took Melody's proffered hanky, swiped her tears away and got to her feet. This was no big surprise. And something she'd simply have to deal with later. Austin blew her a kiss then slipped out of the door.

"You," she said, focusing her glare on Brock who stood nearby, looking sheepish. "You have a lot to answer for so be ready. I love that man," she said, pointing to the empty space once occupied by Austin. "All I want is for him to be happy." She took a long breath. "So help me, Brock Fitzgerald, you are gonna help me achieve that today. Got it?"

He nodded and cocked his elbow at her as the sounds of flower girl music swirled around them, indicating that the bride's music was next. She hesitated, her long-ingrained resistance to this very moment reasserting itself with a vengeance.

"Come on, Evie." He wagged his eyebrows at her.

She frowned, felt herself hyperventilating, sensed Melody at her side, providing support with her presence.

"Let's do this thing, future sister-in-law." Brock grabbed her arm and dragged her forward. He winked then pressed his lips to her damp cheek.

Interesting times ahead. She tucked her hand into the crook of Brock's elbow.

"Relax," he insisted, as he led her into the hallway and the harp music switched to something that made her pulse race faster.

"I can't," she said.

"Yes, you can. And you will. Just focus on Austin, Evie. That's all you need to do. Tell you what. I'll do it too, okay? I think we both need to focus on making his day today."

She took a long breath and did exactly that. "Promise me one thing," she said before taking her first step down the aisle toward her future husband. "Don't ever leave again."

He sighed.

"I mean it, Brock. He needs you just as much as he needs me." She gripped his arm. Their eyes met.

"Okay," he said. "I promise."

"Okay," she said. "Then take me to him, why don't you?"

Chapter One

Ross woke with a start, sitting straight up in bed so fast if felt as if his brain had whammed against the front of his skull before settling back into place again. Sunlight streamed through the windows, piercing him in the eyeballs, not helping the dizzy, unfocused, mushy sensation.

"Ow," he muttered as he swung his feet around to the side of the bed. When his mind registered that he couldn't do that, that something warm was blocking his way, the something made a noise, rolled and exposed a perky pink nipple to his befuddled gaze. At that same moment, someone else touched his shoulder, making him flinch as he stared at the nipple, trying to get his bearings.

Ross licked his lips as the memories rushed back in on him, bombarding his battered, hung-over system with the force of an invading army. The hand on his shoulder became two and together, they slid down his bare torso. As he watched, the lovely nipple disappeared, then materialized as one of a matched set, on a gorgeous set of breasts, suddenly at his eye level.

"Wait," he said. But waiting wasn't on the agenda. The hands behind him tugged him onto his back and into the soft nest of stark white sheets and soft cotton blankets. Ross let his mind fuzz back over and his body take the lead as he reached out and his hands landed on hair. Hair on the head of the woman who had his dick down her throat. He arched his back and let her do her thing while some other chick kissed him, then sat on his face.

Ross wondered for about a half second who these women were, where he'd found them, what he'd said to convince them to engage in his favorite position for a threesome. But the half-second passed, and he no longer cared what the answer to any of those hypotheticals was.

The woman on his face came, then slid off him and onto the bed, purring with satisfaction. Ross swiped the back of his hand across his wet lips and focused on the stellar blow job he was receiving. As he groaned into the sunstruck room and pumped his hips at his climax, something about his life felt one hundred percent wrong. Something important was missing.

And he knew damn well what it was.

"All right, you ladies had your fun. Time to vamoose. I gotta get to work." Ross sat up and sniffed the air, frowning at the aura of pot and spilled booze. "Jesus, this place is a fucking pigsty," he said as he lurched up and stumbled into the bathroom, forcing all thoughts of what was missing from his life out of his head. He couldn't afford to think about it—about her—ever again.

He nearly scalded his skin off in a thirty-minute shower, blessing the gods of tankless hot water systems and his own luck for finding this palatial mansion to rent while its owner was on sabbatical from the University. Once he emerged, he saw that the bed had been made, the crap picked up off the floor and the women, thankfully, were absent. Rubbing his hair with the thick white towel—these owners were obsessed with the whole *tabula rasa* thing—he stood naked at the bank of windows overlooking the mountain view.

Stunning, really. Wish Evelyn could see it.

No, stop. Not going there.

"Hey, sweet buns, you want some coffee?"

He whirled around, heart in his throat. One of the women stood at the large kitchen island dressed in one of his brewery T-shirts, flapping her eyelashes at him.

"Thought you'd left," he half-said, half-grumbled to himself as he headed back to the bedroom for clothes. As he zipped and buttoned his jeans, he forced the anger down and out of his head. It would do no good to come across as an asshole. Who knew when he'd like to have this woman over for another round?

Frowning at himself in the mirror, he made a mental note to get to the barber. Both his hair and his beard needed some professional help. He'd let them both grow out since bolting from Michigan and they were wild-looking, unkempt. Very much unlike him.

Even as he tied his hair back with a bit of leather string, he could hear her voice. "I like your hair long and your beard short," Evelyn would say. Ross blinked at the memory, attempting to banish her yet again from his brain.

His skin tingled, though, and all he could hear was her voice, all he could feel was her soft curves under his hands.

"Ross," she'd whisper in his ear. "Make me come..."

"Shit!" he yelped when someone pressed up against him from behind. "Cut it out." He peeled the woman off him and stomped into the large living room, dining room, kitchen combo room. The space was huge — almost a thousand square feet of open living — fronted by a whole wall of the glass. Smells of coffee hit his nose, calming in that Pavlovian way it always had. He filled one of the professor's stainless steel travel mugs and grabbed his keys off the magnetic rack on the wall next to the fridge.

He could sense his temper lurking, somewhere down deep in his gut. While he didn't want to be a dick to the woman still prowling around in his space, he had no interest in being anywhere near her either. She needed to get the fuck out. But in lieu of telling her that, he left instead, absenting himself from the area she was making proprietary little circles around, like women tended to do on his mornings after.

He shook his head as he climbed behind the wheel of the late-model truck — another perk of renting this house. Something about a night in the playground of his bed always seemed to bring out the clinginess in women. Especially lately. Maybe it was the rarified air up here. Maybe it was his own air. Did he come off as desperate somehow, desperate for love versus seeking to get laid? He needed to work on that, ASAP.

As the truck took the hairpin turns and inclines on his way into town and toward the brewery, Ross had to open all the windows wide to let the cold air clear his head, lest he give in, grab his phone and call her. Hell, to call Austin for that matter.

He'd pulled a classic dick move, and he knew it. And refusing to talk to either of them beyond the basics of, 'Yes, I'm alive. I'm fine. I needed to get out of the way of your happily ever after or I was gonna go nuts' wasn't helping his cause.

"I don't care," he insisted to himself, sipping and driving the truck with one hand, not caring one bit whether or not he made it or if the fucking thing slid off the ever-loving mountain, which would, he figured, put him out of his misery once and for all.

Chapter Two

"Yo, Ross," the not so melodious sound of his boss's voice blared across the brewery floor. Ross winced and looked up from the computer where he was logging the day's brews. "I need you to come here for a minute. There's someone I want you to meet."

He sighed, wiped his hands on a cloth then tossed it toward his assistant. The guy — a kid really, eager to please and super creative in a way that made Ross' head hurt — caught it and took over the computer entries without being asked. "I'll be back," he muttered. The kid raised a hand then re-focused on the work Ross would much rather be doing.

He felt beaten down, dog-tired in a way he hadn't since he'd been learning the craft of beer brewing in his native Munich. That process used to be one on par with a sort of military training — beat them down and build them back up the way you want them. And he'd been so eager to call himself a 'master brewer' as young kid, he'd taken everything dished out to him and turned all his professors into Ross Hoffman fans.

But those nights were some of his longest — sore in body and mind, he'd drop into sleep the second his head touched the pillow, only to wake a couple of hours later, obsessing over some element of brewing chemistry or trying to recall if he'd set the fermentation temps correctly before leaving the brewery classroom. He'd end up falling back asleep eventually but had only averaged four hours a night for those three and a half years of near torture.

Even after he'd buddied up with Austin and they'd

spent their limited extra time blowing off steam by double-teaming as many chicks as they'd been able to get their eager hands on, he'd still run on minimal sleep, maximum caffeine every day.

As he made his way across the cavernous brewery floor now, he felt shoved back into that old life, into the younger Ross' body and mind, wishing for nothing more than a sandwich and a nap—a ten-hour nap. He waved at the assistants who called out for him and attempted to slap a look of interest, or at least coherence, on his face before he shouldered his way into the brewery owner's office. It was situated between the brewery and the main pub, and opened into both rooms. His new boss was the dictionary definition of micromanager but Ross hadn't been able to pick and choose when he'd bolted from Michigan, so he'd leapt at the guy's offer of a job, with housing, and guarantees of 'brewing autonomy'.

He'd kept two out of three of those promises, Ross mused as he prepared a neutral greeting before he realized the someone sitting in the office was...

"Evelyn," he croaked out, his body lurching into flight mode.

The woman kept her back to him, thank Christ for tiny favors. Ross groped behind him for the door handle even as his eyes took in the sway of honey-blonde hair, the voluptuous curve of her hips, the long, lean line of her legs beneath the power skirt. When she laughed at something his tool of a boss said, Ross froze.

That was definitely not Evelyn's laugh. He slumped against the door, head-pounding exhaustion filling the space behind the exiting adrenaline.

"There you are," Brad Jefferson said, motioning impatiently for Ross to approach. Squaring his shoulders, he marched himself across his boss's office, determined to meet, greet, impress, whatever, and get the hell home.

"Well, hell-o there," the woman said as she turned to face him.

If he weren't so smacked upside his head by the sight of her, he'd laugh at how hokey she sounded. Like some B-movie vamp. But he was smacked upside his head, so all he thought at that moment was *Holy brick shithouse. She is fine.*

Her smile emerged slowly as if being teased out of her. Her full lips were deep red, a somewhat shocking contrast to the ultra-white of her teeth. Ross could practically feel his eyeballs rolling inside their sockets as he took her in from blonde head to stiletto-heeled toe. He was acting like a pig, he knew that. But if anything, she encouraged it — hands on her full hips, sticking out one foot, assuming her mating stance.

By the time his gaze had made it back up to her light brown eyes, he realized he hadn't conjured anything resembling an answer to her. The silence that coiled between them felt odd — warm, somehow damp in a way that he liked but at the same time wanted to flee from.

"You'll have to forgive my celebrity brewer, doll."

Ross felt someone shove his shoulder. He blinked, rubbed his arm and dragged his gaze off the woman who was, it seemed, about to suck him straight into her soul — or at the very least between her thighs.

"Sometimes he goes Neanderthal on me," his boss continued.

"Oh, that's all right," she cooed, putting cool, soft fingertips on his exposed lower arm. The gesture was innocuous, friendly even. But he shivered and his whole body seemed to zing to attention, including below his belt. He focused on calculating original gravity for a few seconds, so he wouldn't embarrass himself by springing a teenager-worthy woody. "It's been a long day, I'm sure."

She had a syrupy Southern accent that made her words sound soft and non-threatening. But Ross felt most definitely threatened. And more turned on than he'd been since bolting out of Evelyn and Austin's life. He realized that was a low bar — he'd only been gone for a few months.

But still...he licked his lips and took a breath.

"Hello," he said, holding out his hand. "I'm Ross Hoffman." He glanced over at Brad, expecting an introduction. But the blonde siren already had her hand in his—it was soft and felt perfect but yet not, at the same time.

"I'm Holly," she said, smiling. "Holly Grant."

"Oh, well, hello there," he said, giving her hand a squeeze and letting go of her.

"Holly's the host of Boulder AM," Brad said, surprising Ross. He'd pretty much forgotten the other man was even in the room. "She's here to set up an interview. With you." He gave Ross another shove, which put him inappropriately close to Holly Grant. So close, the tips of her silk-blouse-covered D-cup breasts brushed his T-shirt.

"Sorry," he muttered, taking three steps back, sensing his face flush.

"Oh my Lord, Brad," Holly cooed, not taking her eyes off Ross. "He blushes and everything. Adorable."

Ross ran a hand across his jaw, which reminded him how scruffy he must look. He'd let himself go in so many ways. Including fucking any pussy on two legs. Damn him to hell and back. He must be putting out a serious man-whore vibe. Clearing his throat, he straightened and crossed his arms, trying to assume his mantle of the predator, not the prey.

She seemed to respond in kind, pulling away and withdrawing her advances.

Good. That's a relief.

He smiled at her, keeping it friendly. She tossed her hair back and put a hand to her long, tanned neck. Ross gulped, sensing the equilibrium slip in her direction again.

"So," Brad said, breaking into the tension. "Ross. Holly is planning to have her crew in the brewery tomorrow. She wants you here, giving the tour, talking brews and pubs and shit. You game?"

"Do I have a choice?"

"No," Holly said. Her voice was bourbon-y and tempting.

"Not really. But something tells me you don't shy away from the limelight, do you, Ross?" The slight hesitation between "you" and "Ross" was calculated. He knew it. He frowned at her. She smiled. And the sight of it made his stupid, over-worked dick spring to attention.

Well, her smile, and the sight of her cleavage in the 'V' of her blouse.

You are a craven pig, Hoffman, he reminded himself.

Yep. Guilty as charged, he agreed.

But this woman was practically spread-eagled on the desk. What the hell? How was he supposed to react to such an overt come-on?

Like a grown-ass man.

A man with responsibilities.

A future father.

He shivered involuntarily, hearing Evelyn's voice in his ear and wanting her here, right now, so badly he could taste it.

"All right, then. I'd best get home. So, I can be ready for my close-up tomorrow," he said, unable to resist the temptation to wink at the sexy woman regarding him as if he were a water mirage in the driest desert. "Ma'am. Boss." He made as if to tip an invisible hat, then headed for the office door.

"Um, Ross," the woman's melodious voice intoned.

He smiled, then turned, figuring his little 'ignore 'em until they beg for your attention' trick had worked. He felt oddly revved up, as if he'd gained a second wind from the woman's attention. She hadn't moved from her spot across from Brad. She blinked, slowly. Then, much to his surprise, she licked her lips.

What is she, some kind of a caricature? His skin prickled.

"I'd like to do a little pre-interview…chat," she finally said.

"Fine," he said. "I'll give you thirty minutes. Then I gotta go…home."

Ross hadn't felt this flummoxed and awkward with

a woman in years. He didn't like it. Although, she was intriguing, he'd give her that.

"Great," she said, turning to give Brad an air kiss before shouldering her bag and walking over to where Ross stood, frozen in place by the office door.

"Yeah, great," he said, yanking the door open and stomping out, leaving her to fend for herself.

By the time they made it to a table in the teeming pub, Ross was completely pissed off. He was one hundred percent not in the mood for this full-on seduction thing. He'd buy her a beer, answer her questions and leave. End of story.

He turned when he found the free table, his ingrained politeness forcing him to pull out her chair. She smiled and slid into it. Her movements were fluid, he noted as he sat across from her and lifted a finger to get the attention of one of the waiters. "What do you like?" he asked, squinting up at the huge beer board.

She stayed silent long enough he was forced to look at her. She had her chin in her hand, her full lips pursed as if pondering something—like devouring him. Her eyes were shining.

"It's not a trick question," he claimed. "Beer?" He waved his hand at the blackboard menu behind her.

She glanced over her shoulder, allowing that gaping 'V' in her blouse to deepen. Ross averted his eyes, unwilling to humor her even as sensed his body giving in, hardening in places that sent a different message about humoring her.

"I'll have the Big Boss," she said, tilting her head to one side and pinning him in place with that odd stare.

"The...double Belgian?" he asked, motioning for the waiter again.

"Yes. What do you take me for? A light lager kind of girl?" She pouted, then grinned in what seemed like the first genuine smile he'd seen on her face since meeting her.

"Yeah, actually. I did take you for that. My bad." He glanced up at the harried-looking waiter kid. "The lady will have a Big Boss. I'm having the dopple bock."

He propped his elbows on the table, realizing their knees were touching under the tiny table. "So, you like real beer. Points in your favor."

She frowned at him. "So," she said, pulling a small tablet from her bag and uncapping a fancy fountain pen. "You're German?"

"Um, yes." He leaned away from the table, trying to wrap his brain around her and how his body was reacting to her. And how much he wished his body would grow up and stop acting like a fucking teenager. "Born and raised in Munich. Went to the international high school." He grinned and ran a hand along the scruffy hair on his jaw. "My mother was American. Father was German. They met one Oktoberfest. They were rich but I hardly ever saw them. Was raised by a bunch of employees. When I turned eighteen I chose US citizenship."

"I see," she said.

Ross took a moment to observe her hands. They were small, with slim fingers ending in short, red-painted nails. He let his gaze travel up her arms which were bare, tanned, nicely toned. Her neck was long and tempting. But he knew what attracted him most was her hair — that hair so very like Evelyn's. Long, honey-blonde, thick. Hair that would feel like spun silk between his fingers.

He clenched his hands together under the table and forced himself to calculate the final gravity of the beer he'd brewed today to lessen the stress under his zipper.

Down, boy. This one's not for you. She will eat you alive.
And yet...

He glanced up at her again. Her eyes were fixed on his. She blinked slowly. Ross believed he could hear her long brown eye lashes touch. Those amazing full, red lips were moving again. He gulped.

"Well," she demanded.

He flinched. "Oh, sorry. What did you say?"

She sighed. Their beers arrived, along with a bowl of smoked nuts. He popped a few into his mouth to cover his embarrassment. Holly sniffed her beer then sipped, smiled and took a longer drink. Smacking her lips, she set the glass down.

"Well done," she said. "I'm a tough gal to please."

"Oh?" he asked, taking a long drink of his own, resisting the urge to pat himself on the back over the tricky style. Without trying to be too obvious, he shifted in his seat, attempting without success to alleviate the pressure behind his zipper.

Holly tossed a few of the peppery, smoky cashews into her mouth, drank then blotted her lips with a napkin. "Now, where were we?"

"Talking about how I please you, I think," he blurted out.

She raised one light brown eyebrow at him. He matched it.

"I don't make a point to screw around with my interview subjects," she said, tracing a fingertip around the rim of her glass then putting it to her lips.

"Could have fooled me, Holly," he said, putting emphasis on her name. His lizard brain had taken over and the rest of him was so emotionally and physically drained, it put up little fight. "But that's fine with me. My place, or yours?"

"Mine, I think," she said, draining her beer and tossing down a ten-dollar bill. Ross watched as she rose, her movements like silvery liquid. She stood, hands on her hips, staring at him a few seconds. "You coming?"

"Without a doubt," he said, slamming his own beer and getting up, no longer caring if she could see his boner. She could. And she made a point of letting him know she'd seen it before she smiled and put a cool hand to his hot face.

"I thought as much. Let's go, hot stuff." She gave his beard a tug, turned and sauntered through the crowd.

Chapter Three

Holly Grant looked even better naked, not that Ross ever doubted that she would. She had a skill set just shy of a pro, too, which was nice. But by the time they were done, gasping and sweating side by side in her gigantic bed in front of her own wall of windows facing the Flatirons, the distinct feeling edging out the exhaustion and brain-numbing pleasure of a long-repressed, monster orgasm, was one of despair.

He felt sick at his stomach at his own cravenness. The level of raunchy pleasure he got touching, licking, kissing and fucking her made him want to run for the bathroom and throw up. Which was not a happy feeling to have post-sex and not one he'd ever had before.

For her part, Holly stretched and sighed and rolled away from him before tottering across the room and into the bathroom where she shut the door and remained as long as it took for him to drift off to sleep. When he woke, the place was dark. He sensed a warm body next to him. And the sensation of loneliness, of missing the two people in the universe he cared most about, rolled through his brain like thunderclouds, muttering and dangerous.

You're the one who left, you numb nuts. You bolted and you barely acknowledge their communication attempts with you. You are the one with the problem, whatever the hell it is. Deal with it.

He did, by shoving all thoughts of Evelyn out of his head, wrapping his body around the sleeping curve of Holly's until the good old lizard brain took over and his dick was hard enough to break concrete.

"Hmmm," Holly murmured, arching back so her bare ass

pressed against his eager erection.

By way of response, Ross cupped her breast with one hand and put his lips to her shoulder, sucking in the essence of her, willing Evelyn away from him. He kissed his way up her long neck, pulling that thick fall of hair aside so he could nibble there. She shivered and gave a low moan of pleasure as her nipple hardened under his fingers.

When she tried to reach back and grab him he bit down on the soft skin at the juncture of her neck and shoulder, making her squeal. "I'm doing the touching," he whispered, licking the bite mark until she shivered again. The smell of her lust coiled around in his brain as he kept teasing her skin with his lips and teeth, tugging hard on her nipple until she was shoving her hips and ass so hard back against him he gasped.

"Fuck me, Ross," she hissed, rolling so she was up on her hands and knees, her back arched. The moonlight slanted in and hit her just so, making her look as if she had a white mark splitting her in two. He positioned himself behind her, leaned over and threaded the fingers of one hand in her thick hair.

"Tell me again," he demanded, his voice rough with lust and a strange, emptiness—a distinct sadness at this, at himself, at his piss-poor life choice.

She threw her head back and spread her thighs wider. Ross stared down at the gleaming white of her skin in the semi-darkness, mesmerized by his one hand, in her hair, and the other one, trailing down her back to her ass and to his dick.

"Now," she demanded, her voice filling his head. "Fuck me now, Ross."

He did as he was told, reaching around to flick his finger against her clit, groaning into her shoulder. Her flesh rose under his touch, and she cried out, filling his nose and brain and body with her smell and noise.

He dug his fingers into her hips and pounded hard, watching, and feeling somewhat detached from his dick that was sliding in and out of her, at the way her ass made a heart-shape.

"Oh, God, yes!" she shrieked, dropping to her elbows and giving him an amazing new angle.

He came hard and loud, and kept coming so long he thought he might pass out. But at least that meant he could sleep, and not think about Evelyn for a few hours.

* * * *

The next morning, she was up early, spinning her legs away to nowhere on the bike in the corner of the bedroom. He stumbled into the shower, his sense of emptiness and agony sharper than ever. Cursing, he shampooed and soaped, rinsed and toweled off, then yanked up the jeans he'd had on the day before, leaving his underwear defiantly on her hardwood floor.

Don't be mad at her, you loser. She wanted to fuck. You obliged her.

"I gotta get home," he said. But Holly kept pedaling, going even faster as he watched. Once he figured out she had wireless earbuds in her ears, he stomped around to stand in front of her, his arms crossed, his ears ringing and his heart pounding.

"I'm going," he mouthed.

She held up a hand. He waited, getting angrier by the second for reasons that made zero sense whatsoever. Finally, she stopped and sat up, her legs still going round and round, sweat streaming down her face, darkening the sports bra and highlighting the firm peaks of her nipples. Ross forced himself not to respond, although something about her had him programmed already and he knew it. His dick stirred, unencumbered by his jockey shorts.

"Yes, please go change," she said, smiling and taking a long drink from her water bottle. "I'll have the crew in place…" She glanced at her watch. "Two p.m. Be ready, stud." She winked and dropped her hands to the handlebars, her gaze now trained out on the mountain view, Ross, apparently, forgotten.

He fumed all the way home. As he slammed his way into the borrowed living space, he tried like hell to square his fury with the superb sex he'd had, twice, in the past few hours. What in God's name did he have to be pissed off about?

He drank some coffee and watched the sun rise, then picked up his phone and looked at the screen for the first time since meeting Holly Grant in Brad's office the day before. The texts were in all caps by the end. And they were all from Austin.

Ross' hands shook so hard he dropped the device. It hit the hard wood floor with an ominous crack. He fumbled for it, then managed to hit speed dial for Brad.

"Tell Holly I'm sorry but I won't be available today. I have to go...I have to fly home...to...I mean...fuck."

"What the hell, man? Brad blustered. "How are we going to manage—?"

"I don't care, Brad. Fuck it. I quit."

He hit the end call button, his ears ringing with anxiety and the early onset of remorse.

Quit another job? Nice work. Jesus.

Ah, who cares, anyway? Brad was a tool and a pain in the ass to brew for. He needed to get home. To Evelyn and to Austin where he belonged.

"Ross?" Austin's familiar voice sliced through his brain like a hot knife through cold butter. "Is that you? You have to come home, man. You have to. Shit man, she's... Oh God," Austin's voice broke.

"I'm on the first flight," he said, grabbing the duffel bag he'd unpacked a few months before when he'd moved in and shoving all his belongings into it. "I'm coming, Austin. Tell her to hold on for...for me."

"She's at the U of M Hospital, Ann Arbor, room two-oh-five. Hurry." With that, Austin ended the call leaving Ross standing in the sun-shot great room of his new life, packing up to go back to his old one.

Chapter Four

The four-hour flight into Detroit was a nightmare, and not just because of near-constant turbulence. Ross' guts roiled as he tried to relax, tried to distract himself, tried like hell to pretend that the texts he'd read from his friend weren't true. But by way of penance, or something like it, he scrolled through them repeatedly.

Come home, Ross. Something is wrong.
Evelyn's in the hospital. Her BP is sky high and she's bleeding.
Get your sorry ass here, you fucker. Evelyn needs you! I need you!
GOD DAMN IT, ROSS!

And finally…

JUST CALL ME. PLEASE.

The last one had come through at about three a.m., right about the time Ross had been rough-fucking Holly Grant. He groaned and pressed his aching forehead against the airplane window, the phone still clenched tightly in his hand. He must have slept because the next thing he knew, they were landing with a thump and roar on the wet tarmac at Detroit Metro Airport.

Going against his usual wait-it-out-and-be-the-last-one-off M.O., he yanked his bag from the overhead compartment and stood in the aisle, waiting for the moment that he could power up his phone.

"Sir, please sit down until we taxi all the way to—"

He gave the woman his sternest glare. "I have an emergency. I need to be the first one off."

She blinked in the face of his rudeness. "All right. Follow me please."

He did, and found himself standing in the area between the service carts and the cockpit while the plane trundled along the various runways on its way to the terminal. The jetway extended like an arm out from the building and attached itself to the side of the plane. Finally, after what felt like three contiguous eternities, the door opened and Ross leapt out and ran all the way up to the door before putting his phone to his ear.

"Where are you?" Austin snapped.

"Just landed. Didn't check anything. I'll be there as quick as I can rent a car."

"Make it fast."

"She's... The baby is...?"

"You haven't earned the right to ask me anything yet. Get your sorry ass here, Ross. And see for yourself."

Ross closed his eyes and leaned against the wall. "Austin, I'm—"

"Spare me. Just get here."

It felt as if the entire world had descended all at once upon Detroit, and on the Hertz office in particular. Ross stood in line, his heart whamming around for nearly forty minutes before he was finally handed the keys to a vehicle. As he maneuvered through the traffic in a seemingly vain attempt to get to the freeway, his phone dinged with multiple texts. This time, from Holly.

What the fuck, Ross? led to
You're an inconsiderate asshole.

To

Brad said you quit??!!!!

and

You can't just leave like that!

And finally

Are you all right? Call me.

He sighed and gunned the SUV's anemic engine to join the line of cars and trucks headed toward Ann Arbor. As he focused forward, trying to concoct reasonable excuses for not only the powder he'd taken on Austin and Evelyn's wedding day but for his long string of non-communication with them, the sum total of his fucked-up personal life hit him square in the face.

"Shit," he muttered, balling his right hand into a fist and pounding on the steering wheel. "Shit, god damn, fuck."

A string of red brake lights ahead gave him yet more reason to curse. He sat for a solid five minutes without moving before grabbing his phone and fumbling to re-dial Austin. But the damn thing was already buzzing with a call. "I'm stuck in traffic," he said, his chest tight with anxiety in anticipation of Austin's well-earned fury.

"All I want to know is," the honey-smooth voice of the woman from last night hit his ear. "What's so damned important that you'd get out of my bed, pack your bag, quit your job and leave town?"

"Holly," he said, exhaling as his ever-diligent lizard brain started dumping erotic memories into his brain. "It's… I'm… Shit."

"Well, yes, I'd agree with that assessment."

The traffic started moving forward. Ross shoved the lizard brain back into its hole and stepped on it so he could concentrate.

"Ross," she said, drawing his name out to more than its usual number of syllables. "Honey…"

"I gotta go, Holly. It's a family emergency."

"Well, if you must know, I made sure Brad understood you were having some kind of a crisis and didn't mean it when you said you quit."

Ross sighed. "Not your business, really."

"Maybe not. Maybe not. Listen, do you need anything?"

"I...don't know yet," he admitted, acknowledging the undercurrent of relief that she'd done what she'd done with his boss.

Lame. Triple lame. God but you are a mess.

"But, uh, thanks. For talking to Brad, I mean."

"No trouble, sugar. No trouble at all. I'm here, whenever you want to talk."

He opened his mouth to assure her that wouldn't be necessary, but she'd ended the call.

"Fuck," he spat out as he redialed Austin's number only to have it go straight to voicemail. "Christ," he muttered as he inched forward and tapped out a text. Within ten minutes, whatever was holding up the works on I-94 must have cleared and the line of cars and trucks began gaining speed.

Ross wove in and out of the traffic, waving his middle finger at various honks, terror gripping his entire body, making him rigid and achy by the time he screeched up to the hospital parking garage. The bank of elevators confounded him for a few seconds but he jumped into one and hit the second floor button, praying it would be this simple. He'd find her room, apologize to her and to Austin, make sure the kid—his kid—was still cooking away, or whatever it did in there. Then he could leave again.

That was his special talent—leaving.

He skidded around a corner, reading the room numbers as he fast-walked down the hall. The distinct rubber-plastic-medicinal-piss smell of the hallway made his stomach churn even harder. As the numbers counted down from two-forty toward the target two-oh-five, he slowed, then stopped dead in his tracks when he caught sight of Austin, talking with a woman in blue surgical scrubs.

Attempting to gain some knowledge of Evelyn's status by their body language, Ross watched for a few seconds, until Austin raised his eyes and met his gaze, as if he'd known Ross was there the whole time. The man looked positively strung out. His normally clean-shaven jaw was covered in a week's worth of dark growth. Shadows were gathered under his eyes. Ross hesitated another second, then marched over to him and faced the person he assumed was Evelyn's doctor. He stuck out a hand. "Hello. I'm Ross Hoffman. I am the baby's father. Can you fill me in, please?"

His voice sounded strong and sure. But he was quavering inside. He noticed that the door to room two-oh-five was slightly ajar. Then, he heard it. The thin, strange to him but somehow recognizable sound of a baby's cry coming from the room behind them.

Mouth hanging open like a dolt, he turned to Austin, who nodded and gave him a tight smile. "It's a girl," he said. His voice broke on the last word.

"Mr. Hoffman," the doctor said, pulling his attention back to her. "You are all very lucky. The baby was well-developed for only being thirty-five weeks old. She began breathing on her own after about an hour in the NICU. There's no sign of jaundice at all." The woman glanced down at her tablet. She cut her gaze to Austin, then back to Ross, seemingly confused. "Congratulations," she finally said. "To you both. I'll be back to check on her in a few hours. For now, just support your…ah…"

"Wife," Austin said, abruptly, his brow furrowed. "She's my wife."

"I see," the doctor responded, looking eager to escape this complex tableau. "Well, then, okay. I'll be back soon."

"Austin?" Evelyn's thin voice cut through Ross like a blade.

Austin stopped to glare at him, then ducked inside the room, making soothing sounds that Ross couldn't assemble into words.

The baby.

It's here.

My…baby.

He ran a hand down his face and realized he was taking

steps backward, away from the half open door.

"Ross, join us, please?"

"Yes," he said, straightening up and dragging his fingers through his wild, too-long hair. "Right. Coming."

He strode into the room, reminding himself that this was all right. This was good. Everyone had agreed months ago that the fact that he had fathered Evelyn's child was not going to be a problem.

Until he'd made it into one, of course.

When he caught sight of her, Evelyn, propped up in the bed holding a pink-blanket-wrapped bundle in her arms, all the spit dried up in his mouth. His heart stopped, then thudded forward too fast, making him gasp. She looked up at him, her deep blue eyes full of tears. Her lips trembled. "Ross?" she managed. But her voice was brittle, as if her throat was dry or overused.

Austin stood beside her, his hand on her arm, his gaze fixed on Ross. And it was not a pleased gaze. It was dark and angry. With good reason.

Ross smiled, or tried to, as he walked closer, more nervous than he'd been in his life. The pink bundle made a sudden loud squawk. He flinched and stepped back as both Evelyn and Austin bent over the baby, their faces gone moony and sappy. Ross gulped and put his hand on the edge of Evelyn's bed to steady himself.

This, this whole nuclear family scene, was why he'd left in the first place. There was no place for him in it. They had no business perpetuating some kind of kinky three-way set up as something normal. He was the clichéd third wheel. No matter he had been just as in love with Evelyn as Austin was. No matter Austin had exited her life for a brief period, during which time he and Evelyn had spent getting to know each better — and getting her pregnant.

No matter both of them had insisted to the high heavens that their life would work as 'three'. Austin had even found a house big enough to accommodate them all.

Ross knew better. It was beyond ridiculous — to think

the damn kid could somehow have 'two daddies and one mommy' and they would all live together under one roof.

He glanced at Austin, thinking not for the first time that if he were bisexual and the 'two daddies' thing made sense that way, he might have stuck around. But he was not, neither was Austin, despite their many hours spent fucking women between them. He'd had plenty of opportunity to do a little 'man exploration' as had Austin but neither of them had wanted that. They were just comfortable enough together as friends to share women between them — and they had both preferred it that way.

But now…this…was too much.

He started backing away from them.

"Ross," Evelyn said, finally raising her eyes to his. "Honey. Come and meet your daughter."

He shook his head as his head filled with white noise. He was no good as a father. Austin would have to handle that. He couldn't…

Austin picked the pink bundle out of Evelyn's arms and walked over to him. His gaze was still hard, but his smile softened it a little. He pulled the edge of the blanket away, and Ross got his first look at her. And his heart seemed to burst out of his chest.

"She… She's…" he stuttered like an idiot.

Austin held her out, his smile tightening again. Ross took her — so unbelievably tiny — in the crook of his elbow and smiled down at her, figuring he now wore the moony, sappy expression, too. The baby in his arms yawned and her eyes opened, meeting his. They were midnight blue. Austin tugged back the blanket to show him the shock of reddish-blond hair.

He had the same sinking, out-of-control sensation he'd experienced while watching Evelyn's body grow and accommodate his baby before her and Austin's wedding. He used to love to hold the swell of her belly in his arms and just stand like that, pressed against her back, rocking slightly side to side. Until the hard reality of life crashed in on him.

The whole 'two daddies' thing that would never, ever fly. The poor kid would be stigmatized, no doubt about it.

He loved Evelyn so much, he had honestly wondered if he could share her with Austin. A tiny, greedy part of him had always held out hope that maybe, just maybe, she would choose to marry him instead. Although he always knew that she and Austin were meant to be together. They were *simpatico*, complementary. She and Ross were too damn much alike. They butted heads way more than she ever did with Austin.

And so, to simplify all their lives, he'd left.

But now.

The infant seemed to be studying him, her eyes narrowed as if not quite sure she liked what she saw. The whole world faded for him then. It was him and this child, *his* child. He leaned close and touched his nose to hers. She sneezed, then flailed around again, then she smiled.

"Her name is Rose," Evelyn said.

He glanced over at her. The baby — Rose — was screwing up her tiny face in a weird way. She let out a surprisingly loud burst of sound that startled him. Austin took her, already fully competent, and placed her back in Evelyn's arms.

"She needs to eat," he said, his voice flat. Ross was re-frozen in place, watching Evelyn as she tugged open the string of her hospital gown, exposed her breast, and put the baby to her nipple. He dropped into a chair, mesmerized by it. Evelyn winced, then relaxed as the girl got busy.

Austin handed Evelyn a cup with a straw in it. She sipped then handed it back to him, her face full of the sort of love that Ross wanted to see for himself. He cleared his throat and stood. "I should go."

"Probably," Austin muttered, not looking at him.

"Austin," Evelyn hissed.

"I mean, no, you shouldn't." He glared holes in Ross' skull for a few seconds before he sighed and seemed to slump lower. "Do whatever the fuck you want," he declared in a soft, baby-appropriate voice. "I don't care."

"Well, excuse me but I do," Evelyn said in that same neutral tone. Ross tried not to laugh at them but the whole thing was so dumb, so utterly untenable he had a hard time reigning in a touch of hysteria.

"I'm sorry. To you both," he said, rising to his feet. "But surely you see it's for the best. We—the three of us—would never work in the real world. I'm not gonna saddle the kid with some kind of complex, five paragraph explanation about her 'Uncle Ross' who also lives in her house and sometimes gets to sleep in mommy and daddy's bed." Anger filled his brain, sharpening his words.

They both stared up at him, identical expressions of unhappy acceptance on their faces. His heart sank. Because he knew now—they believed this was for the best. Austin and Evelyn and baby Rose together as the family unit. Ross gone.

He put a hand on the thin hospital blanket over Evelyn's leg. The raw, unfiltered memory of her flesh under his palms, of how she tasted all over, of her laugh, her smart mouth, her brewery-sharp brain, clobbered him, making him blink fast and draw his hand away.

Austin's hand tightened on Evelyn's arm. But the baby remained oblivious to them all, as she fell asleep against her mother's breast, her tiny mouth half open. Ross gulped at the sight. His arms were aching to have her back, to hold her as she slept.

But no. He'd made this decision for all of them. Now he had to live with it. Even if it meant never laying eyes on his own daughter—his Rose—ever again.

"I love...you," he said, trying not to turn the statement into a past tense as he gazed into Evelyn's deep blue eyes for what he assumed would be the last time. "I'm so happy you're okay and the...our baby is healthy and safe."

He focused on Austin. "Can we talk? Outside?"

Evelyn snorted. "You've really been away too long,

Ross. Since when do you guys get to talk about anything that concerns me outside my hearing?" She was glaring at them both as she pulled her hospital gown together and readjusted the baby onto her chest.

"Honey, you're exhausted. You can barely keep your eyes open. Just sleep. I'll make sure he sticks around, don't worry."

"Fuck you, Austin Fitzgerald," she said, before a jaw-cracking yawn. "I hate it when you're right."

Austin cradled her cheek with one hand, leaned down and kissed her, then took the sleeping baby and placed her in a little plastic container thing on wheels next to Evelyn's bed.

"So help me, Hoffman, if I wake up and you're gone again, I will hunt you down and kill you, you selfish bastard."

Ross opened his mouth to respond, but Austin grabbed his elbow and pushed him toward the door. "Sleep, my love. I'll have the nurse check in on the baby."

When Ross glanced over at her, her eyes were closed. That was the first time he took in how thin her face was, how deep the circles under her eyes, how lank and lifeless her usually bouncy, silky hair was against the hospital pillow. He stopped, trying to turn back, to beg her to forgive him, to promise he'd never leave her again.

But Austin was yanking him forward so he kept moving, blinking in the much brighter light of the hallway. "Jesus," he said, wiping his lips with shaking fingers. "That was... hey!"

Hands gripped his biceps and shoved him backward. When his ass hit the railing that ran along the hospital wall, he braced himself. But even then, when the back of his skull whammed into the wall he was shocked. If not completely surprised.

"You," Austin said, his face mere centimeters from Ross'. "You. Fucking. Prick." With every word, spit flew into Ross' face. He tensed, forcing himself not to fight back. He deserved this, and more.

But Austin let go of him then, making him stumble forward. "Screw it. You're not worth the effort." Austin crossed his arms over his chest. Ross took a breath, tamping down his urge to slug the guy, if only to gain a reaction. To his surprise, Austin leaned over and braced his hands on his thighs, as if he'd just run a marathon.

Ross hesitated, glancing at the medical staff people scurrying around trying to pretend the near fist fight hadn't just happened in front of them. His shattered heart seemed to find yet another corner to break off and drop to his feet at the sight of his friend, his best friend, so undone. He reached for Austin's arm but the other man jerked out of his grip.

"You have no idea," he said. "You're out there probably fucking every pussy in Colorado, and you have no...god damned...idea what she's going through."

"I...didn't... I mean..." He stopped and raked his fingers through his raggedy beard. Confusion mixed with anxiety, which just added to his misery. His stomach made a strange noise, reminding him that he hadn't consumed any food in twenty-four hours. His head felt light all of a sudden and the hallway dimmed from the edges of his vision.

"Shit," he said, dropping back to grip the hallway rail again. Austin kept glaring at him. "Austin, I'm... You know it would never work. Shit, man, you don't want me around. Admit it. It's fine when we're sandwiching some random chick after a night out at a bar. We...we can't fucking share her." He pointed to Evelyn's closed hospital door. "And you know that as well as I do."

For the first time since Ross had arrived and seen him, Austin seemed unsure of himself. He ran a hand around the back of his neck, looked at the ceiling, then at the floor. Ross waited him out.

"My gut is about to eat itself. Can we get some food?"

Austin sighed. "Yeah, okay. Fine." He started down the hall, leaving Ross to follow him. They rode the elevator down in silence. Walked across the huge, crowded, granite lined lobby with two feet of air between them. As they stutter stepped their way through the giant revolving door, Ross allowed himself to relax.

The bright sunlight hit him in the eyeballs, surprising him. He'd lost complete track of time, or of the day for that matter. He stopped on the sidewalk and took a long breath. As he opened his eyes, the left hook landed on his nose. He yelled in surprise and stumbled, then recovered and came up punching. His upper cut connected with Austin's ribs with a satisfying cracking sensation.

"You fucker," Austin huffed as he drew back and broke Ross' nose with one punch before shoving him to the ground, landing on his chest and raining blows down on his face.

Someone yanked the man off, but Ross lay on the ground, staring up at the bright blue Michigan sky. He hurt in a lot of places, but the place he hurt most would never, truly heal. He'd never get over Evelyn and the incredible time they'd spent together—both with Austin and without him.

"All right, get up," a voice said. A strong hand gripped his arm and yanked him to his feet, bringing an instant blinding pain to his face. "ER's thattaway," the security guard said, shoving them both toward the big emergency sign. "Beat it. You're scarin' the natives."

Ross spit a wad of blood onto the grass. "I'm fine," he said, fingering his crooked nose.

"No, you're not, ya dumbass," the pseudo-cop insisted. "ER. Now."

Austin was holding his side and wincing. "Come on," he said. "I feel better."

"Well, shit, man, I'm glad one of us does."

Austin gave him a wan smile.

"I'm so sorry, Austin. I didn't mean for you to deal with all this by yourself." He waved his hand indicating the general medical situation. "I really didn't."

"Don't worry about me," his friend said, his eyes softening ever so slightly as they started for the ER entrance. "But I may never forgive you for what you put her through."

Ross grunted and ran his tongue around his mouth, seeking broken teeth. He found one, and spit it into his hand. "You may have just made me better looking," he said, holding up the tooth. "Chicks dig this hockey face thing."

"God, you never change, do you?"

He stopped, processing the deeper meaning of that question. "No. I guess not," he admitted. "I can't stay, Austin. I told you why, and I know you agree with me. We can't...it won't work. I mean, look at us now. It'll only get worse."

"I didn't beat your face in because I was jealous of you, you idiot. I did it because you abandoned her. You made her miserable with worry over your sorry ass. It wore her down. Her blood pressure shot up, she nearly...nearly died." He stopped and put his hands on his knees again, sucking in deep breaths.

Ross touched his friend's shoulder. "I'm sorry. I'll make it clear to her why I'm not going to be involved. No more mystery. No more worry. Ross will be just fine, off chasing pussy all over Colorado." His heart ached at the thought of this reality but he pasted a convincing smile on his face when Austin shot him an unbelieving glare then slowly stood up.

"She won't believe you."

"She'll have to," Ross said as he stepped into the chaotic ER. "She'll be busy with the baby, anyway. I'll just slip away."

Austin turned to him, his bloodied fist raised.

Ross held up a hand. "*After* I tell her why and where I'm going and that she has no reason whatsoever to worry about little old me."

"Fine," Austin said, wincing and holding his side again. "I think you broke my god damn rib, you shithead."

Ross' fake grin widened. As the last piece of his heart that he kept reserved for Evelyn and what they had shared, briefly, a few months ago, broke off and disappeared in the void, leaving him completely empty.

Chapter Five

Ross stood slowly stretching out the kinks in his lower back with a slight groan. The brewery floor was busy, as always. The seeming chaos well controlled. He would know. He controlled it.

He dropped the wrench into the toolbox, then wiped the already spotless exterior of the small fermentation vessel down with a cloth, taking a moment to admire his handiwork. He'd discovered the pilot system in one of the many semi-abandoned areas of the brewery, sitting alone among stacks of boxes full of old marketing crap and outdated six-pack holders. After about an hour's worth of tinkering inside the empty space, he'd decided to haul it out, fix it for real and put it to use.

"What the fuck is that?" his super-encouraging boss asked as he rolled it into the main brewery space.

"What does it look like?" Ross quipped, giving the connections and tubing a once-over.

"Allow me to be more specific," Brad insisted, his voice taking on the tightness Ross recognized well by now. "Why the fuck are you screwing around with a twenty-year-old pilot system while there is real beer to brew in here? You know, that job? That I over pay you for?"

Ross allowed the silence in the wake of that dig grow. Ever since he'd returned from Michigan, resumed his position as head brewer of one of the most successful, still-independent craft breweries in the nation, he'd played a little game with his annoying boss. And with himself. Something that required a lot of self-control on his part.

Which was all part of his New Improved Ross. Self-control

was now his middle name.

He hummed around, poking and prodding and disconnecting the dirty rubber tubes, pondering what he wanted to do with the system, which was like his huge brewhouse, only in miniature. It was how test brews used to get made, before Brad simply started laying out recipes and handing them to Ross with orders for a thousand barrels of this or fifteen hundred barrels of that. Most of which Ross had to adjust in order for the beer to be drinkable.

The five-liter system was high quality, as he'd expect with a guy like Brad. Even starting out he had nothing but the best, given the deep pocketed investors he'd conned into writing him huge checks. The fact that the three thousand dollars-worth of stainless steel had been sitting and literally rotting in an ignored corner of the successful brewery didn't surprise Ross in the slightest. Brad was the sort of guy to simply toss something like this aside and forget it. Which is what he'd done, considering the condition of the thing — eroded rubber connecting tubes and all.

"Are you deaf?"

Ross glanced up from his busy work, having forgotten the man was still standing there, fuming. "Sorry?" he said, muttering 'not sorry' under his breath as he tossed the tubes into the garbage bin he'd dragged over all while ignoring his boss.

"Jesus, fucking, humped-up Christ," Brad blurted out, making a couple of the scurrying assistant brewers stop and stare at him. Their boss's temper tantrums were legendary. Ross couldn't wait to provoke another one. But he waved the young men along. They had a lot to do to meet the demand. All in a day's work.

Luckily, or not, Brad's phone buzzed. With another curse, he yanked it out of his pocket. When his face broke into a goofy grin, Ross realized his opportunity to provoke had passed. And he knew why. Only one thing would turn Brad Jefferson into a moony teenager.

"Gotta go," he said, shoving past Ross. "My woman

awaits."

"Right," Ross said, giving him a jaunty salute. "Give the lovely Holly my regards." He let his hand drop to his crotch, making the brewery staff around him titter. When Brad turned and glared at him, he waved, then returned to his project, forcing a blankness over his mind. So, he wouldn't think about Holly. The evil, manipulative, bitch.

"Down boy," he muttered to his dick as it began to rise to the memory of her. "Made bed. Lying in it now, remember?"

In the five months since he'd left Evelyn, Austin and baby Rose behind for good, Ross had embarked on what could best be described as a monk-like existence. The quick discussion he'd had with Evelyn—the one he'd promised Austin—had been about as awful as he'd imagined but he'd muscled through it. Keeping a fake, wide smile plastered on his face. Giving her the reassurance that she required.

Ross is fine.

Ross is good.

Ross is in no way about to move to Michigan and play three-way house.

Despite the fact that he felt cored out, raw on the inside after the discussion knowing he was doing the exact opposite of what he wanted to do. He did it. And he got on a plane and got his job back. Not tough, considering he was the best fucking brewer out here right now. Brad would be a fool to let him go. And of all the things that Brad was— egomaniac, jerk, asshole—fool really wasn't one of them.

Ross paused, leaning on the table where he kept his tools, realizing those very words had been used against him, fairly recently. And from the lovely, talented mouth of 'Brad's woman' herself. He shrugged. Chick must have a real masochistic streak, he figured. Jumping from his bed straight into Brad's.

"Stop," he muttered under his breath, as vivid images rose in his brain—Holly's mouth and what it could do for and to him. "Just fucking stop."

He turned back to the pilot system, reforming his plan for

it in his head, shoving out all thoughts of Holly, of Evelyn, of women in general out of his aching brain. Two hours later he emerged into the small pub attached to the main brewery, head pounding from the close work he'd been doing, but with a sense of accomplishment he hadn't felt in years.

The bartender nodded and poured him one of the new stouts on nitro without asking. Ross mentally tipped his hat to the guy. He knew his shit. He sat, hunched over his beer, ignoring everything and everyone around him. His new M.O.

After his requisite two beers, he got up and stretched again, noting the various sore spots in his muscles. Part of his improvement plan was to get into the best possible physical shape, so when he wasn't at work, or asleep, he was at the gym or running for miles along the hills of his newly adopted home. As a result, he was in a constant state of sore — which was good, because it served to distract him from his Spartan, sexless life.

At least a little.

He sighed and let his gaze flicker along the bar, noting the various women with a detached, analytic eye. It was an autopilot thing and he knew it. Big difference was, once he would have zeroed in on one, culled her from her chattering group of friends, or even her date for the night and found a spot where they could share some quality alone time.

That, too, was automatic for him and he felt his skin tingle when he saw a potential target. His usual type — tall, full-figured but not fat — he was a tits man, through and through — tight jeans, long, shining hair that he could tangle his hands in when he fucked her silly. The woman in question laughed, flipped a heavy lock of chestnut hair back, turned as if she sensed his observation of her, meeting his gaze with a raised eyebrow.

"Stop," he muttered to himself, turning away and shoving back into the brewery and back into his project, deflecting, distracting, distancing himself as much as possible from the Old Ross. The Old Ross had gotten into that odd, sexy, irresistible situation with Evelyn and Austin and had very nearly lost himself in it.

No good. The New Ross was completely devoid of emotion, of physical needs below the waist. He had to get control of all that shit or he'd lose his fucking mind over missing her, of missing his friend, of giving up what could have been an amazing life.

"Hey, you," he barked at one the many brewery assistants. "Come here and give me a hand with this."

He spent the next four hours putting the pilot system back together and not thinking about Evelyn. Not thinking about Holly. Not thinking at all. Which was the whole point, really.

Chapter Six

The morning of her interview with Fitzgerald Brewing, Elisa Nagel sat at her tiny kitchen table, wide awake and twitching with nerves. She'd managed three hours of sleep from about one a.m., after trying everything she knew to do to relax — an hour of intensive yoga stretching, a half hour of deep breathing, a cup of a chamomile tea mix she'd concocted herself. Nothing had worked.

She'd lain under her covers with her eyes wide open as if they were being propped by toothpicks for a solid hour before giving up and going with an old reliable method — a high alcohol IPA she'd made and stored for a year plus one of her dwindling supply of pain killers. The pills were on the verge of expiring but she'd held on to them, almost as a talisman, ever since… Well, no need to ponder that now. She finished her second allotted cup of mild coffee and made another attempt to focus her rattled brain.

Forward motion, Elisa. Nothing more. Nothing less. This is a big day, but no bigger than any other interview you've aced with breweries just as big as Fitzgerald. She stepped over to the sink, washed, rinsed, dried and put her cup away. The sight of the meager contents of the dish cupboard made her pause. As she put the mug alongside its single companion, a rush of memory made her suck in a breath.

A kitchen, ten times the size of this postage stamp, boasting miles of granite and stainless steel surfaces, the most expensive appliances money could buy, stacks of china, acres of crystal, name brand pots and pans, and — most importantly — the best set of knives any chef might want. All at her disposal every single day. With only one, tiny little string attached.

She shook her head and turned away from her few belongings. It was how things had to be now. It was better. Because that tiny string might have been made of luxurious red silk but it was attached to something—someone—on the other end. Someone she was still running from, still woke, screaming about, and who, she firmly believed, would find her if she didn't keep moving forward, on to the next brewery, the next job. Anything, so he couldn't track her down and drag her back.

Sighing, she berated herself for the millionth time. *Stop living in the past. It's been ten, almost eleven years. Get over it, as the American teenagers say a lot.* Noting the time, she decided that another hour of peaceful stretching might help, so she lit a soy candle, moved the small table from in front of her futon, and unrolled her yoga mat.

As she took her usual mind-clearing breaths to start, the voice—His voice—intruded again. Louder than usual this time, which made her grit her teeth and muscle through the hour-long practice with tears streaming down her face. She spent a longer than usual time in the shower, crouched in a corner of the small, fiberglass enclosure, willing Him out of her head so she could focus on her job interview until the lukewarm water she'd started with turned cold.

This was the usual pattern. She'd been through it before, plenty of times. The past almost-eleven years had been full of interview stress, and first-days-on-the job nerves. She'd never *not* been offered a job, but she had turned down a few. For the jobs she'd taken, once she'd proven her worth as a legitimate brewer, she'd start to feel jittery and begin looking over her shoulder too much. It was always a sign to move on. Like she was doing now, in Grand Rapids, Michigan.

"Forward motion, Elisa," she said to herself in her native German. Then again, in English for good measure, as she applied a bit of powder to her flushed complexion. "You can do this. It's only assistant brewer. You can do this job with your eyes closed." The English words felt funny in her mouth but she forced herself to say them again, doing the mental gymnastics of ongoing translation from German.

She was excited about the interview, as she always got at this stage of a transition. One of her favorite things to observe was how the interviewer's eyes would widen at the first sight of her — five foot nothing, with a deceiving slightness of build she kept well hidden under a buttoned-up professional gray pantsuit, the facial jewelry, her visible tattoos, and her unconventional hair. Without fail, said interviewer would glance at her résumé, as if certain her physical actuality didn't match up with what she'd said about herself on paper.

It was, as they say, a hoot.

She smiled at herself in the cracked bathroom mirror, turning her head to make sure she'd covered all evidence of her face's tendency to blotch red. Running her fingertips along her jaw, she lifted her chin and stared hard at the ink around neck, willing it gone, then acknowledging that it was there for a reason — as a constant reminder of what she'd once believed, whom she'd once trusted.

The small diamond in left side of her nose caught the light and twinkled. She frowned, touched it then the matching one in her eyebrow, and the line of silver balls in the cartilage of her left ear. If she got this job, she'd need to add something else, she mused, clicking the metal in her tongue against the back of her teeth.

After a quick inner debate, she tugged the long strands of her hair to the nape of her neck and fastened them together with a scarf. A few stubborn lengths popped free, framing her face. Deciding that softened her appearance a bit, made her somewhat less alarming, she let them stay.

She'd laid out her interview suit — the familiar gray trousers, sleeveless silk blouse, and short, matching jacket — on her bed hours before. The one pair of shoes she owned that were not work boots or flip-flops were on the floor beside the bed. They were evil — with sharp pointed toes and a five-inch heel that put her a bit closer to most other human beings' eye level. She sighed and picked them up, recalling the last time she'd worn them.

That job had held her longer than any other. She'd felt so at home amongst the brewing staff and had been more than content to work as a 'cellar man' or beer storage manager. This put her in charge of tracking the beer after it was brewed — a job just as important as any other in a brewery as large as that one. They stored, bottled, canned, packaged and shipped out more beer in one week than some breweries produced in a year. It was a busy, fun job. But she'd left after reading something about a new restaurant opening at one of the new casinos nearby.

And now, here she was in Michigan. A state well known for the health and robust nature of its craft beer industry and one she'd avoided until now, on purpose, due to its proximity to Chicago. The west coast had felt safest. But He'd found her, anyway. Him and his damnable *bourgeoisie*, money-printing, celebrity chef franchises.

She'd given her two weeks' notice, suffered through a gut-wrenching good-bye party, ignored one of her fellow brewers who'd tried one last time to get her to go out with him, and driven for three days until arriving in Grand Rapids — a city dubbed 'Beer City USA' and that housed ten different breweries with plenty of related businesses. Thanks to her innate frugality, she'd come away with a fair bit of money saved. She'd been able to sign a lease, pay an exorbitant deposit on a miniscule flat, and start applying for jobs.

With a muttered curse at her inability to focus, she stepped out of her short robe and reached for a pair of panties. Avoiding the sight of her body in the mirror, she stepped into them, then fastened a bra around her, tugging up the straps quickly with the usual thought that she was flat-chested enough to forgo this step but it felt improper to not wear a bra to a job interview.

A glance at her phone's clock confirmed that if she got all

the way dressed now, she'd still have an hour to sit around and stare at the four walls. Too efficient, that was her, to a T. With a sigh, she sat on her bed and pulled her second-hand laptop from the milk crate side table. It opened to the page she'd been studying for a couple of days.

The Fitzgerald Brewing Company was a successful mid-sized operation, with an attached, full service pub, and distribution in twenty US states. Its production had ramped up fast, and continued to climb until the last couple of years. Now, the market was so saturated with IPAs, stouts, pilsners and Belgians, even reliable breweries like Fitzgerald were having to rethink their strategies.

She knew that the owner, Austin Fitzgerald, had recently married and that his wife, Evelyn, was the one who'd be conducting her interview today. She sincerely hoped that this Evelyn knew about the business and wasn't just some kind of acting figurehead replacement for her husband.

That's the sort of sexist bullshit thing you should never think. Don't pre-suppose anything if you don't want anyone to do it to you.

She nodded, accepting the inner reminder from her conscience. It had been less berating lately, more supportive. Which was a lovely break from the norm.

Fitzgerald needed an assistant brewer immediately, according to the ad she'd seen in a trade magazine online. Which worked for her as she was getting tired of draining her savings here in Michigan. This would be her fourth interview in two weeks. And for some reason, this one felt important — fortuitous, fated, even.

Ridiculous. She shook her head so hard some of her hair escaped from the scarf. *It's just because you're being interviewed by a woman who co-owns a brewery with her husband. Stop reading anything more into it.*

As she got up and began to dress, her mind wandered to the other website she'd found — the one for the highly recommended piercing studio. She knew that her penchant for poking holes in her body related to a need to feel pain —

pain only she controlled, and would inflict herself—but she refused to over-analyze it. She was drawn to it the same way she'd been drawn to beer brewing. And she'd spent too many years of her life denying the things she wanted. Even if they hurt.

She slipped her arms into the jacket, relishing the soft inner lining against her skin, even as it dredged up memories of silky sheets, soft blindfolds, softer kisses. All of the things that had fooled her, trapped her, and nearly killed her.

Forward motion, Elisa, the voice snapped. *No backward glances. They're not worth the time spent.*

Elle smiled, realizing that her conscience was starting to sound an awful lot like her beloved *Oma*, the grandmother who'd spent more time with her than either of her parents or her much older brothers.

Chapter Seven

"Come in," a voice said, after Elle gave a light rap on the office door. It opened, revealing a woman who was about as far from what Elle was expecting as might be imagined. "Hello. You must be Elisa." The woman rose from her desk and stuck out the hand she wasn't using to hold a baby.

"Yes, hello. But please, call me Elle."

"Oh, of course. I'm Evelyn Fitzgerald."

Elle smiled at her as they shook hands, reminding herself that even as she was squaring the reality of the woman with her own pre-conceived notions, Evelyn was without a doubt doing the same to her.

"Please, have a seat. I just need to settle her majesty." Evelyn indicated a large work table that took up one side of the cavernous room. "Can I get you some coffee? Tea? Water?"

"Thank you, but no."

The woman moved with a sort of competent efficiency that Elle envied as she put the baby she'd been holding in a complicated-looking seat contraption. The child let out a blat of noise, then quieted. When Evelyn moved the seat-thing closer to the table, Elle couldn't resist a peek into the device that was making a steady whirring noise as it rocked gently back and forth. "She looks like you," she said, running a fingertip along the baby's plump cheek.

"Ah, well, she looks more like her fa—" Evelyn stopped abruptly, making Elle glance over at her in surprise then sit back up, still trying to square what she'd expected and what she was seeing.

"Okay, so," Evelyn said, sitting down across from Elle. "I

hope you don't mind my assistant here." She indicated the seat.

Elle smiled, hoping to put the suddenly flustered woman at ease. "Of course not. I think that only Americans get wound up about bringing babies into the workplace. But..." She pointed to Evelyn's blouse. "I'm afraid that you buttoned up incorrectly."

"Oh, crap," Evelyn said, her lovely face flushing red as she corrected the error. "I probably reek of baby shit and stale milk too." Her bright blue eyes shimmered for a second until she blinked. "This is...exhausting."

"I can imagine," Elle said. "Take a deep breath. I'm in no hurry." She glanced into the seat once more, catching sight of a pair of sweetly pursed baby lips. "What is her name?"

"Rose," Evelyn said.

Elle nodded and tried not to stare at the woman across the table. Evelyn Fitzgerald was over six feet tall in her heels with a full, healthy-looking figure that would be expected after having a baby. She was just shy of stunningly beautiful, with her thick blonde hair, deep blue eyes, and the sort of perfectly proportioned facial features that Elle found fascinating. The faint aura of baby—milk with an undertone of lotion and, indeed, a touch of shit—filled the office space.

Elle glanced over at the huge desk where Evelyn had been sitting, working while feeding her child. It held a giant computer and an open laptop. Both screens were covered in colorful spreadsheets. The chaos of paperwork on the desk rivaled anything Elle had ever seen. But somehow, she had a sense that this woman—Evelyn with her misaligned blouse buttons and model-gorgeous, flushed face—had everything completely under control.

Elle didn't know if she was impressed, or insanely jealous in a way she'd never, ever been about another woman.

"So, Elle," Evelyn said, jolting her out of her thoughts. "Your background is incredible. You've worked at some vastly different breweries." She tapped Elle's résumé which lay on the table between them.

Elle leaned forward on the table. "I know I must look like an odd candidate for this job, Mrs. Fitzgerald..."

"Evelyn, please."

"Evelyn. But I assure you, I'm more than qualified and am eager to make the move from cellar man to assistant brewer. I've brought more references, if you'd like to see them."

"To be honest, I was ready to hire you from your résumé alone. You have a degree in brewing science from Oregon State. Why are you messing around as anyone's cellar man?"

"Ah, well, as you can see..." She passed both hands up and down her front, acknowledging her odd appearance. "I don't always make such a great first impression I suppose. Besides, my last job was pretty...great. I mean, I left, of course." She felt her ears burning hot, a dead giveaway that her face was doing that red blotchy thing in the middle of an important interview. "And, as I'm sure you know, this is a horribly sexist business."

"Oh, boy, do I." Evelyn sighed and leaned back. The hand she used to touch her face was shaking.

"Perhaps I should get you some water," Elle said, her inner, natural caretaker taking over.

The other woman smiled at her. "I have some, right here," she said, pulling a refillable water bottle from the bag next to the baby seat and taking a long drink. "I forget how dehydrated I get when I'm at work."

Elle waited, her eagerness to work for this woman filling every corner of her mind. "I didn't mind working my way up, even with my degree," she insisted, hoping to cover her earlier gaff. "And I've passed up promotions, trust me, because some men are simply impossible to work for. I don't know your brewer that well which means he doesn't have an asshole of a reputation to precede him. Oops," she said, covering her lips. "My mouth. Apologies."

Evelyn laughed. "No, he's not exactly an asshole. But he's

not the most creative guy on the planet, either. The trade-off, if you get me. Are you? Creative, I mean?"

"Very," Elle said. "I was a trained chef before I went to the brewing institute. I was *sous* to a very famous man for a while, before…" She looked down at her hands, cursing herself for saying too much. But somehow, Evelyn Fitzgerald seemed to encourage that. "That's not pertinent to this conversation. Again. Please accept my apologies."

"No need to apologize. You didn't include that on your résumé. The chef thing, I mean."

"I don't consider it relevant anymore." Elle touched the space between her collarbones on reflex, then dropped her hand.

"So, when can you start?" Evelyn stood, holding out her hand.

Elle's heart pounded as she rose and shook her new boss's hand. "Tomorrow, if you like."

"Great. Be here at eight-thirty. I'll set you up with HR and get all that out of the way then introduce you to Bryan, my non-asshole, somewhat boring brewer."

Elle laughed, feeling so comfortable in this woman-space that she wanted to cry instead. At that moment, Evelyn's baby let out a loud wail that sounded sharp and alarming. She turned to the seat, pulled the blanket aside and touched Rose's face. "She's burning up. She's so hot. I… How…? Oh shit."

Elle put a hand on Evelyn's arm. "May I hold her? While you find your phone, perhaps?"

With a shell-shocked expression on her face, Evelyn handed the wailing baby over. Elle held the child close to her lips, all the better to gauge her body's temperature. *"Arme kleine Schatz,"* she crooned. "Poor darling, shush now."

Rose's wails ramped down to sniffles as she tried to process who was talking to her. But her face remained beet red and her eyes seemed glassy. Elle tried to keep her voice level, calling on her old training as an apprentice nurse. "She is very feverish, Evelyn. We should take her to hospital."

"Hospital?" Evelyn burst out, her voice tight. "What do you mean?"

Rose was sucking in air now, as if she couldn't catch her breath. In between, she made mewling, helpless, awful noises as if someone was stepping on her. Elle knew she had to keep the mother calm, but get Rose to medical help as fast as they could manage it. "I think that we should drive to hospital right now. I will drive and you hold the poor sweetling." She kept her voice as neutral as she could. "I am a trained nurse's assistant. It was my first job, in Germany. This child is very ill. We should go."

Evelyn seemed to freeze in place, staring at Elle. "All right," she said, handing over her keys and taking Rose in her arms again. "Oh, my God, she's...so hot. Should we call nine-one-one?"

"No time. Hurry."

Evelyn nodded and followed Elle down the metal steps, through the brewery and out of the back door.

* * * *

They were rushed straight through when they arrived, mostly thanks to Elle's precise description to the check-in staff. Rose was limp in Evelyn's arms by then, her eyes rolled back in her head, her breathing shallow.

"Oh, my God," Evelyn whispered, tears rolling down her face. "She's been fussy all day, but I didn't think anything of it."

"It's all right," Elle said. "My guess is that it's some form of strep since it came on so quickly."

"Strep?" Evelyn repeated. "I didn't think babies got that."

"Not many do," Elle admitted, keeping her palm on Evelyn's arm to steady her. The doctors and nurses hovered over the baby's tiny body. At one point, one of the doctors — who looked to be all of eighteen years old — barked at the nurses to "get the mother out of the room."

"The hell you will," Evelyn said, peeling away from Elle and heading straight for the approaching phalanx of staff before planting herself near the bed. "I'm staying."

Elle moved quickly to catch her when she saw that someone was giving baby Rose mouth-to-mouth resuscitation.

"God damn it, grab her before she concusses on the fucking floor."

Doctors, Elle thought with disdain as she and a nurse got Evelyn up onto a nearby gurney. *Their pompous asshole-ishness knows no borders.*

"Are you family?" the nurse asked as she accompanied Evelyn's limp form into a different, curtained-off space in the emergency area.

"No," Elle said, her eyes on the woman's pale face. "A friend."

"Well, then do you know how we can reach her husband? The baby's father?"

"I'm...um..." Elle backed away, hand to her neck, her mind spinning with a distinct lack of options. She heard the thin wail coming from where Rose had been unconscious a few moments before. She took a deep breath. "I know how to find him," she declared, reaching for her outdated cell phone and hitting re-dial from the brewery's main number. Glancing at her watch, she prayed that it was the sort of place where the front office didn't shut down at five on the nose.

"Thank you for calling the Fitzgerald Brewing Company. This is Alice. How can I help you today?"

Evelyn sent up a quick mental thanks, then said, "Alice, my name is Elle. Elisa Nagel. I'm... I am to be the new assistant brewer."

"Oh, right, yes. Did Evelyn leave with you? I need her to sign—"

"I am very sorry to interrupt you, but I need to know where Mr. Fitzgerald is."

"He's...out of town. Why?"

Elle shut her eyes and slumped against the wall. "Is there

anyone there who can reach him, immediately?"

"Hang on a minute." Elle winced at the sound of a phone dropping onto a surface. "Brock! Come here," she heard Alice saying. There was more shuffling, bustling noises. Then a deep masculine voice said, "Hello? This is Brock Fitzgerald. Austin's bro—"

"Evelyn and the baby are in the emergency room," Elle blurted out, trying not to sound as terrified as she was. "You must come now."

"What? Who is this?"

"It's Elle, Elisa Nagel. I'm the new brewer. We were finishing my interview and the baby…" Her throat locked up. "Please come now, Mr. Fitzgerald. I will meet you at the emergency room entrance."

"Wait, how will I know who—?"

"I'm the short one, with the weird hair. Hard to miss. Bring some extra clothes for Evelyn, if she keeps them there, maybe in a locker somewhere? But hurry, please." She ended the call and pressed her fingers to her lips as a contingent of medical staff rushed past her, wheeling Rose away in a small incubator. The adrenaline rush that had been sustaining her escaped in a giant *whoosh*. Her legs gave out and she slid to the floor, still clutching her phone in one hand.

Chapter Eight

Elle sat in what was possibly the most uncomfortable, pre-formed plastic chair in the entire universe for over an hour, barely moving a muscle. She'd met Brock — a tall, very handsome man who was, she recalled, Austin's twin — and given him the basics of the situation. He'd located Austin in Denver for the annual large beer expo and had arranged to get him on the next plane home. Then she'd been forced to wait, and wait…and wait while Brock sat with Evelyn in her room and they all awaited word of Rose's condition.

The hospital bustled and went about its business all around her, reminding her of her early goals to be a nurse in her youth. At one point, she shifted her hips, which made her lower back sing out in agony, reminding her that she'd been sitting still for too long. It was one of her skills, she thought as she stood up slowly and let the circulation return to her legs. The tingly, prickling sensation made her stumble with the full force of memory.

How many times had she been forced to hold her position — for long minutes, sometimes hours, and once, overnight. She shook her head to clear it of the cobwebs, refocusing on the issue at hand. Aggravated at the level of non-communication that had left Evelyn limp with terror, Elle grabbed the arm of a nearby nurse and used her most important-sounding voice. "Please, may we know something about the — about Rose. Rose Fitzgerald? Her mother has been waiting for over an hour."

The woman glanced down at Elle's hand. She moved it away, realizing that the hop flowers she had inked onto her knuckles probably were a tad incongruous considering she was dressed like a pharmaceutical sales woman, albeit one with unique hair. "I am sorry," she said, holding the woman's gaze, even though that act took a lot out of her. "But we must know something, please."

"Hold on. Let me see what I can find out."

"Many thanks," Elle said, hoping she sounded peer-to-peer professional and not mildly hysterical. She sat, but stayed perched on the edge of the hard seat, her eyes fixed on the double doors between her and the pediatric intensive care unit. Finally, the doors opened again and the nurse she'd spoken to strode out. Elle stood, panic skittering around the edges of her consciousness at the sight of the woman's grim face.

"The child is alive. She has influenza."

"She's…going to live, though?"

"I'm sorry, but I can't say anything more."

Elle grabbed her arm again. "Then please come with me and tell her mother."

The nurse rolled her eyes, but must have sensed Elle's desperation and went with her to the elevator, down three floors, through an incredible warren of hallways until they stood outside the closed door to Evelyn's room. Elle set her jaw. "She's in there. Her husband is not here yet. He is flying home from Colorado."

The nurse, who was, Elle realized, very young, started wringing her hands. "I have to get someone more senior than me," she said, backing away. "I could get into real trouble for saying anything."

When the door opened, the nurse's eyes widened before she whirled and ran down the hall. Elle sighed, then turned, expecting to see Evelyn. But she found herself face to face with Brock. "News?" He jerked his chin in the direction of the cowardly retreating nurse.

"Influenza was all I could pry out of her before she ran off. Is this really how a hospital operates here? It's shameful."

Brock ran a hand down his face.

"Rose? Is she all right? Austin, is that you?" Evelyn's

voice floated out from behind him.

Brock turned into the room. "Evelyn, I need you to be calm."

"Fuck you and your calm. Where the hell is my baby?"

Elle pushed past him. "I'll take this. You go and demand that someone give her some news. Be firm. They'll listen to you more likely than me, anyway."

"Oh, I don't know," Brock said, treating her to a handsome smile. "I find you pretty intimidating."

Elle's face flushed hot.

"Stop flirting, you asshole, and go find a doctor who will talk to me," Evelyn demanded.

"Yes, ma'am." He winked at Elle, the headed down the busy hall.

Evelyn was sitting in the fake leather recliner next to the hospital bed. She looked strung out, wild with worry. She walked over and grabbed Elle's arm. "What's wrong with Rose? Why in the hell am I in this room?"

"She's in intensive care. They had to sedate you after you fainted. You were a bit…hysterical."

"I'm… She…" Evelyn held up her arms, as if surprised to find herself dressed in jeans and a brewery labeled sweatshirt instead of her work clothes.

"I had Brock bring some extra clothes. You struck me as the practical type who'd keep something around in a locker somewhere. You let me help you change."

"Right. Brock."

"And he called Austin," Elle reminded her, leading Evelyn back to the chair.

"Austin," she said, sounding weak. "And Ross?"

Elle hesitated, not knowing whether Evelyn was still fuzzy from the sedative or what, with that last comment. "I'm sure he's coming, too." She patted Evelyn's shoulder. "Is that water?"

"Yes."

Elle poured her a cup and held the straw to Evelyn's dry lips. "Rose has the flu," she said, trying to make it sound innocuous. "They're keeping her isolated right now."

"Flu," Evelyn parroted.

"Yes. She's…okay. But that's all I could get out of anyone."

"Where is she?" Evelyn jumped to her feet, sending the water cup skittering across the linoleum. "I need to see her now."

"All right. I'm sure we can—"

"Take me to her, Elle. Please. She needs me."

Elle nodded, grateful to have a task. She opened the door and checked for nosy staff. Then she led Evelyn down the hall to the elevator. They rode the few floors in silence, exited, and headed down another faceless hallway until they came to a door that said 'Pediatric Intensive Care. Authorized personnel only beyond this point' in shocking red letters. The same door she'd been staring at for so long earlier.

A wave of panicked dizziness washed over Elle. But she sensed Evelyn's hesitation and fear as if it were her own. She rallied, and put her arm around the other woman's waist and motioned for a sympathetic-looking nurse. "Please," she said to the woman. "We need to see her baby."

"I…can't." Evelyn hesitated while the automatic doors into the ICU swung open once the nurse touched her ID to a sense pad. Elle urged her forward. "Austin," she whispered, hand to her throat.

"He'll be here soon. Come on. Let's go check on that sweet baby."

Chapter Nine

Once accepting that she was not going to budge, the ICU staff made Evelyn gown up, put on a mask, booties over her shoes, and gloves on her trembling hands before they'd let her in the isolation unit. Inside, Rose lay in a plastic crib, hooked up to wires, a nasal cannula, and with a needle that looked as big as her arm stuck into her scalp.

"Why…is there a needle in her head?" Elle heard Evelyn ask in a breathy, weak, unbelieving voice as she stood, staring down at her daughter.

"It's the best way to keep her hydrated. The veins in her arms are too hard to get to at this age," Elle said from outside isolation unit, talking into an intercom. "It's normal in the Peds ICU." She smiled. "They're saying that Rose is stable, and her fever is going down. But it will likely spike again, fair warning. That's typical in the first twenty-four hours."

"Oh," Evelyn said, still staring at the child. "Thanks for all your help."

"It's fine. Glad I was there." She sensed Brock standing next to her. She bristled, nervous from his presence. She touched the intercom button again. "Evelyn, you can touch her? She needs you to touch her."

"Can't I hold her? Nurse her? Something?"

"Probably not," Elle said. "She needs to be kept still for now so the staff can control her hydration and medication through the IV in her scalp."

"All right. Okay." Evelyn put her hand on the bed that was dwarfed by the machinery and the sheer emptiness of the room around her. "Rose," she said. "Baby. I'm here.

Mommy's here."

Elle frowned, hearing the helplessness in the woman's voice, watching as she pressed her palms to her breasts. Her anger at the lack of empathy among the so-called medical staff ramped up once again. "Excuse me," she said, catching the sleeve of a staff person. "Can we get a breast pump down here? She's going to need it right away."

Luckily, she seemed to have found someone who gave a shit about a patient's well-being. The woman's eyes softened as she glanced into the isolation room. "Of course. I'll need to head up to maternity for one. Wait right here."

"Thank you," Elle said.

"Please, I need to hold her," she heard Evelyn wail. She turned and saw the woman, tears running down her cheeks. "I have to hold her." The thin sound of the baby's cry tore it for her.

"I'll see what I can do," Elle said and stepped away to flag down a passing nurse right when a loud alarm rang from the isolation unit. Several staff pushed past her as they gowned up before running in and shoving Evelyn aside.

Elle stumbled and sensed herself falling, dropping to her knees. A strange hand gripped her biceps before she face-planted. She looked up and came face to face with a man who had to be Austin Fitzgerald. He was fully gowned and masked, his eyes bloodshot, jaw covered in dark stubble. The distinct odor of beer consumed the night before wafted out of his pores. She nodded, hot-faced with embarrassment and regained her footing.

"Please, don't worry about me. Go to your wife and child."

He nodded and pushed his way into the room, grabbing Evelyn and clinging to her while the staff worked to revive Rose. Finally, the doctor moved away from the bed. The nurses began filing out of the room, ignoring her and Brock, who still stood next to her.

As she watched, Austin let go of Evelyn and moved to the bed. "Give her to me," he demanded. The staff glanced at each other until one of the many pediatricians in room nodded.

"It can't hurt her," he admitted, making notes on a computer tablet. "And it might help."

One nurse picked Rose up, now wide-eyed and breathing normally, but on the verge of crying, Elle could tell. Another nurse had to manipulate the leads that monitored her vital signs, and the thin IV line connected to the needle in her scalp around but neither of them seemed to mind.

"Here, Papa," one of them said. "Hold your girl."

Austin sat in the rocking chair, leaving the rest of them, including Evelyn, to watch.

"My girl," Austin crooned to her, touching his nose to hers. Elle saw the baby shift in his arms, smile and yawn. Elle allowed herself to fully exhale for the first time in hours, then she grabbed an extra rocking chair and shoved it at one of the still-gowned nurses.

"For the mother," she said, furious that she had to point out such an obvious need. The nurse nodded and helped Evelyn into the seat next to Austin. She sat, her hand on Rose's tiny chest, her head against Austin's shoulder.

A combination of exhaustion and hunger hit Elle right between the eyes. Her stomach growled and her eyes burned but she couldn't take them off the scene of mother, father and child before her.

"Is she...all right?"

Elle blinked, confused by the deep, rumbly, German-accented voice to her left. She turned, wondering where Brock had gone at the same time she laid eyes on a man she thought she knew, while at the same time realizing who he was.

"Ross flew back with me," Austin said as he walked out of the isolation room. Elle wheeled around again, feeling woozy and surreal. He peeled off his gloves, then leaned on the receptacle, his shoulders hunched and his eyes closed. "Jesus wept," he whispered, before standing back up and swiping at his eyes.

The two men stared at each other. Elle felt an odd tension between them. Something she'd never encountered — that teetered between fury and support.

"Pardon my rudeness," Austin said in a flat voice. "Elle, this is Ross. Ross Hoffman. He's an...old friend of mine... and Evelyn's. Elle is our new assistant brewer — and the woman who probably saved our — saved Rose's life." He glared at Ross, confusing her further. Then he seemed to slump back in on himself. He turned and stared through the window at Evelyn and Rose.

"I know who you are," Elle said. "I mean, who wouldn't?"

Ross' blue eyes gleamed for a moment, then he, too, seemed to collapse in on himself. He smelled of old beer, as well, but his jaw was covered in a pleasant, red-tinged, tidy beard and his eyes were less bloodshot. He sighed and ran his fingers through his near shoulder-length blond hair, holding out the other hand to shake hers. "Pleased to meet you. Thank you for...today."

Elle tilted her head, allowing herself a moment to study the tall, handsome man before her as he turned to stare through window alongside Austin. When Elle glanced into the isolation room, she caught Evelyn's gaze as it skipped over her, landed on her husband, then on Ross.

The expression on her face made Elle's breath catch. She moved away from the window, hand to her throat, wanting to escape, but for some reason, wishing Ross Hoffman, famous — some would say infamous — artist of a brewer and playboy of the brewing world would put his arm around her as they stood there.

Ridiculous, Elisa. You're delusional from hunger.

"Ma'am?" The nurse she'd found earlier materialized with an alarming piece of machinery.

"Yes, of course. Excuse me, Mr. Fitzgerald?"

Austin turned around slowly. Ross stayed put, both his hands flat on the window separating them from Evelyn and Rose.

"We need to get Evelyn some relief."

He blinked in confusion at the sight of the device, then seemed to recognize its purpose. "Right, okay." He grabbed a fresh set of gloves and entered the room, followed by the nurse with the breast pump.

"Holy shit," Ross muttered, in German under his breath when he caught sight of it. "What are they doing to her?"

"It's a breast pump. *Trottel*," she muttered back in German, feeling strangely comfortable tossing out the insult. She could sense him staring at her. But she wouldn't meet his gaze. A wave of nausea swept through her as a too-familiar panic made her face and ears burn.

"I must go," she said in English, turning away from him and praying she could escape before she screamed, or cried, or did something equally bizarre like jump into his strong-looking arms.

"Wait, *Fraulein* Nagel," he said, making her stop, close her eyes, soothed by the sweet sound of her native tongue, albeit in a countrified Bavarian-style accent. But she unstuck her feet and stomped away, afraid of the force of her own bizarre reaction to Ross Hoffman. Not to mention the even more bizarre way he seemed to fit into Austin and Evelyn's lives.

Chapter Ten

"Hey, um, Evelyn," Ross stood outside her room clutching the bag that the strange woman had thrust into his hands before running off in the other direction as if he'd bite. He paused to contemplate her—the brewer chick Fitzgerald had just hired and who had thought quickly enough to save Rose's life the day before.

"What?" Evelyn's voice jolted him back to reality.

"I brought you some fresh clothes."

He stuck his hand inside the door, since he'd not been invited in and wasn't sure he wanted to be anyway since he could hear the whirr and clunk of the medieval-looking machine that had been milking Evelyn like a Guernsey cow every three hours for the last twenty-four. She snatched it from him without a word.

"How in the world did you know to pack this stuff? There's a nursing bra in here and my comfiest pair of jeans."

Ross pressed his forehead against the door wishing he could kiss her, wishing he could hold the baby. Wishing he could leave and never come back.

"I didn't do it," he admitted on the other side of the curtain as if reading her mind. "That chick, that, um woman, Elisa, I drove her to your house and she packed everything."

"Okay." After a few muffled shuffling noises, she opened the door. She seemed rung out, pummeled by fear, worry, exhaustion. And she was still the most beautiful woman he'd ever seen. She tugged her hair back and into a ponytail with the band she kept on her wrist as he watched, hands clenched at his sides. Finally, she fell into him, forcing him to put his arms around her. "Rose. She's…still all right?"

she said into his chest.

"Yeah." He disentangled from her, and ran a hand down his face then around his bearded jaw. "Austin won't let go of her. They tried to give her a bottle but she wouldn't take it. Her fever spiked again then came back down. I don't know. Shit."

She smiled at him. "You're…different somehow," she said.

"I guess. I lost some weight. I run a lot now."

"Come on. Let's go see her."

He hesitated. "Oh, I don't know. They won't let me."

"They will," she said, tucking her hand into the crook of his elbow. He flinched. "Relax."

He sighed. "I can't. This is…too much."

"This is parenthood. Or so I'm told. Let's go." She tugged at him and they headed down the hall back toward the isolation unit.

* * * *

Evelyn sighed and stretched her arms over her head. The action lifted her blouse, exposing a sliver of the soft flesh of her stomach above the waist of her jeans. Ross averted his gaze, focusing instead on his baby's face.

He had a flight out later that afternoon. Claimed that he needed to leave, to get back to work, but kept putting off the trip to the airport. Surprisingly content to be here, in Austin and Evelyn's house, holding the kid and watching them putter around doing married couple things. Rose made a funny bleating noise and bopped him on the nose with her tiny fist before turning her face toward his chest.

"Give me the baby back," Evelyn demanded as she unbuttoned her shirt. "Time for dinner."

Ross placed the cooing, gurgling infant in her arms. As soon as she sensed her food source near, she turned her head toward Evelyn's breast, opening and closing her mouth. "Greedy little thing, isn't she?" Ross sat on the edge of the bed, watching with wide eyes as Evelyn opened her nursing bra. She didn't have to brush her nipple against Rose's cheek anymore. The girl knew exactly what to do. She latched on hard, making Evelyn wince and motion for something on the bedside table.

Ross couldn't tear his eyes from his nursing child. Austin cleared his throat. Ross looked up. "Oh, uh, what?"

"Hand her the water. Nursing makes her instantly thirsty."

"Oh yeah, sorry." He handed over the water bottle and she drained half of it in one gulp.

"Thanks," she said, closing her eyes.

"So," Austin said in a firm tone. "We need to get you to the airport, I guess."

"Yes, we do," Ross admitted. Evelyn stared at him as he got up from the side of the bed. He opened his mouth to say something crazy like "okay, let's make this work because I miss all of you, especially that baby, and I want to hold her, and I want to make love to Evelyn and I don't care if I am a third wheel."

But Austin cleared his throat, making Ross turn and meet his friend's eyes. The harsh reality rushed back in, reminding him that he didn't want this. He wanted Evelyn to himself but he'd been the one to push her back to Austin. This was how it was meant to be.

"Time to go," he said, his voice rough as he pushed past his friend and headed downstairs.

Their ride to the airport was made in the same tense silence as their ride to the hospital a few days prior. Ross tapped his fingers on his knees, nerves snapping with stress. When Austin's Bluetooth phone rang through the interior of the SUV, he jumped and cursed. "It's just Evelyn," Austin said. "Hang on a sec."

"Yeah, honey, what's up?"

"Oh hell, Austin, is he dropped off yet?"

"No, I'm still here. But don't worry. We're only about five minutes from the airport," Ross cut in.

"Don't be an ass, Hoffman. There's an emergency. At the brewery."

Ross sensed Austin stiffen. He leaned forward and spoke first. "What's wrong, Evelyn? Do I need to stay?"

Please say yes. Please say yes. Please say…

"No, I'll manage it," Austin insisted. "Fill me in."

"It's Bryan. He fell off a ladder. Hit his damn head. Knocked himself out. Elle got him into an ambulance. She's on the other line."

"Elle…" Ross said, staring out of the windshield and recalling his two weird encounters with her.

"Yes, so…I guess you should check in on him, on your way back."

"Okay, but…"

"Elle says she's got a handle on the week's schedule. But we may need to bring back some of those temps we hired last fall, to help manage storage and bottling."

"Fine," Austin said, pulling up the departures gate and putting the car in park. "Hang on a second, honey. Ross is getting out of the car."

"Oh, okay. Bye," she said, sounding about as far away as he felt right then.

He got out, grabbed his backpack from the seat behind him and slammed the door without saying a word to either of them.

Chapter Eleven

"You know," Brock said the next Monday as he leaned on one of the giant fermentation vessels next to the computer where she was working, "you are really something else."

"Oh?" She kept entering the data, trying to block the intense glare of his gaze from her mind. Brock Fitzgerald was not a bad-looking man—quite the opposite of that. He and Austin were a matched pair of tall, dark and handsome. But he was making her nervous with his attentions. She had spent over ten years not dating anyone, not getting close to anyone, and she wasn't about to start now.

"Yeah," he said. "Even though you're a real pro at ignoring me."

She sighed. "I'm sorry, Brock. I'm just not interested...in dating. It's not you, all right?"

His eyes seemed to gleam with understanding. "Oh, I see. I'm not your type."

"No, actually, you would have been, once upon a time." She closed the four files from the day's brews and picked them up, clutching them close, like armor. "But I'm sorry. I just don't...date anymore."

"But..."

She held up a hand. "I don't want you to get the wrong idea. I really like working here."

He frowned, which made him resemble his brother even more. She sometimes forgot they were twins. Brock was light-hearted, always quick with a joke, or a compliment, easy-going in a way that his brother was not.

Not that Austin wasn't nice. He was. And he was devoted to his wife and daughter with the same fierce energy he gave to his company. But it was obvious which of the two was the more serious.

"Until Bryan can return, I'm doing two jobs. And I'm exhausted. If you'll please excuse me." She grabbed the computer tablet and took an obvious step away from him.

He grinned and held up both hands. "All right, all right, message received. Sorry. But I'm around, if you need a friend."

She studied him for a few seconds. He was almost painfully attractive and he knew it. He flirted relentlessly with every woman in the building, old and young, married or single. But he was always the first to jump in and help with any task no matter how challenging or menial. And he had become the unofficial organizer of company parties — going away, retirement, engagement, bachelor parties for one of the bar staff. He was a giver and shared that trait with his Austin.

She smiled, hoping to soften the disappointing news she'd given him. "I will keep that in mind, Brock. Thank you." She ducked between fermenters, her face hot and her mind ablaze with something she had not been able to shake for a couple of months.

The memory of Ross Hoffman — his face, his bright blue eyes, his deep voice when he'd spoken to her *auf Deutsch*, his strangely comforting presence — permeated her world both awake and asleep. It was, in a word, maddening. He was, by all accounts, the epitome of a prima donna master brewer — cocky, arrogant — exactly the type of man she should avoid at all costs.

She had her usual end-of-day report to give Evelyn but had managed to stay a solid forty-five minutes ahead of schedule since coming in early so she decided to take a quick shower and change first.

One of her favorite things about Fitzgerald Brewing was the attention paid to detail on every level. Their dedication to hiring and retaining the best employees was part of that. Evelyn had told her about the seventy-thousand-dollar renovation of the locker and shower rooms she'd insisted upon, and the giant fight she and Austin had experienced over it. But she'd held her ground and so the women's locker room was more like a haven—with soft seating, a television, huge locker spaces, private showers worthy of the nicest spa, the works.

Elle had spent many an hour there, napping on the couches between her long shifts during Bryan's convalescence, having her lunch in blessed, private silence or, as she planned to do now, taking a long hot shower. Intent on this goal, she barely noticed the clump of men hovering around outside the men's locker room. She brushed past them, mumbling apologies. When someone dug their fingertips into her biceps and held her in place, she cursed, and on reflex, stamped down on his foot with her steel-toed boot.

"Ow. Fucking cunt."

She yanked out of his grasp and rubbed her upper arm, her pulse racing at the sight of them—all temporary employees, hired to help keep up production post-head-brewer accident. She'd mostly ignored them, other than to give out the day's assignments as they straggled in to their shifts. But she'd been hard-pressed to ignore one of them, their ringleader, Tim Harris.

He'd been at her from the moment he set foot in the brewery, about two weeks ago. His flirtatiousness was of the aggressive sort—fake lighthearted nonsense about her hair, her tatts, her piercings, that had morphed into the sort of threatening throw-away comments to his minions that might have made other women shake in fear. What this Tim didn't realize was that she knew him for what he was—a spineless bully. She'd faced much, much worse than him. He didn't intimidate her in the slightest, even if he irritated her to no end.

But until now, his pseudo-aggressiveness had only involved words she could ignore. He'd never actually touched her. She stared into his small, dark eyes for as a long as her psyche would allow her to before letting her gaze flick away. As was typical, he'd surrounded himself with his buddies, which she knew gave him a modicum of imagined power over her.

As if to prove this, he moved quickly, standing toe-to-toe, and towering over her. Something most men did, considering, and even at five foot maybe eight inches, he could do a reasonable impression of a tough guy.

"So, little darlin'," he said, daring to put his fingertip to her face before she flinched away from him only to back into a wall formed by his asshole friends. "Thought you might want to know that things are going to change around here, real soon. You might reconsider all your nasty insults and rejections."

"Get out of my way, *arschgeige*," she spat out. When hands gripped both her biceps from behind, Elle sensed the hallway, usually so brightly lit, day and night, dim around the edges. Fear nestled in her chest. It was late in the afternoon. Shift change had occurred and everyone was well occupied, or they'd left for the day. She was alone.

She set her jaw and squirmed but the hands merely tightened around her upper arms. Tim grinned. She smelled his disgusting breath and his foul body odor all at once. "All this ink," the man said, in his somewhat squeaky voice. His finger traced the horror tattoo around her neck. She shivered and had to bite back the urge to throw up. "All this jewelry." He touched her ears, her nose, then yanked open her mouth and leered at the metal ball in her tongue. "I've always wanted a pretty little spinner," he said, confusing her for a moment until she did the translation in her head.

"Fuck you." She spat a glob of saliva at him. It hit his cheek right below his eye and slid down. His dark eyes narrowed even further.

"Oh, I am going to do that, and then some, darlin'," he said, taking her hand and pressing it on his zipper.

She squirmed away, but not before she felt his erection. A small one, she thought, wishing she had the guts to toss that fact at him. But accepting that her position didn't warrant such stupidity.

"First," he said, leaning in close and licking her lips. She spluttered and gagged. "First, we have to take care of a few other pieces of business. I'll be back for you and your sweet ass though. That's a promise."

The hands released her. One of them pushed her forward so hard she dropped to her hands and knees. Memories rushed in as she stared down at the boots of her tormenter. A hand landed on her hair. "I'm gonna have to shave this crap off though. No woman of mine is gonna wear this hippie shit." He pulled it hard enough to make her gasp.

Then, he was gone, along with his backup singers. She took a deep breath then dropped onto her butt and leaned against the wall. This sudden ramp-up of aggression would have to be reported. If not for her safety, for everyone's. She was still half-irritated, half-nervous by his no-doubt idle threats and knew reporting him was the right thing to do, but something held her back.

She got up slowly, rubbing her arms. When she lifted the sleeves of her T-shirt and discovered the fingertip shaped marks which would quickly bruise, fury filled her head, throat and chest. This would not stand. She had to say something about these assholes. And she would do exactly that, today, when she met Evelyn.

She ducked into the women's room, hoping she had time to shower off his stink. After sitting for a few minutes and letting her pulse rate return to normal, she reached into the far recesses of her locker and pulled out the handgun. It was one of the first things she had purchased, after moving back to the US and beginning her brewery studies in Oregon. As a naturalized American citizen, it had taken her a bit longer to get the carry permit, but she'd been patient. In the interim, she'd gone to the gun club and learned how to use such a thing properly.

The dark metal Glock 42 had been an expensive option but worth it. She kept it with her at all times, knowing that when the actual time came to use it—when He found her and tried to drag her back to the so-called life he'd trapped her in before—she'd be able to look Him in the eyes, right before she put a hole between them.

The gun itself didn't intimidate her. The need for it had at first. But now, it soothed her. She kept it scrupulously clean and loaded. It was her little, lethal secret. With a smile, she put it back, got her towel, and headed for the shower.

Chapter Twelve

"What kind of adjustments?" Elle asked Evelyn as they looked over the current week's production schedule.

"We don't have the capacity right now to cover all the current accounts" — Evelyn gestured to the reports — "and send beer overseas. So, we need to cut some of the low-lying fruit. Some of these smaller retailers, maybe some big ones. I've got Brock working on making that call. But I wanted you to know."

"I didn't realize you were planning on exporting," Elle said.

Evelyn heaved a sigh and stood up, rubbing the small of her back. "We have to, I'm afraid. Our sales are slumping and not because Fitzgerald products are bad. Because everybody and their god damned uncle's hound dog thinks they can open and run a brewery. Hence, competition. Most of it crappy. But it confuses the consumer. Makes it hard to break through the clutter, even for an established brand like ours."

Elle frowned. "A dog could open a brewery?"

"Oh, no, sorry. A figure of speech. And a dumb one. What I mean is that everyone thinks that opening a running a brewery is easy, glamorous, around the clock drinking and fun. And while some of them figure out pretty quickly that it's not, enough of them stick around to make it harder and harder for us to keep our loyal customers."

"Well, you and Austin do make it look easy."

Evelyn scoffed.

"But I understand what you mean. When does the first batch get shipped and where is it going?"

"In three months, if we can manage it. Italy, Spain and England."

Elle whistled and made a bunch of quick calculations in her head. The challenge of it excited her, but she understood what it meant for her, as temporary head brewer, and her already overtaxed staff.

Evelyn dropped into the seat across from her at the large work table. "Elle, Austin and I want to offer you the head brewer's job."

Elle froze. Every inch of her skin prickled. Even as her mind shot back to the scary encounter with the *schlappschwanz* in the hallway earlier, she was thrilled. Even as she also knew that she couldn't take the job. It wouldn't be fair to Evelyn and Austin. Because as soon as she got things rolling and settled here, she'd have to leave again.

"I'm…"

"Holy shit," Evelyn blurted out, her eyes wide as she gazed out of the large window down onto the brewery floor.

"What is it?" Elle ran to her side.

She stared, shocked and not quite willing to accept what she was seeing. The brewery floor seemed to move and shimmer as dark liquid poured out from beneath one of their larger fermentation vessels. It was flooding the place with expensive bought and paid for ingredients. It smelled like the chocolate stout. She automatically calculated the malt bill, the hops used, the time spent.

While accidents did happen—a brewery was a factory, one filled with chemicals and other hazards—Fitzgerald had been free of them for years. And now…two of them, back to back like this? Trying hard not to feel paranoid, Elle headed for the door.

"I'm coming with you," Evelyn said.

"Change those." Elle pointed at her boss's high heels. Evelyn nodded, slipped her feet out of the dress shoes and shoved them into a pair of rubber boots she kept by the office door.

By the time they made it down to the main floor, it was clear that the entire fermenter had already emptied itself somehow. Brewers and other staff stood around looking pained as the floor drains did their job, collecting and disposing of fifteen hundred barrels—almost forty-six thousand gallons—of rich, delicious-smelling, carefully crafted beer.

Face similarly drained of color, Evelyn put a hand to her mouth. "What in the hell happened?"

Elle dived under the tank, even as the mostly fermented wort splashed into her eyes. After fiddling around with the connections at the base of the vessel, she found something strange. Giving it a few hard yanks, she stood up, wiping the sticky liquid off her face. "It is sabotage, Evelyn. I am sorry to say."

"Sabotage? What do you mean?"

"Someone rigged the valve to give way. I know this manufacturer and it will not have this sort of failure. Not without human intervention."

"Another accident?" someone muttered behind Evelyn. "Funny, how it all happens now, after our new hire."

Evelyn turned to face the staff. Elle noted that they all met her gaze, not giving away who'd spoken.

"What the ever-loving fuck?" Austin's voice made everyone turn. He ran down the ramp from the warehouse, glaring around at the mess. "Who...what...how...?"

"Sabotage, the new girl says," that same voice said.

Evelyn glared at the young man who'd spoken. But Elle already knew that voice. She stared right at him, surprising herself with her boldness. Tim Harris crossed his arms and glared back at her.

Austin had already crawled under the tank by the time Elle broke the stare-down. He emerged as Evelyn shooed the peanut gallery away and grabbed a squeegee to help guide the remaining sticky remnants of the huge batch into the drains. He leaned against the sink, staring down at the cotter pin Elle had found.

"Well," Evelyn insisted. "Tell me now so I can get the insurance report going."

"I am so sorry," Elle said. "I don't know why someone would do such a thing."

Austin glanced over at her and sighed. He held up the object, which looked like a giant, industrial strength paperclip. "Someone put this damn thing in the valve, all right. Shit." His shoulders slumped. "Someone who knew exactly what they were doing." He turned the pin over in his hand. "It's designed to open up, after being inserted, and it did, which broke the seal. Pressure took care of the rest."

"I've been watching closely and...well...I'm fairly certain I know who it was," Elle said. "I think it might be a guy named Tim."

Austin glanced over at her. "No offense, but he's not smart enough to know how to do this."

"You'd be surprised what you can learn how to do on the Internet." She met Austin's gaze as long as she could manage before focusing down at the tools now in her hands.

"Why do you think that, Elle?" Evelyn asked with a frown.

Elle felt a tremor of panic. All this crap had befallen Fitzgerald since her arrival without a doubt. She hoped the brewery's owners knew it was all coincidence.

"I'd rather not say here."

She caught a glance between Austin and Evelyn. Then he shrugged, and handed over the tiny piece of metal that had cost them something like seventy-five grand in wasted ingredients and lost revenue in an eye blink. "I have a phone conference with the export people in ten," he said, wearily running a hand down his face. "I gotta get back to my office. Can you guys handle this?"

"Sure," Evelyn said, tucking the evidence of sabotage into her jacket pocket. "Elle, let's meet upstairs."

"I need to finish cleaning first, if that's all right."

"We have people for that."

Elle caught the edge of irritation in the woman's voice.

Understandable, but it unnerved her. "I know, but I need to make sure I'm correct about this whole thing. I want a bit more time with this." She put a hand on the offending stainless steel tank. "Before anyone else touches it."

Evelyn blew out a breath, and glanced at her watch. "I have another meeting, too. Can we have this discussion later? Over a beer?"

Elle felt her face flush.

Don't get attached. Don't be social. Not even with your boss. Not even if you think you'd like to have her as a friend.

"You all right?" Evelyn reached out, but Elle recoiled, as if Evelyn's touch would burn her skin.

Stop acting strange. This woman would be well within her rights and sanity to fire you.

But at the moment, she wanted to check one more thing, and needed to get into the men's locker room to do it.

"Yes," she said, as she pulled a set of Allen wrenches from her tool kit. "I will meet you for a beer and give my theory about Tim." Her manner was oddly formal, but then again, it always had been. "Evelyn, I am very sorry for this."

"It's not your fault," the woman insisted but Elle heard the tremor of uncertainty behind her words. "Six-thirty, then. We'll grab beers and talk."

* * * *

At six-thirty on the nose, Elle knocked on Evelyn's closed office door.

"Come on in. As long as you don't mind watching me nurse once Austin brings Rose up here."

"Of course not. It's the most natural act in the universe. I don't know why people get so…how do you say? Hung up? Hung up on it."

"Yeah, I know. So, tell me, what's going on with that Tim guy?"

"Well…" Elle's heart pounded faster, her mouth was dried out from stress. She'd found the pack of similar pins in Tim's locker, after picking his too-easy combination lock. She'd had on a pair of latex gloves but something told her not to touch them—to leave them for the authorities to find. "I really hate feeling like the snatch."

"I think you mean, 'the snitch'."

"Yes. Like a gossip…a *tratschtante*? I'm sorry. My English…"

"Don't worry. You're not a snitch, and your English is fine. I trust you, Elle. It may be strange to say it, but I think I trust you more than almost anyone here that I'm not married or related to in some way."

Elle translated this in her head, feeling relieved once she sorted through the strange turns of phrase. "Thank you. You make me feel very…trusted. Although, I'm afraid I have disappointed one of the people you are related to here."

"Huh? Oh, Brock. Right. Yes, he's used to getting his own way with the ladies. You're providing him with quite the challenge."

Elle rubbed one arm, wincing when she hit the sore places on her biceps. She glanced around the room, uncomfortable all of a sudden in a way she never had been with Evelyn. "I have told him in no uncertain terms that I am not being flirtatious with him. He doesn't seem to get my message."

"Is he really bothering you?" Evelyn kept her voice level, but Elle knew that the last thing she needed was a sexual harassment suit against her brother-in-law to go with all her other headaches.

"It is nothing I cannot handle," Elle insisted. "However, I don't want him to consider me a challenge. I would prefer it if he'd consider me…not anything more than a fellow brewery employee?"

Evelyn opened her mouth to respond but Austin walked in, carrying Rose's car seat and diaper bag. "Get her over here, quick," Evelyn said, as she fumbled with her blouse buttons. Austin picked up the mewling bundle, handed her over and passed his wife a water bottle. "Sorry, Elle. Just give me a minute?"

"Of course. I can come back."

"No, no. Please stay. Oh, ouch, kid! Ah, that's it." She sighed and leaned her head back. Elle watched as that new, strange combination of admiration and jealousy combined in her brain, swirling around like a dark fog.

"Thanks for handling everything today, Elle," Austin said. "I have to head out to cover a beer dinner but I'm sure Evelyn will fill me in on whatever's going on with Tim."

Elle looked at him, then dropped her gaze immediately, unnerved by his intense stare. She knew this tic of hers was weird. But it was a hard habit to break. She'd made some headway in her previous jobs, but some men triggered this knee-jerk response from her. Embarrassing, but it was done now. When she snuck a glance at Evelyn, the woman was watching her closely, her expression between neutral and curious.

Austin cleared his throat, breaking the awkward moment, leaned over to kiss Evelyn's cheek, then Rose's. The baby let go of her mother's breast and gurgled in delight, her small hands waving at her father.

"You're a goner, daddy," Evelyn said, leaning into Austin.

"Yep. She's got me totally wrapped." He smiled at Elle then ducked out of the office door.

"You are a lucky woman, Evelyn," Elle said.

Evelyn glanced over at her. "Yes. I am," she agreed. "But it's not all sunshine and roses, you know."

"Oh, I'm sure," she said, without much conviction. "Men after all, are the more annoying sex. But the child, she's recovered from her flu?"

"Yes. And thank God you were here that day. I don't know what I would've done. I was such a basket case."

"Nonsense. You would have been fine. May I?" She held out her arms.

"Yes, without a doubt," Evelyn said, handing over the sated baby. Rose smiled up at her and Elle crooned in German before draping her over her knees. Then she patted and rubbed her back a few seconds before Rose let out a monstrous belch. Both women chuckled.

"Watch out," Evelyn warned as she laid out a blanket on the big work table. "She usually follows that with a helping of recycled milk."

"Ah, I don't think so," Elle said, leaving the girl on her belly another minute or so before picking her up and rubbing noses with her. "If you let her stomach rest this way," she said, before she brought the girl over for her change. "It's easier on her system." She put the giggling, fist waving child down on the table. "See? No spit up."

"I do see," Evelyn said, as she made short work of the diaper change. "You're an amazing woman, Elisa." She handed the girl to Elle, then she tidied up, repacked the diaper bag and tied the dirty nappy up in a plastic bag to take out to the dumpster.

"I used to be," Elle said, her eyes fixed on Rose's. "I've always loved babies."

"Well, I'm sure you'll have one of your own, someday." Evelyn settled Rose in her seat, pressing her lips to the girl's sweet-smelling forehead as her eyes closed and a spit bubble formed between her full lips. "Let's head downstairs and have a beer. I hear the oatmeal stout's back on tap."

The stout was Evelyn's favorite but the last batch had been less than up to standard, if one listened to the many beer blogger gossips. Elle's first task had been to remedy the problem. She had, and then some, according to the same evil-but-necessary hacks. Elle was eager to taste the first batch of beer she'd ever crafted at Fitzgerald, but at the same time the thought of sharing a social hour with Evelyn was making her ears burn with anxiety, even as she was grateful that the conversational turn regarding babies of her own had come to a dead end.

Chapter Thirteen

"Wow," Evelyn said, licking her lips after her first taste of the deep brown ale. "That is better than ever. Well done, you." She lifted the glass across the table. Elle touched hers to it and they sipped again.

"Thank you," she said, keeping her eyes trained down at the table's scarred top. When three brewery employees appeared at their table, Elle went on high alert, knowing without even looking that one of them was Tim. Evelyn kept her face neutral.

"Can I help you?"

"We'd like to speak with you, Miz Fitzgerald—in private. As soon as possible."

Elle studied his acne-scarred, thin-lipped face while Evelyn made him wait a few seconds for a response. He met Evelyn's glare with one Elle didn't care much for. It made her simultaneously incensed and nervous. It was a sensation she hadn't experienced in a while and certainly not at any of her previous brewery jobs.

Men like this were one hundred percent intimidated by both her and Evelyn. She knew damn good and well that her own talent at brewing pissed him off but he was obviously resentful of Evelyn, too, if his ugly stare was any indication. Being a bully in his shriveled soul, he was eager to show off how tough and bossy he was in front of his buddies. Even knowing that, Elle was shocked by his blatantly nasty attitude, considering who he was glaring at.

Elle's sense of indignation grew. But she tamped it down, reminding herself that spouting off to this hopped-up little jerk would not be a great way to behave in front of customers and her boss.

"Tell you what…Tim, is it?" Evelyn's voice was flat. "Yes. Tim. Stop by Alice's desk tomorrow and make an appointment. She has the best grasp on my schedule. Now, if you'll excuse us?"

We must resume our she-woman, man-hating club meeting, Elle finished in her head on his behalf.

The other two men began backing away at the obvious dismissal but Tim, the jerk-face, stood his ground. His lips got even thinner as he pressed them together. "I said," he began, before clearing his throat and perhaps reconsidering his phrasing. "I mean, I would like it if we could talk now."

"I have a previous engagement," Evelyn said in a stern tone.

The man's dark gaze darted to Elle, then to the half-finished beers between them. "Fine," he said, jamming his sweat-stained hat back down on his head. Evelyn raised an eyebrow at this but he didn't flinch. The man was really pushing his luck, Elle thought, as the sick memory of his disgusting tongue against her lips bowled her over. A flicker of worry on behalf of her boss hit her brain.

"Beat it, already," a female voice called out, breaking their stare down. "You heard the lady." Melody Rodriguez, manager of the Fitz Pub, now stood across from the fuming Tim, arms crossed, her eyes flashing. "I warned you before. No harassing the customers, much less your boss." The woman kept her voice light, as if she were kidding, but Elle knew better.

She watched as Tim's dark eyes flickered down to Melody's impressive cleavage, then back up to her face. Typical, she thought, wondering how in the hell Evelyn had managed to hire such a person. He blew out a breath, turned and walked away, followed closely by his two minions.

"Jesus, that guy," Melody said, smiling at the baby. "If anybody could use a good firing, he could."

"Easier said than done, as you well know," Evelyn said, finishing her beer.

"You ladies want dinner? The soup today is *delicioso*. If I do say so myself."

"Your corn chowder? Sign me up. And I'll take a grilled cheese to go with it. Elle?"

"I'm sorry," Elle said, scooting out from behind the table. "I should go." She wanted to follow Tim and his gang, to make sure they actually left the building.

"Wait," Evelyn said. "Hang on a minute." The honest concern on the woman's face made tears spring to Elle's eyes.

Elle gnawed her lower lip and looked from her boss to Melody and back down at the floor. "Evelyn, I am very sorry. I apparently…have also caused some sort of confusion with that…with Tim as well."

"Confusion?"

Melody's dark eyes narrowed. Elle knew from hearing Evelyn talk about her that Melody possessed an innate desire to help others, to listen and fix things. She was the first to take in stray souls. Evelyn was always finding new employees at the Fitz Pub. People Melody claimed just needed a break to get their lives back in order. She'd hired at least half a dozen super loyal employees that way, so Evelyn and Austin left her to it.

"He is…persistent, as well."

"Persistent," Evelyn repeated. "He's…bothering you too? Like Brock?"

"No, no, not like that. Brock is very sweet about it. Non-threatening. Tim is the opposite of that. He's very much not happy with my unwillingness to join him for a beer or a blow job, which was his last invitation—in the hallway, in front of his friends."

Evelyn's mouth dropped open. She glanced at Melody. "You mean he—?"

"He's a bully. But I'm used to men like this. I can handle it. You shouldn't have to worry about—"

"Like hell," Evelyn blurted out. "Holy shit. He's threatened you? I mean…he's…dear Lord. Elle, you don't have to put up with that sort of behavior. I won't allow it. Neither will Austin."

"I am a shit-face magnet, it would seem. I mean, Brock is not a shit-face. He's just a flirt." Elle touched her neck on reflex, knowing she did it to remind herself of her earlier folly. Evelyn frowned at her. "I'm sorry. My English is sometimes not good."

"So, my dear, what can I get for you to eat?" Melody interrupted.

"I'm all right," Elle insisted.

"Listen, I realize you're entitled to a private life and all that, but I'm going to have to insist that you spill it for me a little." Evelyn rocked the seat when baby Rose bleated out an unhappy noise. "You saved my daughter's life. I think we can consider ourselves friends." She glanced over at Melody who was still hovering, eager to placate the general unhappiness with some of her amazing food. "Let chef fix a grilled cheese for you? His are something akin to a miracle."

"Yes, all right." Elle slid back into her seat. "Thank you."

Evelyn reached across the table and grabbed Elle's hands, startling her so much she flinched. "I want you to think of me as your friend right now. Not your boss. Not married to the brewery founder. None of that. Just Evelyn. I'll listen, and when I'm done listening you're going to file a harassment report against Tim, and tomorrow I will fire his sorry ass."

"I have a difficult time…trusting people. I've been betrayed too many times."

"See? Your first confession to me. I think we're on a roll now." She glanced at Melody. Elle was suffused with a sense of relief she'd not felt in over a decade. "Two grilled cheese, two bowls of corn chowder, and two more beers, please, ma'am," Evelyn said, giving Elle that small jolt of jealousy at her seeming ease with everything around her.

"You got it, *chica*," Melody said, snapping her fingers. "On the double."

"Now," Evelyn said, giving Elle's hands one last squeeze

before letting her go. "Start anywhere. I am all ears."

Elle swiped at her eyes, offered a wan smile, and thought, *Why the hell not?*

* * * *

Three hours later, Elle sat in the dark locker room, clutching her aching head and poring over the myriad reasons why she should not have said so much, revealed so much about her God-awful past. As if needing to touch it to reassure herself of the strict control she'd established — over her own life, if nothing else — she reached into her locker and pulled out the handgun. It felt ice cold, which was strange. Usually it felt, if not warm, at least room temperature. She set it down, uncomfortable with it for the first time since she'd purchased it — un-reassured, un-soothed, unhappy at its existence.

Exhausted, knowing she should go home and at least try to sleep, Elle pulled her legs up to her chest and gripped them closely, face pressed to her knees. She kept the gun on the bench beside her, free of its hiding place. She shifted her hips so the vertical metal bar she'd had pierced into her clitoral hood pressed into her. It felt nice, which made her feel guilty. Which was precisely the point of the damn thing.

The long talk with Evelyn had left her cored out, emptied of everything, a limp rag. Even though she'd left out most of the worst details, things she'd probably never tell another living soul they were so horrifying and embarrassing. How could she have allowed such a thing? She knew that's what Evelyn wanted to ask.

And she had no answer, other than to say, "I'm here now. That's all I've got."

To her credit, Evelyn never did ask. But her eyes had filled with tears more than once. Elle had stared down at her soup, unable to eat a bite as she recited the bare bones of her history to this woman, the only woman she'd ever felt truly comfortable with, for reasons she couldn't explain to herself.

Afterward, they'd gone up to Evelyn's office where she'd made her official sexual harassment complaint against Tim and his four buddies. "Okay, that will take care of him," Evelyn said with grim smile as she printed it, gave Elle a copy and assured her that without a doubt, she would never have to deal with Tim again. He'd be long gone tomorrow.

She closed her eyes, but that only made things worse as the voices — His voice and her own, inner, nagging conscience — ramped up, filling her brain with their useless noise.

"No, that's you, love. You're the useless one. Useless to anyone but me. I'm the only one who will ever give a shit about you. Don't ever forget it," He said for the thousandth time.

"Elle…honey. Get up. Grab the gun. Go upstairs. Do it now. Hurry."

With a gasp, she jumped up, not sure why her Oma's voice was demanding she do such a crazy thing. She reached for the gun but her hand shook so much she dropped it to the sealed concrete floor.

"Calm down, girl," she said under her breath in German. "Chill out," she added for good measure in English.

She reached down and pulled the Glock from under the bench, flicked off the safety, and took a long, deep breath. Then she heard it — a loud shout, coming from somewhere above where she now stood. It was followed by a thump, as if someone had dropped something heavy. She walked out of the locker room, feeling like the world's biggest fool, clutching the gun as if she knew what she was doing.

The brewery space was a cacophony of noise — the bottling line was running, and the clatter, hum and buzz of that operation filled the air, along with blaring, heavy metal rock and shouts of the staff. She hesitated, knowing she had to sneak around behind the main bottling machine with the weapon in her hand.

Gnawing at her lip, questioning her sanity once more, she

flicked on the safety and stuck the thing in her front jeans pocket. It stuck out so obviously, she pulled it out. Deciding to copy what she'd seen on television, she stuck in the waistband of her jeans at the small of her back. Sweating like mad, she nodded at the various workers who called out to her, asking her what in the hell she was still doing hanging around after her long work day.

Finally, after what felt like an hour's worth of traversing the few feet between the back hall and the metal stairs up to the Evelyn's office, she put her foot on the first step. Hesitating, talking herself out of it even as she moved to take the second step, the distinct sound of a woman's scream hit her ears, even over the chaos of the bottling line and music. Someone else behind her shouted but she blocked everything as she took the steps two at a time, yanking the gun from the back of her jeans, praying she wouldn't blow a hole in her own arse as she tried to pull it free.

The office door was open, the knob seemingly stuck in the wall behind it. Elle skidded to a stop, trying to sort through what her eyes took in.

Rose, screaming like a banshee from her baby seat on the large work table.

Evelyn, screaming even louder as she flailed around on the table.

And Tim, holding Evelyn down with one hand.

Elle blinked once, then raised the Glock. She aimed carefully, as she'd been taught for all the months she'd waited for the United States government to give her permission to purchase it.

The noise from downstairs muffled almost everything. But the single gunshot that sent Tim Harris to Hell would echo in her ears for years.

Chapter Fourteen

"Hoffman!"

Ross winced at the way his name bounced around the huge room full of stainless steel. But he was pleased to note that no one looked up at the sound of it. He had the staff well-trained, Brad Jefferson did. He was eighty percent bluster, fifteen percent bullshit and five percent businessman. He'd lucked into the craft beer business by being at the right place with a giant trust fund, not too far off Austin's story, really. Big difference being Jefferson was a shitty brewer while Austin was pretty good. Not as good as Ross of course, but not many people were.

He grinned at himself in the spotless surface of the giant kettle where thousands of gallons of Brad's Finest IPA were brewing away under his watchful eye. Since returning to Colorado after Rose's flu scare he'd jumped right back into his austerity measures — work, workout, sleep.

No women. No partying. No sex.

He'd toned up his body even more and had never felt better, except for the 'no sex' thing. He was pretty certain that he wasn't wired for that particular life choice. But his options remained scarce since he didn't put himself in a position to pick up women anymore, other than the ones constantly eyeballing him at the gym. So, he was going with it, channeling his pent-up energy into lifting more weights, running more miles. Hell, he'd even started reading books again.

"God damn it, Hoffman I know you can hear me."

Ross began whistling as he waited for the monitor to flash so he could add the final ingredients to the boil. He really hated this hands-off, computerized brewing. But when dealing with batches as large as these, it was the only way.

Brad ran up to him, breathing heavily.

"You ought to lay off the beer cheese, dude," Ross said as he shoved past the man to grab the dried moss, the ingredient that kept the wort from boiling over. As he shook the carefully measured grayish powder into the recesses of the kettle, he kept his eyes on the dark swirl of almost-beer in the tank below him. Brad waited, knowing that Ross wouldn't pay a lick of attention to him while he was working on a batch of their best-selling brew.

"Now," Ross said, as he tossed the pail into the large sink next to the brew house. "What can I do for you, Bradley?"

The man's face was bright red around his brewer-hipster, carefully trimmed beard. His eyes blazed with fury. Ross raised an eyebrow, wondering what in the world would have gotten the guy so worked up.

"What did you do?" his bossed half-whispered to him.

"Not sure, other than brew yet more of this super boring, very average IPA."

"God damn it. I mean to *her*."

"To...whom?"

But he thought he knew who. And, as it turned out, he was correct.

"Holly. She just dumped me."

"Oh, I'm sorry." Ross patted the man's thick shoulder. "Want to sit and eat a pint of ice cream together?"

"Fuck you, Hoffman. I know it's your fault."

"Hardly," Ross said, as he pecked out a few commands on the keyboard, setting the concoction's temperature for the next couple of hours. The brief memory of Holly's hot ass, tits, and mouth made a shiver run down his spine. But he clenched his jaw and forced himself to turn back to his boss. "I mean, I haven't talked to her or seen her or anything since I got back from Michigan. Scout's honor."

"Your honor isn't worth shit to me. I know it's you. She told me."

"Well, she lied. Big surprise there, eh, champ?"

"No, I think you're lying."

Ross felt a meaty hand clamp his left biceps. He glared down at it, then over at Brad's flushed face.

"You're a lying, cheating, woman-stealing shithead," Brad declared, his face beet red.

"Once upon a time, perhaps," Ross said, peeling the man's fingers off his arm before he lost his cool and did something even stupider than he'd done so far in this job. "But you'll have to find someone else to blame this time, I'm afraid. Or you could blame your fat, lazy, self."

"You...are..." Brad hauled back and Ross braced himself. The guy packed a fair bit of muscle under his bulk and he quite possibly deserved to get decked for that last crack. But the blow never came. "You're fired."

"Aw, you don't mean that," Ross said, wiping his hands on the towel he kept tied onto his belt loop. "Don't go away mad. Let's get some fudge ripple and binge-watch *Sex and the City*."

Brad double flipped him off then turned and stomped away, muttering under his breath. Wishing the guy had whacked him one so he could've laid into him and released a bit of his pent-up energy, Ross caught the eye of a few of the other brewery staff and shrugged. "Boss man's got lady trouble," he said.

Within a few hours, he'd forgotten the whole incident. As he was packing up to head home, his phone buzzed with a message. When he saw who it was, he repressed the urge to delete without reading it.

Man up, Hoffman. You can't ignore her forever. He dropped into the couch he'd liberated from the employee lounge his first week as head brewer. *It's Evelyn. You like her, remember?* With a sigh, he read her message.

I think we need your help here for a while. Can you manage to break away from The Diva out there for a few weeks?

Realizing that now might indeed be a great time for a break from this place, let Brad cool off and remind himself why he'd bolted from Michigan with a dose of Austin-Evelyn domesticity, he grinned as he replied.

Sure thing. I call my own shots out here anyway. If he doesn't like it I'll just quit again.

Or get fired.
Whichever.
He picked up the phone, recalling something that had nestled in the back of his brain ever since he'd returned. Elisa Nagel — the strange-looking *fraulein* with the ice-gray eyes, skinny body, and wild-ass hair. Why in God's name an odd bird like her would stick with him as long as she had, he had no earthly idea.

What about your new lady brewer? She might not like me coming in and bossing her around.
He stretched out, staring at the screen, waiting for the reply. Waiting too eagerly, of course. Evelyn Benedict Fitzgerald always had that effect on him. When nothing came, he stamped out the tiny flame of disappointment and resumed shutting his space down for the night. The brewery ran on a twenty-four-hour cycle, so he passed by the brew house to check on things before heading out of the back door, hopping on his borrowed motorcycle and pointing it toward the house he still rented from the on-sabbatical prof.

The night was cool, and smelled oddly of lemons and engine exhaust. He took deep breaths as he made the hairpin turns up the mountain without even thinking too hard about it. Memories of Evelyn flooded his brain, aggravating him, turning him on, pissing him off.

Damn woman. He'd never be shed of her.

A small voice rose in his head reminding him that if he didn't even try to find someone else, that would be a hard fact for the rest of his life — and his own damn fault, to boot.

He parked in the driveway and slammed the kickstand down, furious with himself, and his dick which was already half-hard at the thought of her.

Maybe he was over-valuing this whole monk-like existence. Maybe he should go out and get himself laid, knock off his edge.

Because he really couldn't fathom spending two or three weeks working alongside Evelyn without losing his ever-loving mind and perhaps expiring from blue balls. Embarrassing for a man of his age and general experience level.

Resolved to take his usual ten-mile run, even in the near dark, then go out to a bar, find a girl and fuck her brains out, he shoved open the door to the kitchen. He froze, realizing in a split second that something was off...that a hell of a lot things were, actually.

As he put his helmet on the kitchen table, he took it all in. The place was spotlessly clean for one. Not the condition he'd left it in to be sure. He wasn't a slob, but it looked like an entire battalion of maids had swept through the place. The damn kitchen faucet sparkled for crying out loud and the place even smelled good.

"Hello?" While he wasn't exactly nervous—he'd never heard of robbers doing a white tornado cleaning job—he had a sneaking suspicion about what might be going on. And while part of him didn't want any part of it, another part—the part now straining the crotch of his jeans—had a different opinion. "Down boy," he muttered, shifting his junk around so he could breathe. "Who's here?"

He dropped his backpack and pulled a water bottle from the fridge, figuring she'd show herself eventually. Finally, he turned and was treated to the view his brain didn't want but that made his dick practically leap out of his pants. "I thought it might be you," he said, letting the water bottle dangle from two fingers.

Holly smiled and leaned into the doorway against one raised, slender arm. The action highlighted her tits, which were barely encased in a black, silky-looking blouse. "I'm here to call a truce," she said, holding out two glasses of dark beer. "What do you say?"

He sighed, took the beer and clinked glasses with her. "Fine," he said, before downing the thing in a few gulps. "You can go now."

"Don't be like that, Ross baby," she said, leaning forward and giving him a clear cleavage shot. "Let's be friends."

"I'm not your..." he stopped, realizing that his tongue seemed to be stuck to the roof of his mouth all of a sudden. "Shit," he said. Or at least he tried to say.

Holly moved closer, put her finger to his lips. "Shh, no more talking," she said, her face doing a freakish wavering thing in front of his eyes.

"Bitch," he said. Or thought he said as several sets of soft hands seemed to be guiding him out of the kitchen.

That was all Ross remembered for a while.

* * * *

He woke to the great-grandmother of all headaches. Groaning and gripping his throbbing skull, he rolled away from the mass of bodies piled all around him. The sun illuminated the room, hitting him in the eyes with the force of a sledge hammer. Stumbling around, he managed to make it to the bathroom and empty his bladder while leaning against the wall so he didn't fall into the toilet. A shower seemed like the best idea on the planet so he cranked the water to blazing hot and ducked under it.

He stood, hands propped on the tiles, letting the water hit him square in the face. When he tried figure out why he was so damn sore, he saw bite marks and tiny burned spots on his chest and stomach. Wincing, he touched his dick which felt scraped completely raw. His lips were raw too. His neck stung when the water hit it, cluing him in that it was probably in the same shape as his torso. But nothing compared to the utter pounding ball of agony that had replaced his noggin.

With another loud groan, he dropped his hands to his knees and focused on not puking his guts up all over the shower. Slowly, carefully, as if he might shatter into pieces otherwise, he plucked a towel from the rack and patted himself dry before wrapping it around his waist, yelping in pain when the fabric touched his stinging cock. Forgoing that particular modesty, he walked out into his bedroom naked, then into the hall, listening for sounds indicating the orgy ladies still lingered.

After brushing his teeth — which also hurt — for nearly five minutes, they still felt coated in slime. "Bitch drugged me," he muttered swiping a shaking hand down his face. Finally deciding that he didn't care who was around, if he didn't get some water into his system in the next ten seconds he would keel over and die, he stomped past the scene of the debauchery and into the kitchen. Two huge glasses of water later, he stood, gasping, and staring out of the window.

When he processed that the buzzing sound wasn't coming from inside his head, he picked up his discarded jeans and tugged the phone from his pocket. Austin had been calling and texting him for the better part of the last — he squinted at the first message — eight hours.

"What the fuck is it now," he muttered, scrolling through to make sure the kid was all right before giving up and putting the phone to his ear.

"You really know how to make yourself scarce, don't you?" his friend said by way of greeting.

Ross grunted a reply as he sat gingerly down into a chair at the kitchen table. The sunlight blaring through the window pierced him right in the eyeballs. It shoved the spike of pain nice and deep into his brainpan, blinding and deafening him for a few seconds. "What? Sorry. I'm a little fragile this morning."

"Whatever, dude. So, can you come?"

"I already told Evelyn I would." He couldn't keep the snippy tone out of his voice. It was all he could do at that moment not to puke all over the expensive hardwood floor.

"What? When did you talk to her?" Austin sounded frazzled. But he'd sounded that way ever since Rose's birth.

"Shit man, I don't remember. What the hell day is it anyway?"

"What happened to Mr. Pure Living?"

"He got gang banged by a pack of succubus, all right? Cut him a break."

"Nice," Austin said. Ross couldn't tell if he were amused or honestly pissed off.

"Whatever. So yeah, I told her at some point I'd help you guys. I'm somewhat *persona non grata* around here all of a sudden, anyway." He rubbed his eyes. "Seriously, what day is it?"

Austin's heavy sigh set Ross' sensitive on edge. But he sat still, willing the clanging agony in his head to stop, knowing getting angry would only exacerbate it. "It's Wednesday morning, eleven a.m. where I am, which makes it nine where you are."

Shocked at the lost twenty-four hours, he lurched forward, which sent a jolt of nausea up his throat. "Oh, shit."

"Yeah. So, I guess you heard it all, then. If you talked to Evelyn?"

"I, uh, don't know," he hedged as he stumbled to the kitchen sink just in case. The silence on the other end of the line made his pulse race. His good buddy was getting a tad bit bossy and Ross was in zero mood for it. "Guess you should tell me whatever the fuck it all is. Since the last I spoke to Evelyn it was Monday night. Tuesday seems to have been sucked away, along with every ounce of my—"

"Spare me."

"Dude, just fill me in. Holly showed up here that same night and I'm pretty sure she drugged me or something."

"Poor little snowflake," Austin said, amusement clear in his voice this time.

"Yeah. I sure as hell wish I could remember any of it." He touched his sore dick before pressing fingertips against the many, tiny burned spots and gouges on his chest. "So, anyway, what's going on now, drama king?"

"Oh, not much I guess. Other than my wife was nearly raped and killed by a psycho almost-ex-employee before he got popped between the eyes by my strange new German lady brewer."

"You really shouldn't mess with me right now." Ross kept his head lowered, waiting for the inevitable over the sink.

"I'm not."

"Evelyn was…is she all right?" He poured another glass of water and forced it past the rising gorge in his throat.

"Yes. Thanks to Elisa Nagel, she is. Although that woman is now in custody and I gotta go post a two hundred fifty thou bail and get her scary ass in front of my lawyer."

"Elisa…who?" The room had commenced spinning so he squeezed his eyes shut. "Oh, right. The Berliner brewer chick." But he knew damn well who she was. Fronting with confusion was his reflex to counter the surge of emotion that had muscled past his pain at the sound of her name.

"Not to mention Evelyn's office window overlooking the brewery is coated in blood and brains. And some got on Rose." His voice got tighter and higher. Ross opened his eyes and took a long breath.

"Rose is all right, though?"

"Yes. No worse for wear."

"Austin, you're serious about this."

"Fuck, yes, I'm serious. Why would I make up a story like this and interrupt your fragile, post-succubus recovery period with it?"

Ross sat slowly so as not to jar his head. There was something like a million pains all over his body now — so many he couldn't pinpoint exactly where any of them were, specifically. "Okay, I'm sitting down now. Tell me again. All of it, please."

"There used to be an employee here named Tim, who, apparently was seriously harassing Elle, the lady brewer. Evelyn convinced her to file a complaint the same day somebody—Tim, we now believe—sabotaged one of the biggest fermenters, sending something like fifteen thousand gallons of beer swirling down the fucking drain. Evelyn had a heart-to-heart with her, got a lot of bizarre details about her life, had her fill out the harassment claim, then was in her office packing up when this...this...asshole showed up." Ross could hear Austin's throat clicking as he swallowed. "He, uh, tried to attack her. Our Evelyn, Hoffman. He was going to...to rape her right in front of the baby. Oh, Jesus."

Ross leaned forward, elbows on his knees, willing himself not to react. If he lost it, he believed that his head may very well pop off his neck like a zit and roll across the kitchen floor. Part of him wished it would, if it meant the pain would stop. He waited Austin out, the silence between the two men as long as the actual miles.

"He ripped off her blouse, yanked out some of her hair. She told me...that she was ready to do whatever he wanted just so he'd leave the baby alone. Rose was crying I guess and so this fucker picked up her car seat and put it on the god damned table. Then he...he...he..."

"Enough," Ross choked out.

As if he hadn't heard Ross speak, Austin kept going. "He was... He had her pinned to the table and was... It..."

"God damn it, man," Ross roared, leaping up to pace the room, monster headache be damned. "God fucking damn it."

"Yeah, so...literally just as he was about to rape her...the door flew open and there stood our little vigilante." Austin sucked in a shaky breath. "She walked in and blew Tim's sorry brains out without a word, Evelyn said. She grabbed the baby and they ran down to the brewery floor. It was a bottling night so all their noise was covered up. But Elle had one of the brewery assistants call the cops while she helped Evelyn get herself...her clothes...back together in the locker room."

"Holy... I... I don't even have a word."

"Right, so…now my head brewer is still laid up with a concussion and my second-in-command is facing assault with a deadly weapon and manslaughter charges. Evelyn's all right, I mean, as all right as she can be. And we just signed a wholesaling agreement with a super aggressive exporter. Follow me?"

"Yeah. You need me."

"Exactly. So, when can I expect you here?"

"Well…" Ross ran a hand through his hair. He felt sweaty, sticky, and the clanging in his skull had only gotten worse. "I gotta talk to Brad first."

"Fine. Do what you have to do and get here. Please, Ross. I'm tearing my hair out and really need your help."

"Okay. I will. Sorry about…all the mess. You sure Evelyn and the kid are all right?"

"Yes, they're fine. Now, get the hell off the phone and get on a plane."

Ross opened his mouth to reply but the line was dead.

Chapter Fifteen

By the time Ross made it into the brewery, he had an inkling that something strange was up. His first hint being Brad Jefferson walking up to him as he was checking the overnight brewing logs, tapping him on the shoulder and crooking a finger, indicating Ross should follow him back to his office. He had noticed that no one would meet his eyes. But he'd never gone out of his way to make buddies so he hadn't thought much of it. He'd lost an entire day thanks to his impromptu orgy, and had an excuse in mind already as he followed Brad's broad back through the brewery and its busy, gaze-averting staff.

As he flopped into his usual seat, wearing his usual up-yours expression, the sense of things being ever so slightly off intensified. He watched as Brad futzed around with the piles of crap on his desk, checked his phone, and made himself comfortable in his big leather chair. Ross' head was still a tad echo-y, even since he'd had a hot shower and eaten some bland food and felt a thousand times better. But this whole scene was setting him back a few hours.

It would be nothing, he figured. Simply a good opportunity to broach the subject of an extended leave of absence. While recovering at home after Austin's shocking phone call, he'd spent some time shuffling the schedule, making sure he could cover Brad's distribution targets. He'd never up and go without having a plan for this brewery in place. He may be an asshole but he'd never let the beer suffer.

Brad smiled a little wider than usual. "You're fired," he said. The big man leaned back, plunked his show-off, steel-toed boots on his desk and laced his fingers over his ample gut.

"Yeah, yeah, we've been through this," Ross said, waving a hand. "Listen, I do need some time off, though. I've got the floor covered for the next two weeks."

"I'm sorry. I guess you're deaf as well as stupid."

Ross blinked, realizing that something was, indeed, amiss. As he attempted to keep his cool, he leaned back, matching Brad's causal stance. "Well, no I'm not deaf. But you know, I figured we were just fucking around. Did I miss something?"

"Let's see," Brad said. He flipped on his laptop, clicked around for a few seconds, then turned the thing so Ross could see the screen. "I thought I recalled you denying that you were with her, but, apparently, you are a liar, in addition to being deaf. And stupid."

Ross leaned forward, squinting and trying to process what he saw on the screen. When he realized it was him, naked, along with some pretty hot chicks, similarly undressed, he groaned.

"We can't have this sort of crap floating around, now can we, Hoffman?" Brad grinned wider, making Ross think of a gargoyle. A fucking fat-ass gargoyle.

"I didn't…I mean, it wasn't something I…" Ross sighed, then clicked his boss's computer shut and stood. "You know what? Fuck it. You're just jealous you never scored a party like that."

Brad's cheeks and forehead flushed red. His feet *thunked* to the floor but he remained seated. "You're a god damned pig, Hoffman, and I want you out the fuck out of my brewery. Don't come back this time, either."

"With pleasure," Ross said, shooting a jaunty little salute, even as his heart thudded. Panic and residual detoxing from whatever drugs that bitch had dosed him with swirled in his veins, making his vision dim. He could sense the man's fury rolling off him in waves as he headed for the office door. "Oh, and by the way," he said, turning back to face the fat asshole one last time. "Holly told me about your little problem." He put on a fake sympathetic sad face. "You know, Brad, I hear that even your cheap-ass insurance program will cover having your micro penis enlarged, ya *schlappschwanz*."

"Get out!"

Ross ducked to avoid getting brained by a flying chunk of metal—one of the half dozen awards his beers had garnered for the self-aggrandizing jerk. It smashed through the upper glass part of the door and bounced off the wall opposite, taking out an impressive divot in the drywall. "Sheesh, dude. Temper, temper. I'd hate to have you pop an aneurism. Calm down. I'm going."

"Don't even stop at your locker. I've already burned all your shit. Get out and don't look back or I will call the cops."

"Whatever," Ross muttered under his breath as he made his way through the large, successful brewery, his home away from home for a damn long time. No one spoke as he stomped across the brewery floor then slammed the metal door behind him. Gulping in a few lungs full of air, he wondered what, exactly, Holly had done to him. Realizing getting pissed off at her at this stage would constitute a waste of everyone's time, he climbed on his bike and fired it up, relishing the power and noise of it.

He sat a few seconds, pondering the back of the brewery where he thought he'd really, truly made it. His brain felt pinched from the effort not to yell, curse, to track that silly bitch down and shove her face into the wall.

No, Hoffman. Of all the things you are, a woman-beater isn't one.

"Enough, now," he said to himself, hitting the throttle and screeching the bike out into the street. "Fucking, enough. Go home where you belong." But home as he knew it, the way he referenced it, meant more complications than he even wanted to contemplate.

Chapter Sixteen

"Traveling light these days?" Austin eyeballed Ross' duffel bag as he shouldered it off the luggage-go-round in the airport.

"Yeah. I'm very Egyptian that way," Ross said, unwilling to admit that all he had to pack were his few clothes, a laptop and a toothbrush on his way out of Colorado. He'd been tempted to track Holly down and have a not-so-friendly conversation with her — especially once he'd looked up that fucking blog with photos of his sky-high, naked, self on it. Bitch hadn't even given him a good angle. Nor had she shown his full face, he supposed, to her credit.

But he was disinclined to give her credit for anything other than costing him a job at that moment. So, he'd run into the professor's house, thrown a few things into the single piece of luggage he owned, left the bike — also the professor's — in the garage with a full tank of gas and caught a taxi to the airport.

Light as air, that was Ross Hoffman. Never connected or tied down or otherwise attached.

Until now, it would seem.

The ride to the brewery from the airport was made in total silence. Austin kept a death grip on the wheel and Ross kept his gaze out of the window. He'd forgotten how desolate Michigan could be, even in the early spring months. It was still mostly iced over, it seemed. Old, dirty snow was piled in drifts everywhere. Brown tufts of grass poked through in forlorn patches. He sighed and pressed his forehead against the window.

"Don't sound so excited," Austin quipped as he pulled

into the Fitzgerald Brewing parking lot.

"I didn't say anything."

"That's sort of my point." Austin parked and sat, fingers still wrapped around the wheel, staring out the windshield as if in a trance. "This has been a nightmare. I don't even know if it's a good idea for you to jump in the middle of it."

"No, it's fine." Ross put a hand on the man's shoulder. "It's what friends do."

Austin shot him an odd look. "Right."

Ross' anger flared. "Listen, I know it's been hard. I know I bolted. I realize all of this. But I'm here now. Let me at least have a shot at making it right."

Austin's shoulders slumped. His forehead touched the steering wheel between his hands. "Fuck," he muttered. "Fucking mother humping fuckstick."

"Wow," Ross said. "You're quite the poet these days."

"All right, so here's the deal," Austin said, leaning back and turning to face Ross across the SUV's console. "I'm gonna let Bryan go. He's too unreliable."

"Okay," Ross said, letting his friend take his time.

"We have to get up and running, like, yesterday. I've committed to export deals on the IPA and stout to start and we're something like twenty thousand barrels behind already."

"Twenty thousand…"

Austin closed his eyes. "I know. It's a mess."

"Twenty thousand…" Ross' brewer's mind was already calculating man hours, ingredients, all the details. He was excited about it, truth be told. It might even allay his looming anxiety over being around Evelyn again. "What about the gun-slinger?"

"What? Oh, right, Elle. She's here—in there."

"Out on bail? Headed to trial? Can I work her into the schedule?"

"Likely won't be a trial, if my lawyers get their expensive way. And she owns the schedule. You're here as a consultant to help her out. She's the head brewer now."

"Fine." Ross opened his door, then turned back to Austin. "Well, shit, man, I've got work to do. What are we waiting on?"

"Thank you. I know getting away from Brad's operation is no mean feat."

"Yeah, well, it was easier than you might think." Ross averted his gaze. He wasn't ready for that true confessions moment yet. "Down to business — what're you paying me for this little vacation?"

"Your usual fee," Austin said. "Plus a bonus if you get us to the export barrelage target. Same as Elle's."

"Great." He hesitated. "We going in there, or what?"

"You should know that Elle is, um, off-limits."

"Who? Oh, the gun-*Frau*? No sweat. I'm swearing off chicks. One of them cost me my —"

Austin raised an eyebrow when he hesitated.

"Never mind. Tell ya about it later. Let's go. I need to get my hands dirty. I have a bonus to earn and a boss-lady to meet." Unwilling to engage in any more heart-to-heart, he jumped out of the truck, shouldered the bag containing everything he owned in the world, and grinned at the smell coming off the building. He took a big sniff. "Ah, I love the smell of a mash-in in the morning."

"It's four o'clock in the afternoon, dumb ass." Austin walked by him and opened the metal door. The odors of the second shift of a brew day got stronger. "Come on. Let me introduce you to your new boss. She's eager to get going, too."

Ross nodded, ducked inside, squinted through the steam rolling from the huge brew kettle and spotted the small figure, above him on the catwalk between the brewing vessels. She was facing away, hands on her hips, yelling something that it took him a half second to register was in German. He was reminded of her petite stature from that hospital horror but now, dressed in her sweat soaked brewery T-shirt, cargo shorts and rubber boots — the usual brewer's uniform — he saw the strength in her wiry arms and legs.

The steam cleared some, giving him a better view. The noise of the busy brewery faded from his ears as he caught sight of that bizarre mass of blond dreadlocks, currently piled up and tucked under a loose cap. He took a step forward, trying to ignore the strange, tingly sensation in his scalp as he watched and listened to her bark orders in mixed English and German while she marched back and forth on the raised metal path.

Someone shouted her name. She turned and looked down, meeting his eyes. Hers seemed to shine out from the steam — the oddest mix of blue and gray. Ross stumbled backward at the force of her exotic beauty and the realization that he had, indeed, been obsessing since meeting her the first time.

The small-featured, perfectly proportioned face that should have been overwhelmed by that bizarre hair-do was, instead, complemented by it. Her tight, compact body was likely a full foot shorter than his, if not more. She frowned, as if trying to place him, then stood straight, arms crossed. The light caught the small gem in the left side of her nose. When she tilted her head, he caught sight of the barbell in her eyebrow.

A shiver of raw, terrifying, primal lust shot down his spine, making him stumble forward a step or two. He'd bet his first consulting payment from his friend Austin that she was pierced in other places — places on her that he wanted to see, to taste, to feel so badly at that moment he realized he was breathless.

He could make out the tatts on her arms and knuckles — oddly matching his own. As well as a slash of black around her long, porcelain-skinned neck. The sight of that made his chest hot and tight. The full effect of her made him feel so completely weird — somehow dizzy in a way he didn't like at all.

He heard Austin clearing his throat somewhere to his left and realized he and this creature had been staring at each other for a full minute in silence. He dropped his gaze first.

"Elle," Austin called up to her. "This is Ross. Ross Hoffman. He'll be…"

"Your humble assistant," Ross barked, needing to move or speak or something to shake the way his body had reacted to her. "As of now." He grinned up at her. Her frown deepened. His dick stirred at the sight of it.

Well, that's just great. I'm obviously losing my mind. She's the opposite of everything I like about the female form – short, wiry, angular and hard-looking and that hair…

"Hoffman," she said, her voice as sharp as she looked. "Welcome to Fitzgerald Brewing Company. It's about time you got here. Now, move your sorry ass and get to work. We're behind, in case you haven't been informed already."

He blinked up at her like a dolt. She'd spoken clearly enough, but in citified, Berliner-accented German. His smile widened. She smiled back for a brief second, then moved away from the railing. Something about that—her sudden, almost reactionary shift out of his line of vision—caused a strange sort of protectiveness to surge through him.

Yep. I've gone 'round the bend for sure. Or I'm suddenly so homesick for the Fatherland, the sound of some chick speaking German is making me horny.

"Ugh," he muttered under his breath as he re-shouldered his duffle and looked at Austin. "All right, boss man, point me toward a computer so I can figure all this shit out."

Austin was staring at him, fully noting the strange exchange, Ross knew.

"What? She's weird-looking, all right? Plus, she's trigger-happy? God. I'll avoid her like the plague."

"Right," Austin said, shaking his head as he walked away. "Come on. We're in for a long set of weeks."

Chapter Seventeen

"God damn you, Hoffman," Elle growled under her breath, in her snooty Berliner accent.

"Fuck off, bitch," he said, cheerfully, in his native Bavarian.

After a few days of establishing that while she might be head brewer, he was just as in-charge as she was, he'd continued using their native tongue, figuring she couldn't pretend not to understand him that way. She glowered down at him from the top of the platform where she was supervising a batch of stout. "You overshot the ingredients," she insisted, crossing her arms. "I told you that was too much crystal malt. But you're an asshole male human. I should know better than to tell you anything."

He held up both hands. "*Ach*! Don't shoot!"

She rolled her eyes, and turned away, giving him a pleasant view of her tight little ass in well-worn jeans. Cursing to himself, he headed to the lab to prep the additives before they moved the wort to the kettle.

In a way, settling in at Fitzgerald Brewing hadn't been as hard as he'd thought. Evelyn was busy with the kid and the export plan. He and Austin had worked side by side the first couple of days, planning the aggressive brewing schedule. And Elle had proven to be one of the most naturally astute brewers he'd ever encountered. She was so small in stature it surprised him, given that she was German. But her attitude more than made up for it. She was equal parts irritating, amusing and alarmingly sexy.

He'd tried to go easy with her—to be funny, friendly, unthreatening. But she either saw him as an interloper for a job she was more than capable of handling alone, or as some kind of lame-ass 'friend of the boss' know-it-all determined to make her life a living hell.

Either way, they clashed from the get-go.

"Hey, Hoffman," she called across the brew house platform. "Get up here and you'll see what I mean."

The rest of the staff had fallen into line. The incident with Tim, and Bryan's subsequent firing, had rattled the tight-knit group. They knew Ross' reputation and seemed to be grateful for his help — or at least they made a show of acting like it. He didn't really care. As long as everyone did what they were supposed to do, when they were supposed to do it.

"I'll be there in a minute," he said. He'd admit that dropping back into German was a relief. Even though he spoke flawless English, he still translated in his head. Not having to take that extra mental step made him feel more at home. Even if it was mostly insults woven in around the brewing terms.

He smiled as she muttered, "*Trantüte*" under her breath as he stalled.

Once he'd satisfied himself with the original gravity calculations, he climbed the metal steps, hip bumped Elle aside and opened the mash tun lid, filling the air around him with the rich, malty odors of a Fitzgerald stout in the early brewing stages. "What?" he said, looking over at her and trying not to pay too much attention to the long, slender line of her neck, or the way her odd, blue-gray eyes flashed.

"Look. There." She shone her flashlight into the huge vessel of dark liquid and grains. With a grunt of frustration, he grabbed the light from her so he could reach deeper into the tank. "Do you see it? Are you blind, or just stupid?"

He sighed and held out a hand. "Safety glasses?"

Once he had had them on, he stretched farther, gripping the edge of the open door with one hand. "Holy shit," he said. "Are you serious?"

"I told you," she said, from somewhere to his left. At that

moment, the condensation caused by the steam they were releasing through the open door made his hand slip. For a split second, he pictured himself boiling alive inside the one hundred twenty-some-degree mash. And his thought wasn't for his safety, but for the ruination of this critical batch. If they could get this one through the process in time, they'd almost be caught up to the export goals. Almost.

"Mother fucker," he blurted out in English as his fingertips let go and his brain tried to readjust to the sudden shift in his equilibrium.

A strong hand grabbed his forearm. Fingers dug into his muscle, gripping tightly, yanking him free of certain deadly burns. He found himself pressed against Elle's compact form, her fingers still wrapped around his arm as she leaned back against the railings at the top of the brewing platform. She was so small, he thought, apropos of nothing at that moment.

So small and…so gorgeous.

He allowed himself a few moments to feel her body against his. She was strong as a damn ox. She'd managed to haul his hundred eighty-five pounds of mostly muscle right out of that kettle. But her strength was subtle, and sexier than he'd ever encountered.

"Get the hell off me, you bloody oaf," she shouted, shoving him away. Which allowed him to squelch the sudden urge to kiss her.

He stumbled, still staring at her, still wearing the safety glasses. She frowned, causing the cutest little crease between her eyes. He itched to touch it, to ease her stress.

Good Lord man, you need to get laid and get over this chick.

"So, before you nearly ruined all that future beer, did you see the problem?"

He blinked, then stood up straighter. "Yeah," he said, swiping the sweat off his face. "I saw it. Speed up the sparge," he said, pointing to the keyboard attached to the computer. "That should unstick it."

"Can this equipment do that?"

"Yeah, it's top drawer. Just try it. I'll keep an eye on it."

She raised a pale eyebrow. "Without falling in, *bewegungslegastheniker*?"

He grinned. That was the thing about German — the insults were so much more poetic. "I may be *bewegungslegastheniker*, but I know how to work this machinery. Go on. Do what I asked for. There." He pointed to the computer again.

She turned from him and started punching in the commands to increase the sparge — the speed at which the water was tossed on top of the concoction of nearly spent grains and almost-beer in hopes that it would filter through faster, and loosen a section of stuck mash that she had, indeed discovered. Once again, Ross found himself fantasizing about her. Her small but firm-looking breasts. Her slim waist and hips. Her nice, rounded ass. Her pert, Cupid's-bow lips. Her compact, deceivingly strong arms and hands and legs that would wrap very nicely around him.

"Hello? Anyone home up there?" Elle snapped her fingers in front of his face. "I've been talking to you for the past ten minutes, but you seem to have checked out."

Ross startled, and turned away from her so as to hide the clear results of his brief imaginings of her pale skin under his hands and lips.

"*Off-limits,*" Austin had said, without further explanation. There hadn't been time.

Evelyn had hinted that there was something bad in her past but she hadn't gotten around to expanding that, either. And in the meantime, he'd been mostly put out with her bullshit attitude, anyway.

Once he had his half-hard dick back under control, he turned to face her again. Her attention was focused on the computer screen. He fixated on the odd tattoo circling her neck, fully revealed as she had her crazy-ass hair bundled up on top of her head and covered with a hat.

The black ink seemed darker than usual this morning. It was ugly. Like a scar. For the first time since meeting her and being rocked back on his heels by her unique, compelling, beauty — so unlike his usual, more obvious, over-the-top type — he studied all the ink he could see on her.

Ross had his own tatts, of course. He had hop flowers on his right knuckles, too. There was an intricate hop vine snaking up his biceps that wound across his upper back and down the other arm. He'd also recently added one. His daughter's name, Rose, in a small heart. It was on the left side of his ribcage, hidden and private.

But that thing on Elle's neck right above the angle of her collarbones seemed somehow evil. As if it were dug deep into the delicate skin there. Meant to be painful upon application and remain that way, as a torture. Without thinking, he reached out, wanting to touch it and see if it felt as hot as it appeared to be. They were only separated by about eight inches up on the tall metal platform between the brewing vessels so it wasn't a huge gesture. But to Ross it felt mammoth, a life-changing move.

His fingertips grazed the nape of her neck, near the soft curls under her thick blond dreads. Her skin was ice cold. Strange, since there were up here amidst all this steam and she'd just literally dragged his klutzy ass away from potential disaster. She must not have noticed his first touch.

When he let his finger trail along the ugly ink across the back of her neck, she yelped and whirled to face him, her eyes wide with something his brain refused to process. Since it was an expression of abject terror.

He stuck the offending hand into his jeans pocket as his face flushed. "I'm sorry," he said, lapsing back to English as he turned away from her again. Her breathing was loud and rapid, but not in a sexy way. He worried her heart might explode from fear. Of him?

No. But someone had harmed her badly enough to make her as skittish as a rabbit, pinned and frozen under the shadow of a hawk through an open field. Ross had never considered himself particularly protective of anything. He kept things separated in his mind and heart — at least until he'd met Evelyn, of course. He squeezed his eyes shut, cursing himself and that particular weak period of his life.

A period that had resulted in another human being now breathing air on the planet. He'd surrendered the fatherly duty thing to Austin but thoughts of Rose were all tangled up in memories of his time with Evelyn. And so best left un-thought, in the grand scheme of things.

Austin was in charge of being protective of the baby, and of his wife. Ross had forcibly let go of those urges, purging them first with as much pussy as he could bang for a few months, then later with his monk life. Forcing abstinence down his own throat like his own ugly tattoo of punishment.

But now.

Now.

Now, something new and hot was coursing through his veins. He recognized it, of course. His new-found obsession with the skinny-sexy, German-speaking smart ass woman who was easily as talented a brewer as he was, had blossomed from something distracting, to something massive, all-consuming.

Something he needed to avoid like the fucking plague, as he'd promised he would.

Because on the hot tide of that desire to see her naked, to press his tongue against the deep cleft between her collar bones, to cup one small, pert breast while sucking the other no-doubt sweet pink nipple into his mouth, came something new to him. A raging, boiling fury at whoever had turned a strong, able, strong woman into the quivering prey across from him right now.

He took the few inches of space between them, looming over her in a way that probably didn't help. His hands hovered over her upper arms. Not quite touching, but close enough to sense the coldness of her skin. She met his eyes once, then dropped her gaze to the floor between them.

Confused, since she'd never done that before—had always met him more than halfway with her left-handed compliments disguised as mild criticism of his methods—

he tilted her chin up. The experience of looking down at her, of wanting her so fully, while at the same time wanting to shield her from whatever horrors roamed her backstory, choked him into silence. She blinked fast, then jerked her chin out of his grasp and took a short step back, connecting with the metal railing and gripping it with both of her hands.

"Don't fucking *touch* me," she whisper-yelled in English. "Ever."

"I… I'm…" It took everything he had in him not to grab her and yank her into his arms. To hold her close, so she could press her face into his chest and feel safe. He shook his head. He must be totally losing it. Her eyes seemed bluer at that moment and he realized they were brimming with unshed tears. "Elle… Elisa…listen."

"Don't *ever* touch me. Do you understand?" In English again. Such an ugly language.

"Yes, but…" His hands were positively burning with the need to touch her. He had the odd urge to lick his index finger and scrub it against that horrible thing circling her neck. To wipe it off her skin and out of her memory. Alarmed to realize he was doing so, he reached for her, in a sort of slow motion. The steam from the mash swirled around them, giving the whole scene a bizarre surreal aura.

She flinched away from him, turned and stomped down the metal steps. He leaned over the railing where she'd been standing and saw her turn. Her hand went to her neck, touched the disgusting ink that must be representative of the 'something bad' Evelyn had hinted at a few weeks ago.

"I am not for you, Ross Hoffman. I am not for anyone. Not anymore." This, said in German, hit his brain and buried deep. Her small hand seemed to tighten around her own throat which brought that roaring, furious, protective monster to the forefront of Ross' brain.

"You say that now," he said, matching her in their native tongue. "But you might change your mind. I'm told I have that affect." He kept his tone neutral but his throat was so tight it hurt. The steam cleared, giving him a view of the single tear sliding down her face before she turned away and disappeared into the stainless-steel jungle of the brewery.

With a loud exhale, Ross slumped back against the mash tun. The increased spray of water that he'd ordered made a comforting, rhythmic *whish-whish* sound behind him. The sounds of the busy brewery filled his ears again, replacing the noise of his pounding heart. He looked down at his hands, surprised to find them clenched into fists, so he opened them slowly, inspected his palms with their familiar scars and imperfections. He turned them over and studied the hop flowers on his knuckles.

Someone had hurt that woman. Hurt her so badly she thought she would never be happy again. They'd transformed her into something that ran opposed to her natural, strong-willed personality. He'd realized that the moment she'd dropped her gaze to the floor when he'd stood over her, glaring at her like some kind of an asshole.

He yanked his phone from his pocket and tapped out a quick message to Evelyn.

I want Elisa's whole story. Tonight. I'll be over and bring pizza for dinner. No excuses.

Her reply came while he was transferring the thousands of gallons of liquid from the mash tun to the boil kettle. As he wiped his face with the towel he kept tied to his belt loop, he felt the phone buzz.

I promised her I wouldn't tell anyone. Sorry.

Cursing under his breath, he shot back —

I don't care what you told her. I want to know so I can kill the fucking bastard who did whatever he did to her.

It's a little more complicated than that, she replied.

I can take the complexity.

He took a drink from the water bottle he kept handy, trying to come to terms with the odd sensations racing around his mind. After he hollered for one of the assistants to come babysit the kettle, and gave him strict instructions on when to add which ingredients, he stomped away, heading for the flight of steps up to Evelyn's office.

It was a space he'd managed to avoid so far. With good reason. The moment he was halfway up he was blindsided by memories — most of them X-rated — of his life here, with her. With them, together. Of all the times they'd shared — working, laughing, and fucking like their lives depended on it.

He stopped, hands gripping the metal rails, head dropped low, willing his mind clear so he could focus.

"Ross." Evelyn's voice circled around his brain, clogging it like smog. "Come on up."

He lifted his head and met her steady, blue-eyed gaze. At that moment, something heavy seemed to lift off his chest. Something he'd been dragging around ever since he'd forced Austin and Evelyn back together and had decided to leave, to give them the space they deserved. It was as if it had been tied around his neck, albatross-style and the string holding it there had broken the minute he looked at her.

He smiled, and walked the rest of the way up the stairs. The hug they shared was easy, friendly, comforting.

"Thank Christ that's over," he muttered into her hair.

"What?" she asked letting go of him.

"Nothing. Nothing at all. So, are you gonna spill it or do I have ask her myself?"

Chapter Eighteen

"Fucking girl code," he muttered as he finished adding the yeast to the giant fermenter of stout he'd begun that morning. "Fuck that shit."

Sweat streamed down his face. He reached for his towel but couldn't find it. Cursing a blue streak, he hauled the yeast container onto the 'gator so he could drive it across the brewery and back to the cold storage. When he turned to complete the process then clean the area, a small white towel met his gaze. He looked at it, then at the person holding it.

"Thanks," he grunted, grabbing it from Elle's hand and applying it to his face. Every cell and molecule in his body was aching, sore and exhausted. He'd been at this, without direct contact with Elisa after their odd encounter for a solid five days now with little sleep. Either brewing himself like he'd done today to spell the staff, or pitching in with bottling and packaging around-the-clock to catch up after the series of disasters.

He wanted nothing more than to fall into his hotel bed — he'd declined Austin and Evelyn's invitation to stay at their house — and sleep for a solid ten hours. After he ate a giant steak, some potatoes, and drank a few pints.

She stood there, hands behind her back, staring at him. He could sense her nervousness as a visible shimmering movement in the air around them. It was akin to the kind of sexual chemistry he'd experienced before, but milder, slower to act. And in its own way, pleasant.

She'd come to him, he figured. So, he was gonna jump right in to this. Something was urging him forward. And if it were the same something that had allowed him to let go of his unhealthy obsession with his friend's wife, then he was by-God going with it.

"So," he said, tucking the towel into his belt loop where it belonged. "I think you owe me a beer. At the very least for ignoring me for the past week." He spoke in German, figuring it might ease her anxiety as much as it did his.

She blinked, and lifted her hand as if she were going to touch the tattoo he now hated so badly he could taste it in the back of his throat—slippery and metallic, like blood. He kept his eyes on hers and she lowered her hand slowly.

"Nothing more than that," he said, crossing his arms and willing her not to drop her gaze. "Just a beer. And a nice little chat between…what did you call us? Oh, right. Colleagues."

"I'm…I don't drink with colleagues."

"I think those are the best people to drink with. I'll see you in the pub in an hour." He didn't formulate it as a question but also tried to keep the bossy tone out of his voice. He turned away from her to fiddle with the fittings on the tall fermentation vessel. "Are Rick and Scott cued up for the next brew? We must keep to the schedule."

He looked up and saw her still frozen in place. Her hand was at her neck now, which infuriated him for reasons he couldn't explain. "Go on," he said, more gently this time. "Check and see if those guys are all set. I know the brew house is ready, thanks to the second cleaning crew you made Austin hire."

She worried the ball that was pierced into her lower lip, making Ross wish he were doing that exact thing.

God damn, I am turning into a full-on sap.

Fuck it. He wanted to at least find out what had happened to this strange, alluring woman. Even if nothing ever came of it.

He raised an eyebrow at her, keeping himself low, still checking that he'd closed all the connections, recalling that this batch of stout was one of many he'd brewed to make up for the sabotage at one of these very vessels. But he also knew he was staying low for another reason. He didn't want her to feel threatened by him, and he'd figured out that looming over her like some kind of ogre would do exactly that.

"All right. I will check with them." She turned away as if to leave, then glanced over her shoulder at him. "I'm not certain that we should be fraternizing. I don't think that's a good idea for either of us."

"Really?" He stood, wincing at the pain in his back from the last week of non-stop brewing. "Allow me disagree, just this once?"

She frowned but sort of smiled at the same time, giving him hope that she'd pop off with something smart ass and the stupid tension between them would be broken. "Fine," she said in English, making his heart sink. "I will allow it. And meet you for one beer in one hour, and nothing more."

"I'll take what I can get," he said, smiling. But her frown seemed embedded onto her face now so he figured he'd best leave it for later. Wondering what, exactly, he wanted from her later, he resumed the final tasks of his brew.

Once he'd supervised the mash-in for the third brewing shift, he took a quick shower in the locker room and redressed in a clean pair of jeans and plain gray T-shirt. He pondered his image in the foggy mirror for a few seconds. The relief he'd experienced a few days earlier, when the whole Evelyn obsession had slipped away from him was still the most prominent thing in his mind. He ran fingers through his wet hair, then tied it back with a bit of leather string as he let that new, but very pleasant sensation suffuse his bloodstream.

While he wasn't positive that the reason he'd had that burden lifted off him didn't have a direct correlation to his new obsession with the German brewer lady, and that *that* might prove even more difficult to shake down the road, he was nothing but grateful for it. He even felt the urge to hang out with them, to hold Rose and be a part of their family, but in a safe, uncle-type way. He brushed his teeth, then grabbed his backpack, whistling his way around the back of the still-busy brewery to the pub.

"*Hola*, Adolf," Melody called out. "How's it hangin'?"

"Low, heavy, and to the left, *chica*," he answered. "Hey, shouldn't you be cleaning my hotel room right now?"

"Go fuck yourself," she replied merrily as she poured him a beer without asking what he wanted.

"Ah, if only I could. Then I could retire on proceeds from my Nobel Prize." He took a seat at the bar, blew her a kiss after she set the glass in front of him.

"Food?"

"Maybe," he said, feeling his stomach growl when the delicious odors wafted from the kitchen.

"Angus beef burger is particularly delish today," she said, leaning forward on the bar and wincing.

"What's the matter, doll? Feet hurt from running across the border?"

"Shut up, genocidal Nazi."

"Touché," he said, lifting his glass and polishing off the hoppy IPA in two long drinks.

"I'll order up a burger for you. Rare, right?"

"*Si, por favor*. Almost mooing."

"Disgusting Kraut," she said, smiling. "Oh, hello there."

Ross sensed her before he saw her. The hairs on the back of his neck and on his arms trembled as that uncomfortable combination of lust and extreme protectiveness coated his brain. Melody flicked a coaster, landing it square in front of Elle — or Elisa as he was starting to think of her. Ross kept his eyes forward, watching while the woman pulled them both a pilsner, once again without asking. Funnily enough it was the perfect chaser to the astringent pale ale he'd already consumed.

"Can I put in an order for something for you, Elle?" Melody's tone had gone soft and mushy. Her mother-y voice, Evelyn called it.

"No, thank you very much. This will be fine. I won't be

staying…long."

Ross glanced over at her when she spoke the last word.

"Shall we?" she asked, in German, indicating an empty booth away from the busy bar filled with eager-for-gossip ears.

With a shrug, he got up and followed her, keeping his eyes anywhere but the tight ass of her dark jeans. She'd also changed, he noted, recalling that she'd been wearing cargo-shorts earlier. All the better to house wrenches, measuring devices and pens, he mused, admiring her all over again.

He slid in across from her, determined to get something resembling a back story out of her and wondering what it would take. Typically, he had little trouble making small talk, which then ended up being a full-frontal assault of unwanted personal details from women he was trying to pick up in bars. But right now, at this precise moment, sitting across from the most interesting woman he'd ever encountered in his entire life, he was dry-mouthed with stress.

She sipped her beer, patted her lips with a napkin, put it neatly in her lap, propped her elbows on the table, and met his gaze. "All right. I'm here, having a beer with you. And what are we to chat about? Do you want study the bottling line output? I have that right here." She reached into a pocket of the sleeveless denim vest she was wearing over nothing, best he could tell.

Stymied, he gulped down some beer then coughed for the next few seconds when it went down his breathing hole. She had, he saw, matching circles of thorns around each biceps, high up, near her spare shoulders. There was also a series of stars running up the inside of one arm.

Shocked when his mouth actually began watering at the thought of how her near translucent skin would taste, he cleared his throat and leaned away from the table. "Nice ink," he said, by way of super-awkward segue.

She nodded, sipped and put her elbows back on the table, waiting him out.

"Well, um, no I don't require a bottling line update. But we will have to check in on it first thing tomorrow. Make sure it's keeping up. I know there was an issue with it last week."

"Yes," she agreed, sipping again, her gaze wide and expectant but somehow guarded at the same time.

"Your eyes," he blurted out, likely surprising them both. "They're a very unique shade of blue."

She shrugged and looked down at the table.

"Don't do that," he said, his voice low and soft.

"Don't do what?" she asked, picking up her glass. Her hand shook so hard she had to put it back down. "You need to leave me be," she whispered to the table top.

Confused by this honest comment, Ross stayed silent, studying her. The thick ropes of her dreadlocks were piled high. The tiny bands holding them together were all different colors, he noted for the first time. As he watched, one slipped free and fell over her face. He reached slowly across the table, and held it between his thumb and index finger. Marveling at its silky texture, given the somewhat brittle appearance of them, he allowed himself a quick fingertip graze to her cheek. She flinched, but not nearly as violently as she had earlier.

In a matter-of-fact way, she took the rope of hair from him and tucked it up into the mass on her head. The action exposed her bare armpits to him and Ross was jolted by the sight of them. Dear Lord but he was definitely losing it if the sight of a woman's pale, delicate underarms was making him pop a boner harder than concrete.

He greeted the server who'd brought his dinner, thankful for the distraction. Grinding his teeth and feeling like a god damned teenaged boy on prom night, about to get his first feel of actual pussy, he downed his beer and clunked the glass on the table so hard the people next to them glanced over at him.

"I am telling you again, Ross Hoffman, we do not need to be anything but colleagues."

She spoke this in stilted English, giving it a formal finality he didn't like.

He took a breath, cleared his mind ever so slightly, and smiled over at her. "Well, why don't we see how things progress?" he replied in German, popping a tater tot into his mouth. "Mmmm, want some?" He turned the plate around so the pile of strange potato products he loved were facing her. "I love these damn things."

"What are they?" She picked one up and rolled it over in one small palm, sniffed it, then took a tiny bite. "Tastes like *frites*," she said, finishing it off. "Sort of. But different."

He dredged one through ketchup laced with hot sauce. "Try it this way." He handed it to her, letting their fingers touch on purpose.

Teenager! Next thing you'll do is yawn and reach for her boob.

"My God! That is delicious." She grabbed another one and dunked it in the red sauce, then another. She grinned across the table at him and Ross honestly believed his heart may have skipped a quick beat. He took a huge bite of his burger to cover his discomfiture.

Elisa wiped her lips. Ross reached over and touched his fingertip to a splotch of ketchup she'd missed, then put it in his mouth. She flushed. And his dick got hard again. So hard he felt his zipper bite into it which made him flinch and put the burger down.

This is too weird. She is so not my type.

He caught her staring at his burger. "Don't you start too," he said before taking a long swig of beer, wondering how he could politely extract himself from this before he did something truly stupid.

"I am very sorry to break this to you, Hoffman, but I'm not quite sure that animal is dead yet. Shall I stab it for you? Just to be safe." She brandished a knife.

He frowned. "So, Elisa. Tell me about that tatt around your neck."

She froze, knife still raised in mock burger-stabbing mode. Her face, so prettily flushed, drained of all color in an instant. "This is none of your business," she said, her voice strained. "I've finished my beer. Thank you for the round *pommes frites*. Now I must go. Oh, and it's Elle, as you well know."

He exhaled, cursing his sudden inability to be subtle. "Okay, I take it back. Sit. Stay. Good girl. And why not Elisa? It's a lovely name. Fitting."

He patted the table next to her beer and treated her to his best, charm-the-panties-off-'em smile. She hesitated, half-standing already. "What is this strange face? You have indigestion? Weren't you taught to cook the meat before you put it in your mouth?"

Ross picked up the burger and took an obnoxiously large chomp, letting the grease and hot mustard ooze out the sides of his mouth. Elisa rolled her eyes. But she slid back into her seat, even though her stance was wary again, guarded, afraid in that way that made Ross want to punch somebody. To beat them until they couldn't walk.

This was going to take longer than he'd bargained for. But hell, it wasn't like he was going anywhere. The beer blogosphere had been apoplectic by his ignominious firing from Jefferson's brewery. Brad had made sure some of the more salacious but not quite grossly explicit pictures Holly had taken of him, pissed off his keester and being serviced by two girls at once got wide distribution. He'd had to cancel his Facebook page, thanks to all the attention. Much of it from chicks who had zero qualms shooting him wet, split beaver shots in his personal message inbox.

Bizarre and somehow titillating at first. But after a few hours perusing them, he felt sad for the women, and disgusted with himself. He'd saved some of the better tit pix of course. He wasn't a monk after all.

The server brought them both a stout. Elisa thanked him and asked for two glasses of water while Ross made short work of the bloody hamburger. Finally, he groaned, wiped his face with his napkin and shoved the decimated plate away from him. She kept her icy gaze on him as she sipped the dark brew. "This is very good," she said.

"Thanks," he said, taking his own sip.

"I am not complimenting you, fool. I made this batch, with Bryan, the clumsy asshole."

Ross grinned. "I know. I was just testing you." Determined not to spook her again, he set his beer down and contemplated his next conversational gambit.

A shout hit his ears, jarring him. Elisa craned her head up, trying to see around his shoulder. He turned, annoyed by the interruption.

"Hey, Hoffman," Melody called. "You guys are needed in the main brewery. Now."

They both jumped up, ran behind the bar and into the back of the pub then across the parking lot. Ross slammed the door back, taking in the chaos. An out-of-place aroma hit his brain just as he looked down and spotted the thick ooze of propylene glycol. Before he could stop her, Elisa ran past him, headed for the corner where the stuff was stored. Fitzgerald didn't use much of it, since they only had a few lagers requiring non-stop glycol cooling. But there was enough to cause a mess, just like the one he was staring at.

"No, Elisa, stop!" He reached for her but caught nothing but air at the precise second both of her booted feet hit the stuff. Her fall was in acrobatic, slow motion, sending her feet up and her head down. She landed hard on her butt right in the middle of the worst of the spill, and bounced the back of her skull on the concrete.

The damn stuff was more than a little caustic, even in the low concentrations they kept, so even as he yelled for Rick to run over and turn off the power to that part of the brewery to stop the leak, he scooped her up in his arms and ran for the locker rooms.

As he ran, he yelled orders, telling someone to call Austin, and someone else to start diluting and squeegeeing the thick liquid down the drains. She struggled, using that surprising strength of hers to try to escape. But he figured since he had eighty pounds of muscle on her, he put it to use, gripping her tighter as he shouldered his way into the ladies' locker room. There were only a few straggling employees, mostly pub staff on a shift change.

"Out," he barked. They scattered.

"Let *go* of me, you giant oaf," she screeched. "Oh, my God. Oh, my God. My skin..." She began to whimper in a way that freaked him out. Elisa did not strike him as a whimperer.

"Sh. It's all right. Hang on." He leaned into the shower and turned on the water, then climbed in, still holding her in his arms. The water hit his face first so he turned, keeping her under its wide spray. One of the things Evelyn had demanded was an upgrade to these facilities, insisting that since so many people used them post shift or sometimes early in the morning to get ready, she wanted them to be top-notch, the level of a high-end gym. Ross thanked her mentally for that, grateful for the strong, wide swath of hot water sluicing the viscous fluid off Elisa's exposed skin.

She shivered and clutched his neck, keeping her face buried in his chest as they were both soaked through to the skin. He kept making nonsense sounds, trying to calm her, trying not to notice that he had a full view of her left nipple in the gape of her wet denim vest. At some point, she looked up at him, water streaming across her face so he did what he'd been wanting to do all day.

Her lips were full, firm under his but he went slow, easy, hoping not to scare her. When his tongue found the hard, gold ball in her tongue, he groaned, turned on even more. Not wanting the kiss to ever end. But it did, leaving them both gasping. Ross looked down and saw that the small, rosebud pink nipple he could see was rock hard. His dick slammed against the back of his zipper once more. But he held on to her, sensing this was what she needed of him right now. Nothing more.

"You're a pretty good kisser...*armleuchter*," she claimed with a small smile.

"Oh, my heart," he said, over the sound of the water.

"You break it with your sweet talking."

"Then put me down," she said, pushing against his chest. He let go of her. When her feet hit the tiles, her legs buckled so he caught her under her arms, pressed her against the shower wall, and decided to show her how good he really was at the kissing thing.

Chapter Nineteen

Elle's inner nag raised her voice the moment Ross' lips touched hers for the second time, striking up a distracting mental conversation.

"Elisa Henriette Nagel, you promised."

"I know I promised. Now, shut up, bitch, and let me enjoy this. My God, this man... Such a man... Such a..."

"Ja, and such a man as this destroyed you. Drove you from your home. Forced you to start all over again. Landed you here...with this man... Oh my God, he can kiss!"

"I told you so. Now go away and let me have this for a few more seconds before you remind me that I am making another huge mistake."

She gasped and drew away from him, heeding the inner warning voice, even though everything else in her was urging her forward. She put her hands on his chest, gulping in air and framing her argument—mostly to herself. Realizing she had her damn legs wrapped around his hips like some of slut, which provided her with the sort of friction the lady who'd pierced her hood had promised would blow her mind. She wiggled free and stood. "I think I'm cleaned off now." Her voice sounded weak. She hated that but had gotten used to it in the years since...since Him.

She shivered so hard her teeth rattled. Likely mistaking it for the fact that they were still standing under the shower fully dressed, Ross cursed under his breath and turned off the water. As he turned back to her, she ducked under his outstretched arm and ran into the locker room for a towel. Her mind was spinning. Her body revved up in ways it hadn't been for years.

Losing control was not an option. It was what had ruined men for her. Or so she claimed to herself. Repeatedly.

As she watched, the Viking god of a man emerged from the shower. He tugged his hair free of the tie-back and shook it like a dog, spraying water everywhere. His bright white grin shone through the red, close-clipped beard like a beacon of hope.

"You are nothing," a different, much harder-edged voice insisted in her ear. It was a voice she'd managed to suppress for the past few weeks. But now, it was back. And it was loud. Tears burned her eyes as she and Ross stared at each other across the locker room floor. *"You deserve nothing. You deserve to sit in your own shit. To lie in your own piss. To lick the mud off my boots. Now get over here, on your useless hands and knees and suck my…"*

"Stop!" She gasped and slapped a hand over her mouth when she realized she'd screamed like a crazy person. But crazy people hear voices, right?

Right.

"Elisa."

Ross. Ross was saying her name. She opened her eyes, forgetting that she'd squeezed them shut. He was mere centimeters from her now. So close she could trace the outline of his musculature under the wet brewery T-shirt. Could almost reach out and lick the water on his neck, bury her hands in his thick hair, lose herself in him.

"No," she said, holding out both hands and locking her elbows. He frowned, but stopped.

"What's wrong?" he demanded, crossing his arms and getting that line of stubborn between his deep blue eyes. The line she'd come to recognize, respect and love.

No, Elisa. No more.

"I'm soaking wet and freezing. That's what's wrong. Are you blind in addition to being a mouth-breathing fool?" She tried to keep her tone light but her teeth were chattering so hard it made her sound scared — which she was, of course.

They stood in their odd tableau, him pressing against

her outstretched hands, both of them in dripping clothes. She could sense the frustration rolling off him in waves so palpable they were like a hot wind, buffeting her, pressing her back until she dropped to her butt on the wide wooden bench along the wall of lockers.

"Go," she said, her voice stronger now. "Leave me alone. I won't do this. I can't. You... You have to leave me alone."

She dropped her face into her hands, willing him gone.

Willing him to stay.

His hands were warm on her arms, pulling her to standing, sliding up the back of her neck, tugging her close. She resisted. God help her she did, including trying the stiff-arm thing she'd used a few seconds before. But even though he was as soaking wet as her, he was warm. He was a comfort. His arms were strong and they were around her.

"It's all right," he whispered in her ear, confusing her for a second until she realized she was sobbing. Great, loud, snotty sobs that would be embarrassing. But somehow, she wasn't embarrassed.

She put her arms around his waist, pressed her face into his firm chest and let the tears flow. Ross made more soothing noises, crooning to her in German and English, stroking her hair, keeping his touch light and innocent.

Finally, he pulled away and tilted her chin up. His smile made every nerve ending she possessed zing with pleasure. But it also triggered the voice. His voice. Reminding her of her basic unworthiness.

She disentangled herself, swiping at her still-streaming eyes. He handed her a towel and she wrapped it around her shoulders, keeping her gaze fixed on the floor.

"You are like a piece of shit on my shoe. Don't you ever forget it. You'll never amount to anything more than what I want you to be." The voice—something she'd once craved like a junkie—filled her brain, drowning out everything else. *"Now, spread your legs and shut up."*

And she had. Because He'd trained her that way, the sadistic fucker.

She turned away from Ross and glared at her reflection in the mirrors over the row of sinks. The ink He'd paid for around her neck stood out against her blotchy red skin like a scar. He'd claimed it was the sign of His devotion. That because she wore His collar permanently, she was safe, forever.

Well, she had been safe from anyone else, anyway. After that, He'd started to isolate her, demand that she account for her every movement outside of the restaurant and their small apartment. Not long after that, He'd raped her for the first time.

That's not what He'd called it, of course.

Ross' hand on her shoulder made her yelp and whirl around. As she gripped the towel tightly in one hand she held up her other. "I thank you for that…moment. Now, you must go."

"I'm not going, Elisa," he said, his jaw clenched. "Not until you tell me what the fuck that thing is around your neck and why…" He hesitated, swallowed hard and softened his glare. "Tell me why you're afraid."

She dropped her gaze again. A purely involuntary gesture, but one she'd had drilled deeply into her psyche by The Monster she'd once trusted with everything. Ross stayed silent. Finally, she looked up at him. He was smiling, which put her on guard. The Monster used to smile too, while He was doing some of the worst things to her. By the time she'd run, with nothing but the clothes on her back, her passport and a whole wad of His cash in her pocket, only the very worst things would get Him hard, much less get Him off.

A sudden surge of nausea filled her throat, forcing more tears down her face. Ross' shoulders slumped. She shoved past him, ran for a stall and slammed the door. Pressing her forehead against the cool metal, she realized that The Monster had won. Even though she'd escaped him physically and geographically, He'd made His mark. Left His scar. And not only around her neck.

"Go, Hoffman," she blurted out. "I mean it. I don't like

you. I don't want you around me." She saw his work boots under the stall door. "God damn it, you're an idiot. Leave me the fuck alone!" She slammed her palm against the door once, twice, so many times she lost count and her hand stung. She sat on the toilet, still dressed in her wet, cold clothes, shivering and cursing her stupid life until she heard the locker room door click closed.

"See? Now was that so hard? You know it's for the best. No man can be trusted. Not even that one. No matter how much you want to or think he's worthy. You're not worthy of him. You're shit. You're a whore. You're useless."

"Shut up," she whispered, as she rocked back and forth, arms wrapped tight around herself. "Shut up. Shut up. Shut up."

"Elle?"

The actual voice coming from the other side of the bathroom stall door startled her out of the semi-trance. A soft knock made her jump up and wipe her eyes. She had made a complete mess of this place. She should go and leave these nice people to their normal lives.

"Elle, open the door." The Spanish accent came through, revealing the nosy parker as Melody, the pub manager. "Come on now." The door rattled.

With a sigh, Elle opened the door. It creaked open revealing the attractive, dark-haired woman. "*Mi Dios*, come on." She grabbed Elle's hand and pulled her out. "Do you have spare clothes?"

"Y-y-y-yes." Elle pointed to her locker and gave the combo. Melody opened it, poked around and emerged with a clean pair of jeans. "I don't have a clean shirt, I don't think."

Melody looked around, then grabbed a Fitzgerald branded sweatshirt draped over the bench nearest the door. "Here, I had this on earlier. Get out of that wet stuff. Do you have undies?" She stuck her head back in Elle's locker and pulled out a small bag Elle usually kept hanging on the hook that contained her extra underthings.

She took the bag and stood there, feeling sheepish. Melody stared at her, then slapped a hand to her forehead. "Sorry. I'll wait outside."

"Thank you," Elle said, unable to even comprehend any of this—of her near-visceral reaction to Ross' earlier kiss, of the wrenching reality of her life, of anything that had happened to her in the past few weeks.

Her mind flew to its usual perch, worn down by her mental workings of it. The gun she kept—that she'd bought in a pawn shop with the last of her cash. The gun she'd use to kill The Monster when he found her, because He would find her. Of that, she had no doubt. If He snuck up on her and snagged her, she'd use the gun on herself. Death would be preferable to what passed as life as His emotional prisoner.

The stupid gun that had come in handy, as it turned out and that she no longer owned, thanks to what she'd done.

With a groan, she slumped on the bench, taking deep breaths and forcing Ross—his hands, his lips, his arms, strong chest—out of her mind for good.

Chapter Twenty

The next morning, she slunk into the brewery, the dread at having to face him like a noxious smoke filling her chest. Perversely, she craved the sight of him, the sound of his country-Bavarian accent when he spoke to her in their native tongue. All the while knowing that he didn't deserve to get caught up in her shit. Period.

But that kiss... Dear Lord, if anything were more wonderful in this world, she was hard pressed to know what it might be.

She sighed and hid behind a row of fermenters when she heard him barking orders at some hapless brewery assistant. Her scalp tingled and the tiny hairs on her arms rose as she listened to him.

"Don't do it, Elisa. Don't trust him."

She heard Austin holler for him from upstairs and breathed a sigh of relief when he replied that he'd be right up, leaving the main brewery floor free for her. Ears buzzing, she tried to make herself even smaller than she was — a trick she'd learned well during her time spent as a so-called submissive to The Monster.

A few hours of work calmed her jangling nerves. The smells and sounds of a brewery always did that for her. As she was checking the specific gravity of the IPA, pleased with how it had turned out, she sighed and allowed herself to relax. Whatever Austin had needed him for, Ross had stayed scarce for most of the day, thank the Lord in heaven.

"Hey," he said from right behind her.

She screeched in shock, flinching to violently the hydrometer went flying up into the air. After juggling it a few times, she held it to her chest and turned to face him.

"Nice catch." He smiled.

Her heart wanted to melt. But she kept a tight grip on it, refusing to give in to that ever again. "Persistent? Or perhaps just—"

He held up a hand. "I know, I know. Mouth-breathing idiot." He leaned against the stainless-steel sinks. She tried not to let it, but her gaze was drawn to his shoulders, his arms, his chest…and lower. Gulping, she focused on the floor. When he cleared his throat, she met his deep blue gaze. "All right. I have a plan." His tone was light and easy-going.

"Oh?" She set the expensive piece of brewery equipment beside the sink and turned on the water so she could wash out some of the stacked-up containers. Ignoring him, or at least attempting to, at the same time. "Does this plan involve the two of us? Because if so, you can forget it."

"It does. And I won't. Because I am persistent."

Fury nearly blinded her. She turned to face him, hands on her hips. "Do you want to fuck me?"

He blinked fast, and took a small step away from her. "I… I'm…"

"Because I can accommodate that. And then we can stop all this foolish…flirting or whatever. Let's clear the air." Her knees were shaking so hard she had to grip the edge of the sink for balance. "What do you say?" She jerked her chin up, trying to look brave. "A quick screw in the locker room, maybe? It's what you wanted last night, I think."

It's also what she wanted, but that was beside the point. He would be the first man to touch her intimately in almost eleven years. Also beside the point, because she was not going to let it happen.

"Stop it," he said, his brow furrowing into the familiar stubborn lines. "I am here to ask you out on a proper date. Like a nice guy. But if you want to fuck…" He lifted his chin. "I can accommodate that."

In a heartbeat, he'd pulled her close, his grip around her

arms gentle, but firm. He slanted his lips over hers, grazing her cheeks with the roughness of his beard in a way that drove her half mad with lust. His tongue parted her lips and she let him, wrapped her arms around his neck and went way up on her tiptoes. She had never, ever felt this way about any man. Her need to have him, to be with him, to have him all over her, inside her, was so strong it took her breath away.

"That's right, little whore. That's what you want to do. You fuck that big Viking and see what happens to you when I find you and get you back where you belong. Just wait."

She gasped and struggled away from him, slapping hands over her ears. His gaze wasn't angry, or reproachful. It was soft and sympathetic.

"Okay, now that we have that out of the way, how about that date?" He raised an eyebrow, making her drop her hands to her sides and sigh.

"I am...how do you say...one hot mess. You don't want any part of me." She said this in English, something she always reverted to when she was trying like hell to reject him.

He thumped his chest with his fist and his grin widened, filling her with that ill-considered, yet oh-so comforting sensation of hope. "I am a big strong man. I like hot messes, especially yours." He reached out and touched the corner of her lips with his fingertip. She closed her eyes, turned her face away and grappled with herself a few seconds.

"Fine," she snapped, grabbing a towel and wiping down the counters for something to do with her hands. "I will make you dinner tomorrow night. I am a French-trained chef, after all." Her voice was brisk, matter-of-fact.

He leaned to the side, remaining at the perimeter of her vision until she was forced to look at him. "That sounds lovely. I think."

She threw the towel down and faced him, hand out. He shook it, solemnly. She rolled her eyes and let go of him. "Give me your mobile, fool. I'll put my address in it."

He pulled the device from his jeans pocket and handed it over. She put in her address, part of her regretting every letter and digit, then gave it back to him. He had his head cocked, as if studying her.

"Don't stare. It's rude. Now, we have work to do, I think?"

He stayed still. She frowned, not allowing herself to give in to the compulsion to throw herself at him. Instead, she snapped her fingers in front of his moony-looking face. "Let's go, Hoffman. Beer to be brewed."

He blinked again, as if emerging from a daydream. "Right. Let's hop to it, Annie Oakley."

"Who is this Annie, and does she brew beer as well as me?" She marched past him, letting their arms brush ever so slightly, berating herself for being so stupid and needy. That very feeling had gotten her into a giant fucked-up tangle with a man once, and she would be damned if it happened again.

"Oh really? Then why did you invite the Viking God to your shabby apartment where you will seduce him with your cooking? Huh? How's that gonna work out, Elisa?"

"Shut up," she muttered.

"What's that?" Ross asked, turning as he climbed the stairs to the kettle.

"Nothing," she said, once again trying not to fixate on his ass. "Nothing."

"Really? Then why are you staring at my bum?"

"Because it's big and fat and in my way," she lied. "Get a move on, or I'm telling the boss you're a lazy, mouth-breathing arsehole."

He grinned, making her heart pound even faster, then turned and ran the rest of the way up the steps ahead of her.

Chapter Twenty-One

"Hey, *Mamacita*, you got a minute?" Ross slid onto a stool in the Fitz Pub. His face felt hot. His ears were buzzing. The events of the past two days had him reeling and antsy — sleepless, and non-stop horny.

Melody appeared from the kitchen wiping her hands on a towel. He leered at her. "You have a nice rack," he said, conversationally, smiling at the bartender who'd placed a dark stout in front of him.

She flipped him off and leaned in the doorway. "Yes, I know. Now that you're through harassing me...may I please get back to work?"

"Seriously, Melody, I need to talk to you about something."

She leaned back into the kitchen and said something in rapid Spanish, then approached him, looking wary. "Seriously? You're actually serious about something?"

"Yes," he said, before taking a sip. "Did you get your family all settled back there?"

She propped her elbows on the bar in front of him. "I'm busy doing my grown-up job. What do you want?"

"Sorry. You're too easy to tease. But I do have a serious topic to broach with you." He looked around, suddenly nervous. This was, to put it mildly, a delicate subject. But he knew she knew a thing or three about it, at least based on what Evelyn had told him about her new boyfriend.

"Is this about Elle?"

He nodded, feeling half foolish, half hopeful she could shed some light on a few things for him. She sighed. "We need to go somewhere more private for this talk."

"Are you coming on to me, *Señorita*?" He put a hand to

his chest in fake shock.

"Fuck you, Adolf. Do you want to talk about that poor girl, or what?"

He grabbed his beer and followed her behind the bar, through the kitchen, where the cooks and other staff called out to him. He hollered back greetings until Melody yanked on his T-shirt to get his attention. "Come on, Chatty Cathy. I don't have a ton of time."

"*Adios, amigos,*" he said, waving and following Melody until they got to her small office.

"Sit," she said, closing the door behind them. After taking her seat behind the small, metal desk covered with various receipts from food vendors and employee time sheets, she clasped her hands on top of it all and leveled her dark gaze at him. "So, if you want to know what I think..."

He nodded, sipping, content to let her lead the conversation.

"I think that the tattoo around her neck is a form of a collar." She touched her own neck. Ross saw the necklace she'd been wearing lately—a thin, rope-like, silver chain with a funny-looking charm on the front. He squinted and leaned forward.

"Is that a...?"

"It's a lock," she said, holding it out. "This is a type of collar. It was a special gift. From my...from Trent."

"Yeah, so? He has weird taste in charms. What does that have to do with the thing on Elisa's neck?"

"Trent and I are together, as Dom and sub. The collar is a public symbol of that private relationship."

"Dom and sub," he repeated, stroking his beard and pondering that for a minute. "So, you guys are kinky in the bedroom. He ties you up and shit like that?"

She rolled her expressive eyes. "It's not quite that simple. However, since you are a simple man, I'll try to keep it that way for you. In a healthy D/s relationship, there is nothing but trust. A hundred percent trust. Each partner, the Dom and the sub, give something up to the other as part of the give and take. And it's not about being kinky…all the time, I mean. It's not about abuse, either, or who's 'in charge'." She hooked her fingers around the words. "Unfortunately, I've discovered in my research that plenty of psychotic abusers hide behind being a Dom to find victims. I'm not saying that our Elisa is a natural victim. If anything, she strikes me as the opposite, in a way."

"Yes, I agree with that." Ross' protective hackles rose even higher, making his throat tight.

"I think that she was drawn into a fake D/s relationship. She gave her most important thing—her trust—and was subsequently abused once he—the abuser—gained that from her. It's the worst sort of a betrayal, really."

"So, this thing around her neck, it's the collar? The symbol of the kink or the lifestyle or whatever?"

"*Si*. She was in her trusting stage with him, got the ink, then I'm willing to bet my last peso that he started abusing her after that. I don't know this. She's not said a word to me about it. But Trent says…" She stopped and blushed under her olive skin, making her even more attractive, if that were possible. Ross waited her out. After clearing her throat, she met his gaze again. "Trent says that I have a sort of a sixth sense about people. I've always been that way. Able to tell what's on a person's mind or somehow know what's wrong when they're sad, you know?" She rose. "Anyway, I admire you for wanting to dive into that. Because God only knows what kind of abuser he was."

"Kind? Is there more than one kind?" Ross remained seated, trying to wrap his head around all this, and not lose his mind with fury at the same time.

"Yes. And I have a feeling that she got both barrels— emotional and physical abuse." Melody touched the odd, lock-shaped charm on her necklace—her collar, Ross thought.

"Yeah. That would account for a lot."

"Oh, *mi amigo*. You love her, don't you?"

It was his turn to blush. "I'm… I don't… I mean. I just

thought I'd… Oh, fuck it. Maybe. Are you happy now?"

She smiled, which was impossible not to match. "You're not without your own baggage, eh, ya big ugly Kraut? I mean, considering?" She hooked her thumb at the wall. Melody had been witness to the whole Ross-and-Evelyn-without-Austin-thing as it unfolded. And she'd been there when Evelyn had married Austin—the day Ross had bolted like a damn fool. He sighed.

"No, *chica*. I am not." He finally rose. "Thanks. I really appreciate you filling me in on this."

"I don't know how it will help, since you don't really understand the dynamic of it. But…"

"But I'm glad to know you back me up on my hypothesis."

"Be careful with her, Hoffman. She is seriously broken."

Ross hooked his fingers in his belt loops, feeling like he wanted nothing more than to run out into the brewery, scoop the woman up and cart her off to his lonely, long-term hotel suite and spend days deprogramming her…in the most pleasant ways possible.

"I never thought I'd say this, but…I think you might be the exact thing she needs. And vice versa." She came around the desk and gave him a one-armed hug. "Go easy, though, Adolf. Not every woman can handle you the way Evelyn did."

Ross turned the hug into a real one, giving her a tight squeeze before releasing her with another fake leer. "Nice tits, babe. Don't tell your boss man I said that. He could probably kill me with one blow, eh?"

"God. I knew I never should have said anything nice to you, pig. And yes, he could."

She opened the door. He saluted her and headed through the kitchen again, thinking he might do a bit more research before jumping into the private dinner.

One thing was certain—he knew, with every cell, nerve and molecule in his body, that he wanted Elisa Nagel. And not just in his bed, either. While he'd never been the most introspective guy on the planet, he knew one thing for a

147

hard-core certainty — he was going to bring her out of her brittle shell, prove to her he could be trusted, and that he would protect her, forever.

Around the bend you go, Hoffman.

He grinned to himself and started whistling, anticipating how pleasant that trip might be.

Chapter Twenty-Two

"You're a fool. An idiot. You've avoided any kind of attraction or connection for how long? Ten years, that's how long. Ten years, Elisa. Why are you letting this…this Ross in now?"

"Shut up," Elle muttered under her breath as she put the finishing touches on a way too ambitious Black Forest cake. She'd been soaking a batch of Michigan cherries in kirsch for a while, for reasons that were unclear until that morning, when she'd woken in a panic over her 'private dinner' invitation.

The Monster's evil voice had, of course, been the first thing she was aware of. *"You couldn't make a proper genoise if your shitty life depended on it, you know."* His tone would be solemn, as if He were delivering sad, but necessary news. He rarely, if ever, raised his voice.

By the time He'd turned from her Dom to her abuser, He'd had her so well-trained that yelling wasn't ever necessary. His declaration of her horrible cake-making abilities would likely be followed by a reminder that He'd dragged her sorry ass with him from Paris to Chicago. And that she'd repeatedly failed Him ever since — in every sense. She was no longer any use to Him in the bedroom — unless He was drawing blood, or her loudest, most agonizing screams. She'd been declared utterly useless as His so-called *sous*-chef so He'd demoted her to pastries at the famous restaurant that had hired them as a package deal.

But she knew damn well that one of the two things she could make the shit out of was a melt-in-your-mouth Black Forest cake. And by hell she was going to do it today. The other thing was beer. But that had come much later in her life. Her life on the run. Her life taking every other second to look over her shoulder, to follow The Monster in the news, see what He was doing, what restaurant He'd saved, which buxom, D-level starlet was hanging off His arm.

As she rolled out of her bed and put her feet on the cold floor of her apartment, she allowed herself a split second's worth of happy anticipation. She had an actual date. One she wanted. Not that she hadn't wanted to go out with men in the past almost-eleven years. She just hadn't wanted it enough. Ross Hoffman was more than enough.

She wanted him, bad. And while that terrified ninety-five percent of her, the other five percent was getting loud and persistent. So, here she was — the day of her first date in years, all tingly like a schoolgirl.

Sighing, she rose, stretched and took a quick shower to try to wash away the dread and fear that was rushing in behind her happiness, threatening to smother it with a blanket. An hour later, she'd shopped and unloaded all the ingredients, having managed to use thoughts of recipes and dinner to force both The Monster's voice and the sound of her own, nagging *Oma*-voiced consciousness out of her head.

Stepping back as far as she could in the miniscule kitchen, she admired her handiwork. The cake was magazine cover-worthy. She straightened one, ever-so-slightly crooked cherry by its stem, then placed the cake stand on the kitchen table so it was out of the way.

Still in her cooking trance, she cleaned up, then glanced at the time to determine how she'd go about the dinner prep. Since she'd gone super-heavy with the dessert, somehow convinced that a Bavarian boy like Ross would devour a Black Forest cake cooked like his *Mutter* used to, she'd decided to go meat-free for the meal. As she stared at the butternut squash, second thoughts almost forced her to throw on her jacket run out for a steak. She had miniscule grill on her equally tiny balcony she could use to prepare it.

No. Everyone loved her homemade ravioli and *Herr* Hoffman would just have to forgo his not-quite-dead cow flesh for one night. Elle gnawed her fingernail, as the two voices kept up their low-level murmurings in her head. Both voices were reminding her of the same thing, essentially. But while one was looking out for her, the other was berating, chiding and threatening.

"Shut up," she said, firmly as she tossed together the ingredients for the pasta, squeezing them through her fingers in a way that brought back more memories than it suppressed. As she draped a damp towel over the bowl and set her phone timer so the dough could rest, she realized that, for the first time in many years, she'd maintained her general happy feeling for almost four hours straight.

A record.

"Bitch," The Monster's voice was so loud she winced and pressed her floury hands over her ears. *"Whore. You're nothing but a convenient hole for the Viking. He wants to see what it feels like fucking someone so small. Nothing more. He'll scrape you off his shoe soon enough. Just like I did."*

"Perhaps," she said out loud into the kitchen in German. "But I want to see what it feels like to have a real man between my legs for a change. A man who kisses like that one does. So fuck off, you god damned freak. Get the hell out of my head. Now."

She ducked on reflex, as if avoiding a blow to her face. She'd had her nose broken no less than three times by The Monster. Had stitches in her scalp twice. Nursed broken ribs, a shattered ankle and a concussion—among other things—the first time she'd tried to escape their vast flat overlooking Lake Michigan.

But no blow came. The Monster had not followed her the second time, for reasons that had made her frantic the first couple of years as she'd looked over her shoulder while learning how to brew beer on the west coast of America. Then she'd settled into a steadier emotion—a low-lying anxiety that never left her, no matter how normal she might feel.

After rejecting the trip down memory-hell lane that had

been the last years of her life, she stood, hands on her hips and yelled the last words again for good measure, "Get the hell out of my head, you god damned freak!"

The silence in her space after that was almost as deafening as her caterwauling. And it was the most glorious sensation she'd ever experienced. It was nearly, but not quite, as good as an orgasm. Something she'd not allowed herself since managing to slip past the front desk guard of the Chicago building with her passport and a bit of cash, after lacing His evening Scotch with the pain pills she'd been saving for months.

But no. No more of that. She had a date. A real date. With a real man who wouldn't hurt her. He'd already promised that much.

"*Little fool*," her *Oma's* voice whispered. But she shut that down by cranking up her favorite rock and roll oldies station on her phone, streaming it through a cheap, Bluetooth-enabled speaker. "*All men hurt, one way or another. You know that better than anyone. When will you learn?*"

"Shut up," she repeated, as she began washing the fresh spinach she'd chosen at the farmer's market, picking out the dirt and pebbles, then setting the mound of rich green leaves on a towel to dry. She surveyed the kitchen with its broken dishwasher, four-burner electric stove of which only two worked, the single, stainless steel sink and the ancient white fridge. The three-layer cake with its homemade whipped cream frosting garnished with the brandy-flavored cherries livened up the table. The mound of green spinach, two fat butternut squash, and her bowl of ravioli dough took up all the available counter space. And she was happy.

Chapter Twenty-Three

Ross stared up at the ugly brick building that matched the address Elisa had programmed into his phone, then glanced at the two liters of beer he'd brought — both of his own homebrewed recipes — as his contribution to the meal. They sat on the passenger's seat of the boring sedan he'd been renting, alongside the obnoxious bouquet of red roses. The smell of the flowers nearly overpowered the fake-new-car spray they used in these pieces of shit rentals.

His head spun. He felt nauseated. His pulse raced, then slowed, then raced again, galloping along and making him breathless. The tingling sensations he'd been having all day that started in his scalp and raced down his spine, settling in his lower back, then gradually working around to his dick were distracting in the extreme. And now that he was within shouting distance of her, they were ten times worse.

He, Ross Hoffman, master of any immediate female universe, was as nervous as a sixteen-year-old boy on his first date. Which was a one-hundred percent new feeling, since he'd lost his virginity at fifteen and a half to one of his mother's colleagues and had spent an entire summer in a sex-soaked haze of worship at her feet. He'd hardly looked at girls his own age after that. And a 'date' to him meant fucking some girl's ever loving brains out, bestowing the skills that the lovely *Frau* Schmidt had spent many hours teaching him, then getting off and getting the hell out of Dodge.

He sat very still, coming to terms with this honest-to-God nervousness. He hadn't even been nervous at any point around the one woman he had allowed himself to love. His relationship with Evelyn Benedict Fitzgerald had started a natural progression in his life as a double-team expert with Austin, at least at first. Purely sexual. And incredibly sexual at that.

Then, he'd gone and fallen for her, like the mouth-breathing fool Elisa claimed he was.

And now here he was — a shaky, half-puking, half-horny, anxiety-riddled mess.

Something he had no frame of reference for — and did not like one bit. "Get a grip, man," he said under his breath, forcing himself to take long, deep breaths. "It's just a girl — a woman. She has all the same parts as every other woman you've experienced. Sure, it's cool because she's a brewer. And she's the most intriguing female you've ever encountered. And your need to protect her is so strong it almost chokes you most days… Oh fuck, just get out of the car already."

He grabbed the bottles and the flowers and climbed out of the nondescript Oldsmo-buick, squared his shoulders, checked the crooked sign indicating the direction of the various apartment units, then headed upstairs. It took him thirty seconds to catch his breath, not from the stairs but from the refreshed, sickening surge of anxiety that slammed into him at the sight of her door. "Get a grip," he repeated to himself. "Get a — oh, hello." He took a step back, trying like hell not to gape, mouth-breathing style, at the sight of Elisa in the now-open doorway.

She wore the tiniest scrap of silky black fabric, held up by thin straps at her shoulders. That wild-ass tangle of dreadlocked hair was pulled back and up, with a single strand of it hanging down to one shoulder. The god-awful ink at her throat glowed at him, seeming to taunt him, until he forced his gaze away from it. He stared at her upper arms, from the thorny vines, down to the small hops, not unlike those that ran across his upper back and down his arms.

Woozy, he focused on her other adornments, the ones that

turned him on more than anything he'd ever experienced with a woman. Tiny black dots sparkled in her impossibly small earlobes. The diamond in her nose and the matching jewel in her eyebrow plus that small silver ball in her lip made his mouth dry out. The memory of the hard ball of metal against his teeth and tongue nearly blinded him.

He gulped, and turned his horn-dog thoughts away from the other places she'd likely be similarly adorned. He had never seen an actual woman with a hood piercing but he'd heard about them, seen plenty of photos in his time. Ross licked his lips, already tasting her there.

The dress, he noted, was not terribly revealing. The dip in front was modest. The skirt length about mid-thigh. But it clung to her perfectly, highlighting her small waist, contrasting with her slim, but womanly hips. When she held out her right arm, indicating he should enter and stop gawking from the hall, he spotted the series of stylized star tattoos again, running up the pale white skin of her inner arm, from wrist to near her armpit.

She was, hands down, the oddest female he'd ever been attracted to. But the attraction was so powerful, it was painful — a dryness in his throat, heat behind his eyes, and a distinct tightness in his trousers that embarrassed him.

He entered the main room, his eyes adjusting to the low, candlelit ambiance. A cacophony of delicious odors hit his nose and brain all at once. He turned slowly to face her. She'd shut the door and now stood there, hands on her hips, her head tilted slightly to one side, regarding him. Her feet were bare. Her toenails painted black. He gulped, trying not to keel over from lust and terror.

She held out one hand. Ross stared at it, hearing soft strains of music — Django Reinhart if he weren't mistaken and he didn't think he was — and completely unable to move. She crooked her fingers at him. He looked at them, down at her feet, then back up at her bemused expression. Before he knew it, she was in front of him, filling his nose with her unique scent — a waft of vanilla with distinct undertones of something spicier and exotic—like cardamom, or cloves. She peeled his petrified fingers from around the wrapped stems of the roses, then plucked both plain brown bottles from his arm and hand.

"I wish I had my camera," she said, her voice low and soft.

"Um, huh?" He winced. "I'm sorry. I don't normally act like—"

"A befuddled caveman?" She smiled. She'd put a touch of something shiny on her lips. He wanted to kiss them so badly he had to clench his fists at his sides to stop himself. "I'll put these in water," she said, brandishing the roses. "Thank you."

He nodded, shoved his shaking hands into his jeans pockets and cursed his lameness. She moved around the tiniest kitchen he'd ever seen—which matched her in a way that seemed just right, to his mind. After grabbing two glasses and a plate of something, she returned to where he still stood, frozen, feeling like a lumbering elephant in the middle of English high tea.

She put the glasses and plate down on a table in front of a futon, then sat, tucking one leg under her. "Pour one of those," she said, pointing to the two bottles sitting on the small kitchen table next to something that made him do a double take.

"Is that...?" He approached the kitchen. "Dear Lord in heaven, it is." He gazed down at a Black Forest cake worthy of a photo shoot.

"Don't touch it yet, pig," she called from behind him. "Pour us a beer."

He grabbed the bottle with the red stopper, turned, took a deep breath and smiled. She smiled back. This was going to be all right. He could handle it. He would have to exercise caution and he knew it. No rushing straight in, picking her up and dumping her onto wherever her bed was so he could prove to her how he felt about her.

No. This was different. And a scene he was determined to

master, somehow. Maybe.

He opened the bottle and poured them each a measure of liquid. The rich, smoky odor filled his nose as he handed her a glass. "*Prost,*" he said, holding his up. She touched hers to it, sipped once, then took a longer drink. The soft groaning noise she made, along with the sight of her exposed skin pebbling with goosebumps made Ross' eager dick so hard he had to bite back a grunt of surprise. He leaned forward and plucked a bite of cheese from the plate to cover his discomfort.

She leaned forward then as well, which draped her across his lap in a way that did not help his condition in any way whatsoever. He closed his eyes so as not to fixate on the back of her long, porcelain neck. She retrieved the bottle and poured herself more of the *Rauchbier,* a special German style, whose distinctive smoke flavor was imparted by using malted barley dried over an open flame.

"Rye? Seriously, Hoffman? You smoked rye for this… you…crazy asshole."

For lack of anything better, he held up his glass to her. She rolled her eyes, sipped more, made that horrifyingly sexy noise again, then set the bottle on the table. Ross tried to smile but he sensed it faltering.

Keeping her gaze on his, she took a small piece of cheese and put it to her lips. He watched, utterly mesmerized by her fingers, by their black-glazed nails, the hop flowers on her knuckles, as she took another morsel of cheese and what he thought was prosciutto. The flash of metal inside her mouth forced him to stifle a groan. To his surprise, she stretched her fingers across to him, bringing the food to his lips. He blinked, like an oaf, he knew.

She raised the pale eyebrow that had the diamond in it, her blue-gray eyes shining with amusement. He opened his mouth, grazing her fingers when she placed the food on his tongue. He saw her shiver at that connection but before he could comment, she pushed his elbow, bringing his glass of beer up to his mouth. "Go on, combine these. It's incredible."

He did. And she was right. He took another bite, another sip and felt himself slowly but surely unclench.

"So," she said, leaning back and tucking her other leg underneath her so she sat like a little kid on her knees. "Tell me about your child."

He choked on the beer, spluttering and drooling and shocked to his core. "My…uh…what?"

"Rose Fitzgerald. The baby you had with our mutual boss."

"I'm… You… How did you…? Shit." He looked down at the bottle. "It's a complicated story."

"I can handle it," she said. "I mean, if you want to tell me about it."

Ross had never once revealed this fact to anyone. As far as he was concerned, the only ones who knew were himself, Evelyn and Austin. But it was completely stupid of him to think that. Everyone at Fitzgerald knew he and Evelyn had been together for almost a year. Austin and Evelyn had broken up and he'd had to run his newly deceased father's food supply business, leaving Evelyn and Ross in charge of the brewery.

Then, all of a sudden, Evelyn and Austin were back together, then married, and Evelyn had waltzed down the aisle visibly pregnant—but with his child. His throat closed up. His face burned. Something strange was going on with his eyes. He frowned at her, unwilling to let her do this to him. During his seemingly eons-long reflection over this bizarre conversational gambit, she'd remained silent, sipping her beer, curled up in her corner of the futon.

"Do you love her?" she asked, rocking him back even further on his emotional heels.

"Of course I do." Without thinking about it, he lifted the front of his carefully pressed white dress shirt. Her eyes flickered from his face to the small heart he'd had inked on his ribcage with the word *Rose* inside it in simple script. He let the shirt drop, embarrassed all over again.

"I meant Evelyn," Elisa said. Her voice was calm, non-confrontational. It soothed him in an odd way. He'd never quite felt the precise combination of emotions churning through him. She sipped. He stared at her, willing himself to talk.

"I…don't. Not anymore. I mean, I did. Who wouldn't?"

"Yes, Evelyn is an amazing woman. I can see how you would."

"It drove me away," he said, sipping without tasting. "I let it. I know that. It's not her fault, or Austin's. I still consider them my very best friends."

"I can tell."

"We agreed that…" His throat clicked, betraying the sort of emotion he hated — despised — to feel, much less to reveal to anyone. "That Austin would be Rose's father. I suggested he legally adopt her, making no questions down the road, no complications. You know?"

"But he didn't, of course," Elisa said, matter-of-factly.

"No. Stubborn fool." He shook his head and poured himself more beer, letting the high alcohol bite calm him.

"She is a beautiful child. Looks like her father."

"Her mother isn't hard to look at, either." He lifted his glass. "Since we're being honest." He let a beat of time pass. "Are you jealous of her?"

She sipped, keeping her gaze on him, then put her glass on the table. Ross hoped she might crawl into his lap. How he'd hide his raging erection then, he had no idea. But she stayed in her corner, making herself even smaller by wrapping her bare arms around her knees. He caught a flash of hot pink underwear. A bead of sweat popped on his temple, rolled down his face and made a wet spot on his shirt.

"Ask me something else," she said. "I'm not ready to answer that one."

He leaned back, musing on this revelation. "What was his name?" he asked.

He'd done his research after talking with Melody and still

didn't understand the appeal of the BDSM thing at all. He got it that everyone had their own level of kink. But trying to imagine the super feisty, smart, strong-willed Melody Rodriguez on her knees in front of some guy—even if it was Trent Hettinger, the super-cool gazillionaire owner of bars and liquor stores—to picture her bound, gagged, nipple-clamped, red-assed from being spanked, eating glass or licking piss or any number of other horrific things he'd read about online, was outside the realm of his understanding.

It was Elisa's turn to blink. Keeping his gaze as neutral as possible, he asked again. "What was his name, Elisa?"

She gulped and pressed her forehead on her knees. She muttered something.

"I'm sorry I didn't hear you."

"Nolan," she said, clear as day. "His name is Nolan."

"And how did you meet him?"

"He was my instructor at *L'ecole Cordon Bleu*."

"Your instructor." He sipped, noting that his hand was shaking like mad.

"Yes. He was the head chef, as a matter of fact. He seduced me, flat out. I was a child, of course. Barely nineteen. A silly virgin."

Ross' hand shook so badly he had to set his glass down at that little bombshell. "And you were with him how long?"

"Almost five years. He took my virginity three months after I started at *L'ecole*. A rather clinical experience. We had some…nice months together. But it was, all in all, pretty awful." Her eyes were blazing. She'd unfolded herself from her crouched over position. As she slowly rose, sinuously, like a dancer, Ross had to suppress the compulsion to pant like a dog. She stood over him, filling all his senses, making him dizzy. "Let's eat," she said, before heading into the kitchen.

He sat for a few seconds, pondering the goddamned chaos he was about to jump straight into, then he rose, grabbed the empty bottle and followed her.

Chapter Twenty-Four

The sound of blood *whooshing* in her ears as she crimped the edges of the ravioli focused her, allowing her to ignore Ross' massive, overwhelming presence in her cramped space. He'd settled himself into one of her two mismatched chairs at the table that held that over-the-top stupid cake. Keeping her back to him, she worked away, more than a little dizzy from all the things she'd said, all the words that had come out of her mouth, including The Monster's name.

As she set the butter in the cast iron pan, she felt as if she had gotten a bit of her equilibrium back. She turned, and found him sticking one of the cherries in his mouth. "What do you think you're doing!" She pulled the cake away from him.

Without a word, he snagged another cherry by its stem, wrapped his fingers lightly around her wrist and pulled her to him. He smelled of beer, and a little like leather and outdoors. Like a man should smell — not of silly colognes or perfumes. She wanted to kiss him. But she waited, smiling when he pressed the cherry to her lips. She opened them and ate it, relishing how its tartness was enhanced by the kirsch she'd kept them in for a month. It burst into her mouth, slid down her throat, and filled her entire being in an entirely inappropriate, purely sexual way.

She kept her face close to his, waiting for another of his toe-curling kisses. But he let go and jumped up. "The butter is burning," he said, taking one short step over to her stove. She put a hand on his arm, loving the play of his muscles under her palm.

"It's supposed to burn. Sit. Let me handle the cooking.

And keep your paws off the *gateaux*." She gave him a shove. The kitchen was small enough so that when she moved past him, their bodies brushed. She sensed how he pulled away from her, as if she'd burned him.

Focusing on the pan of browning butter, she let the meal prep distract her as much as she could. She dropped the pasta pouches stuffed with puréed butternut squash, truffles and light spices into the hot pan, moving them around so they cooked evenly.

"Would you mind taking the salad from the cooler?" She pointed to the fridge with her wooden spatula. "It's already dressed."

She tossed the ravioli a few more times until the nutty scent of the scorched butter mixed with the pasta into an ideal mix of aromas. She took two warmed plates from the oven and scooped three of the large ravioli out onto each one, sprinkled them with fresh parsley and thyme then reached for the expensive chunk of parmesan.

She smelled him before she felt his body against her back. The combination of leather, grassiness, malt and hops was something she already loved about him. But to feel both his arms around her, his large hand over her small one as she picked up the cheese, to see him take the grater in his other hand and angle it over one of the plates, was almost more than she could take. She leaned into him, letting him cradle her in his arms as they slowly grated slices of Parmesan together on first one, then the other plate of rich ravioli.

"I like a lot of cheese," he whispered, taking extra time over the second plate, the action more erotic than anything The Monster had convinced her to try. Reluctantly, she set the cheese aside and the grater down.

Instead of stepping back, Ross wrapped his arms tighter around her. He stood in silence for several minutes, resting his chin on her head, and providing the sort of intimate comfort she'd never received from anyone in her entire life. To his credit, Ross didn't let his hands roam anywhere. He simply held her. A single tear slipped down her face.

"Dinner is getting cold," she said, wishing he'd never let her go, but knowing he must.

"You're a convenient hole, my sweet little slut, my darling spinner. He'll fuck you and run. As he should. Because no one wants you but me. So you deserve to get fucked and left in the gutter."

Ross hadn't moved, as if sensing her desire for him to hold her a while longer. She sucked in a shuddery breath. "I hear His voice in my head. He is telling me the things He used to tell me the last years we were…together. In Chicago."

"What things?" Ross asked, letting go and turning her around to face him. "Look in my eyes, Elisa. You have no reason not to look at me."

She met his gaze, even though everything in her screamed at her to focus on the floor, lest she get a hard slap across the face. "He was… He is a monster. He did terrible things to me. And I let him."

"Yes, but at first, he was something else to you, right?"

"Yes," she said, her voice small, fighting the compulsion to lower her gaze. "He was…my Sir. He was my Dom. I was his submissive. It was…exotic and sexy — or so I thought. I didn't know any better. He was so much older than me — had so much more experience. He was never really gentle. He liked to…" She gulped and looked down.

Ross let her have a few moments to collect herself, then he lifted her chin. The sight of his bright blue eyes, of those full lips surrounded by the sexy red beard, his square jaw, his broad, strong shoulders made her knees turn to jelly. "He was rough with me from the beginning. But I was dumb. I thought it was how things were supposed to be. I thought the older, handsome, head chef wanting puny little, funny-looking me was worth the pain."

"Ach," Ross said, gathering her close again. She fit right against him, her face in line with his chest just below his collarbones, pressed into his pectoral muscles. She was shaking from lust and terror that she'd told him so much. She'd never told anyone all of it. Not even Evelyn, although

she had given her the basic outlines.

He let her go rather suddenly, she thought. But he dropped into the kitchen chair and pulled her to him, holding both her hands in his. He pressed his luscious lips to each of her knuckles, then to each of her upturned palms, then her wrists. Elle had never felt the sensation before but was certain that her panties were soaking wet.

She placed her palms on his bearded cheeks. "Let's eat, Hoffman. I worked hard on this meal. And I think we should talk a bit more before…" She bit her lip when his smile widened in a way that made her entire scalp tingle.

"All right," he said, grabbing another cherry off the cake. She yelped and smacked his chest, then picked up the plates and took them back to the futon and coffee table.

"I'm sorry I don't have a proper dinner table."

"I like this one," he said, bringing out the other bottle he'd brought, along with the vase of roses.

She went back for the salad plates and utensils, blushing harder when she spotted the cheese and grater. If nothing else ever happened with Ross Hoffman, she would never again feel the same way about such a simple kitchen chore.

She picked up the cloth napkins with the utensils and headed back to the living room. Ross was gazing at her wall of books, pulling one, then another off then sliding them back. "Like the scary books, eh?" He held up the latest, German-translated, Stephen King blood and gore-fest. She shrugged.

"I guess I like to think there are worse things in the world than what happened to me." She sniffed the open liter of beer, shocked all over again at his prescience with the beers. "Great choice," she said, pouring them each a portion of mild brown ale.

He shrugged, put the book back and fiddled with her phone. The music changed to piano classics as he sat on the floor in front of his plate. She frowned. "You can sit on the futon," she said.

"No, this is better." He grabbed a thin pillow and tossed it to the floor next to him. "Join me." Before she could protest, he pulled her plate closer, so she was at right angles him instead of at the other end of the table. She sat, noting the way his sharp blue eyes followed her every move, as if he were afraid she might bolt. He picked up his glass. "*Prost.*" She smiled and clinked and sipped, admiring his brewing artistry.

"Crystal malt," she said, smacking her lips and holding the light brown liquid up to the candle light.

"You have an excellent palate," he said, cutting a corner of the ravioli and taking a bite. She observed him, eager and nervous. There was nothing quite like watching people enjoy something you'd made for them, be it food or beer. He closed his eyes, chewed, swallowed and sighed with pleasure. Without a word, he devoured one of the large pasta pouches, then he sipped. "Not hungry?" He pointed to her untouched food.

Startled, she looked down at her plate. "Yes. But I like watching you eat."

He blushed, which made her almost faint with longing. When he reached over and cut a corner of her pasta and brought it to her lips, she took it from him, chewed and swallowed. "I like watching you, too," he said, before he repeated the process until one of her ravioli was gone. He sat back against a second-hand armchair, his face gone pensive.

"What?" She covered her lips with one hand, self-conscious and borderline embarrassed by how wonderful she felt, right here, right now, with this man.

"How did you get away from him?" he asked.

She cut a corner of another ravioli on his plate, and held it up until he leaned over and took it off her fork. Then she speared some spinach and a two pomegranate seeds, holding her fork up for him to eat from it. The sheer intimacy of this action made her warm all over. So she let her guard down.

"I tried to escape from Him, from our so-called home,

once before but He found me. I hadn't gotten far enough away fast enough. I paid for that." She leaned away from him and put her fork down, her eyes moving down on reflex at the frustrated anger on his face.

"Don't look away from me, Elisa. Please."

"I'm sorry. It's ingrained in me."

"I realize that. I also realize you have to try to fight it and I'm going to help you with that." He sipped his beer. "Tell me the rest."

"Why?" she demanded, angry all of a sudden at his incessant nosiness. Why couldn't they just enjoy this night, their first date, and what would no doubt be a very pleasant time together afterward. "Why do you want know all of this...awful...shit about me?"

He reached over and tucked one of the stray dreadlocks behind her ear, touching her earlobe and her jaw before he settled himself once more. "It's not shit, Elisa. Stop thinking that."

She sighed and averted her gaze again, biting her lip. "About seven months after...that first time, I was able to drug Him. I used some pills I'd been hoarding a while, dumped them into His nightly triple pour of Scotch. I'd spied on Him using the safe in his office enough times I thought I knew the combo and thank heaven I did so I was able to get my passport and some money. That's all, though. Everything else I had I left behind. Not that I would want any of it. It was all of the things I associated with Him. With The Monster."

"What made you run the first time?" His voice was tight. She glared at him.

"I was pregnant," she said. "And I wanted the baby. I knew he didn't. That he'd make me have an abortion. That was the only reason. To protect my baby."

His brow furrowed. She reached out and touched the stubborn line, smoothing it off his face. "Don't, Hoffman. Please," she said. "It's over."

He gripped both her wrists, sending a bolt of alarm up

her spine. Her flight instinct kicked in, making her struggle against him. He let go immediately. "I'm sorry. I'm not mad at you. I shouldn't have…" He ran a shaking hand through his hair.

She sat back, rubbing one wrist, then the other, her rage growing into something she couldn't control. "You want to know it all? Really? All of it? Fine." She stood and yanked her dress up over her head. Ross sucked in a breath. "This," she said, pointing to a long scar from her left hip to her lower right rib. "This is where He cut me with a blade, punishing me just enough, just deep enough to scare me and make me bleed. This is where He almost bit my god damned nipple off." She held a hand under her right breast, letting him see the full mangled glory of the body that she no longer believed was hers.

She lifted her chin and put her hand to her neck. "I got this collar in Paris, before we moved to the US, before He turned on me. But this," she turned so he could see her backside, pointing to her left cheek. "This is what He gave me after the first time I ran, after I told him I was pregnant." She could practically feel his fury, could taste his anger — not at her, she understood that. But part of this was her fault. She had let The Monster bend her over his knees and burn his fucking initials into the soft skin of her ass. She'd never lose that — the fact that he'd branded her like a prize heifer.

She crouched down to the floor, no longer able to hold herself up on her wobbly knees. In an instant, she was transported back to the times He'd make her stay on her hands and knees for hours — once for an entire day, well into her pregnancy. In the old days, he would soothe her after that sort of torture. He'd apply ointments to her abraded skin, to open candle wax burns, to her extended nipples. But something about being in Chicago changed Him, turned Him from a mildly abusive asshole into The Monster.

She felt a blanket drape around her and let Ross pull her

to her feet. But she yanked herself away from him, tugging the edges of the blanket close. The blanket, like every other damn thing in her life, she'd either been given by her brothers after running all the way home to Germany at first, or she'd bought at some second-hand crap store, saving as much of the money from her *Oma's* inheritance and her many brewery jobs as possible.

He stood, hands at his sides, looking utterly miserable. But that was too damn bad, she thought. He asked for it.

"How long since you ran?"

"Ten and a half years," she said, picking up her dress and slipping it back down over her naked torso.

"And he never found you, never confronted you, nothing?"

"No," she said, draping the blanket over the back of the futon. "And for the record, I didn't get an abortion either," she said, glaring at him.

His mouth dropped open. "But…"

"But what? You can count, I assume. I was with him another seven months. He kept at me, of course, doing everything he knew to do to cause me to miscarry. It was… the worst seven months of my life, but…I would have the child. In the end, I would have my baby." She sank to the couch, wrapping her arms around herself.

Ross remained where he was, halfway across the room, open-mouthed and horrified, no doubt. "I had the baby in the hospital, but He… He… He gave it away. He sold my baby to some childless couple, in New York, He said. But who knows where, really. I saw him…my son, once. They laid him on my chest after his birth and I touched him, then they took him. They all thought I was in on the adoption thing, of course. He made sure of that."

Ross sat beside her and tried to drape an arm over her shoulder but her ears were ringing and her heart pounding as an inexplicable rage filled her. Rage at The Monster, at herself for allowing those years of ridiculous behavior, for letting Him take her child, for allowing His violent manipulation of her for years.

But mostly at Ross, for daring to dredge it all up and out of her like so much disgusting vomit.

"Leave," she croaked out. "Go. I don't want you here anymore." When he tightened his arm around her, she wrenched herself away, grabbing the blanket and wrapping up again. "I hate you for this," she whispered, shaking so hard her teeth rattled. "I hate…this. I hate my life and I don't want to fucking talk about it."

He tried to hold her but she ran to the one other room in the flat and slammed the door shut. Her chest heaved with sobs. Tears burned tracks down her face as she leaned against the door, palms flat against it, willing the last thirty minutes back.

"Elisa," he said. "Open the door, please."

"Go the fuck away!" She screamed this last, meaning it. Not meaning it. Not knowing what she meant anymore.

"Elisa, open up."

She turned the lock, then backed away from the door, dropping onto her thin mattress and curling up in a ball, hands over her ears until she was certain he'd left.

Lightning flashed through the crooked blinds. Thunder boomed, making the whole building shake. A deluge of rain smacked against the single window.

Great. The very weather to enjoy a solitary dinner and that stupid, fucking cake all by yourself.

Chapter Twenty-Five

"Silly whore," The Monster whispered. *"You'd never be a decent mother. That boy was better off well clear of you."*

Wiping her eyes, she sat up, realizing she must have dozed. She felt drained, exhausted in body and spirit. Damn Hoffman, dragging all that out of her like some kind of a pseudo psychologist. She'd managed this far without therapy, or a man's touch on her body, any other lips on hers—she'd just have to continue down that road. She had her piercings, of course. The pain of them, then their reassuring presence as something she'd done to herself, at her own discretion.

But she didn't want to leave Fitzgerald Brewing. She'd run from every other brewery, always feeling like she stayed one step ahead of The Monster. Never knowing for sure, but counting on Him to find her and, likely, kill her if He ever did. She shed the dress and dragged on her comfy jeans and a sweatshirt with the neck cut out so one shoulder stayed exposed. Ever since her escape, she couldn't bear anything around her neck above her collar bones. She always cut her brewery T-shirts, avoided turtle necks or sweaters too close to her face. Hours spent with actual shackles around her neck had left her with that particular phobia.

No, she wouldn't leave. Ross would. He was only here for a consult, anyway, while that fool, Bryan was recovering from his concussion and when Austin and Evelyn needed help bringing the inventories up so they could export. Relieved, and at the same time depressed by that thought, she picked up their partially eaten food and carried the plates to the kitchen. Damn the man for wasting this good food, too. She ate a few bites, but everything tasted like soggy cardboard.

She shoved the plate away, fighting the deluge of memories her verbal regurgitation of her shitty backstory had caused. The cake caught her eye—the cake missing three decorative cherries. She smelled him then—not The Monster and his sickly, Euro-trash colognes, but Ross with his rich malty, leathery manliness.

What had she done? Why had she behaved like that? Ross was a kind, lovely man and he wanted to help her, to hold her and protect her and she'd turned into a screaming banshee, ordering him out of her house.

A surge of longing for him filled her soul, choking her throat, making her want to scream, to cry, to shove her fist through the wall all at once. The Monster had ruined her for men. But one man wanted to pull her out of that mire, to bring her back to the land of the living, breathing, sexually healthy women. And she'd shoved him away.

Without thinking, she stuck her finger straight into the cake, pressing against the soft *genoise*—the chocolate sponge cake layers. She pulled her finger out, observed it a few seconds, then stuck it into her mouth.

"Shit," she spat out, in English, which surprised her. Since she thought in German and had to translate every time she spoke, having Ross around to converse with in her native tongue had gone a long way toward easing her into a level of comfort with him. That was probably why she'd opened herself up. But no matter why, she knew she had to fix it. It was up to her to go to him, now.

"Don't do it," her nagging Oma-sounding subconscious insisted. *"Don't trust any man, ever again, remember?"*

"Fuck that," Elle declared, covering the cake so it wouldn't go stale, then sticking her feet into flip-flops and grabbing an umbrella. "Wait, Elisa. You don't even know where…" She snapped her fingers and grabbed her phone. Ross had obviously turned off the pleasant dinner music on his way out her door. As she was typing out a text to Evelyn, she gave up and hit call.

"Hello, Elle? You all right?" Evelyn's voice hit her brain, bringing on a rush of reality. She dropped onto the futon, boneless with anxiety, hand over her lips.

"Evelyn...I..."

"What is it? Do you need me to...?"

"I need to know where Ross is living, or staying, or whatever he is doing."

"Oh." The woman's voice died off in an odd way. Elle bit her lower lip, recalling that she'd declined to answer Ross when he'd asked her she was jealous of Evelyn. "Hang on, let me ask Austin."

After a few minutes spent second-guessing this whole thing, Elle heard Evelyn's voice again, sounding back to normal. "He's at the Residence Inn over on Sumner. I'll text you the address if you want."

"Yes, please." The pause extended past a polite period. "Evelyn...we..."

"I can't think of a better suited couple, Elle. I mean, I guess you know about...us. About me, and Ross...and Austin."

"Well, I know some of it. I know Rose is Ross' biological child."

"Oh." Another long, awkward pause. Elle waited, knowing they would have to get this figured out sooner or later. Because she had no intention of leaving Fitzgerald, and every intention of making Ross Hoffman something more than just her fellow brewer.

"It's all right, Evelyn," Elle said. "You have a history. We all have one of those, remember? Besides, Ross is —"

"Ross is a great guy. An amazing man, really. You're... You should go for it. You're perfect for him. And he will be the sort of man who'll protect you, forever."

"I know. I'm not sure we're... Well, let's say we're working some things out."

Evelyn chuckled. "Yes, I can just imagine. Listen, Elle...I want you to know that I consider you more than an employee. I mean, obviously, since you saved my life and all. You know what I mean."

Elle smiled to herself, getting that warm all over feeling she'd gotten earlier — sans the girlie tingles this time.

Friends. She had actual friends. She hadn't had those since...well, since ever.

She was the only daughter, the youngest child, of a reclusive set of parents who divorced, more or less leaving her to be raised by her elderly grandmother as her brothers had already gone away to University. She'd always been small, pale and weak until she figured out that she'd better get strong to protect herself. Her Oma had been rich and had loved her, in her way. She'd even paid for the French cooking school.

When the woman had died the month after The Monster had dragged her to Chicago, he'd not allowed her to return to Germany for the funeral. And of course, He'd kept her completely isolated from anyone she might consider a friend.

"Elle?"

"What? Oh, sorry, Evelyn, I was drifting."

"Anyway, listen, once you and Ross...uh...figure yourselves out, please know that Austin and I support you completely. Since Ross lost his job out west, we were considering...well, hoping really, that he'd stay with us. Which has to be good for you...I mean, right?"

"Right." A thrill of possibility shot up her spine again. "So...I'm going to go now. To find him. I owe him an apology."

"Have fun. See you on Monday." She ended the call before Elle could respond.

After sitting and staring out at the ongoing deluge, relishing the power of the lightning and thunder, Elle packed up all the leftovers, including the cake that now sported a finger-sized hole, grabbed her keys and ran down the metal steps to her car. She sent up the usual prayer of crappy car owners everywhere that the thing would actually start. When it did, she gave a little yip of nervous pleasure, checked the directions on her phone to Ross' hotel, and pointed herself that way.

She knew she was fully capable of chickening out, so she forced herself up and out into the pouring rain, cursing her lusty forgetfulness over the umbrella still in the closet of her flat. But the thunder had mostly subsided and the rain, while steady, wasn't pelting. It actually felt good when she tilted her burning hot face up and accepted its caress on her cheeks, lips and forehead.

She'd parked in front of the building where Ross, apparently, had a set of rooms at the top of a single flight of wooden steps. She stared up them, contemplating how drastically she wanted her life to change, and the fact that if she walked up those steps, it most definitely would.

She went up fast, not giving herself a chance to turn and run away. But when she raised her fist to knock, she hesitated. The voice was screaming at her now, blocking out the sound of the rain. She put the bags down and slammed her hands over her ears, crouching for a few seconds, willing it silent. Finally, her mind cleared, and she stood. Taking a deep breath, she raised her fist and banged hard on the door. "Hoffman! Open up!"

By the time he finally did open the door, she was soaked all the way to the skin but she felt energized—reborn. Slick and wet and eager in ways that confused her. Even the line of stubborn between Ross' eyes didn't deter her. She smiled, held out her arms and yelled, "Can I come in? It's a tad damp out here."

He stood inside the door, arms crossed over his bare chest. She stared at his pecs, at the thick black hop vine tattoo that matched hers, at his visible ab muscles.

"Eyes up here, please, ma'am," he said. "I'm not a piece of meat, you know."

She held up the bags of food. "Do you have a microwave?"

He nodded, but didn't move, continuing to block her way in. She dropped her arms, letting the rain pelt her, sensing his gaze taking her in from her dripping hair to her wet shoes. "You are a crazy bitch," he said, conversationally, as if she weren't standing right there, getting pelted in the rain while he remained dry less than a foot from her. "I'm not positive I want any part of you."

She blinked, then forced herself forward and into his arms, dropping the bags as she wrapped herself around him. "That's okay. I want us enough to make up for your lack of enthusiasm."

He yelped. "Shit, you're—"

"Yes, wet to the skin. I know. We seem to be like this a lot, don't we? Now, shut up and kiss me before I—oh."

He did just that, transporting her to what she'd come to think of as her only happy place—in his arms, with his mouth on hers, his tongue breeching her lips, forcing her to give in to him. She wrapped her arms around his neck and let him drag her inside. He picked her up, soaking clothes and all, continuing to kiss her all the way to the bedroom at the back of the mini-apartment.

He was gentle and tender as he undressed her, kissing every inch of skin he revealed, teasing her at the back of her neck and along her bare shoulders with his lips and teeth. He turned her this way and that, taking her all in, running his long fingers down her torso, cupping her breasts, licking each of her nipples, giving extra care to the still deformed one all the while muttering to himself in German.

He seemed especially fascinated with her piercings. He kissed her nose, her eyebrow, sucked the tiny ball in her lip into his mouth for a few seconds, rolled his tongue against the metal she'd placed there.

The line of balls in her ear cartilage got special attention. Each one of them touched with his fingertip, and his tongue.

Elle stood, eyes closed, letting him do what he wanted and loving it, loving him, if she were honest with herself. He ran his hands down her hips, around to her ass, across the evil puckered skin where she'd been burned. He was on knees now, his lips pressed to her stomach, then lower as his hands slid down the outside of both legs. His touch

175

tickled, taunted, made her breathe fast as she tried to relax.

With shaking hands, she untied the leather string holding his hair back and slid her fingers into its silky depths, grazing his scalp with her short fingernails. He looked up at her. His eyes were bright with emotion. "You all right?" he whispered. "This is okay?"

"It's very much okay. Please…more?"

He nodded and stood. He'd answered the door wearing nothing but a pair of shorts, as if he were going to exercise. She'd attempted to ignore the sheer magnificence of his body, but its size was enough to take her breath away. He was at least six foot four and obviously spent plenty of time at the gym. The light covering of blond hair across his upper chest was matched by a darker line of it below his navel. She touched his ribs, inside the tiny heart with the word Rose. His skin pebbled at her touch. She trailed her finger up to the hard, bronze disc of his left nipple, then higher, sliding her palm against his bearded cheek.

He took her wrist, kissed it, then planted tiny kisses on each of the inked stars on in the inside of her arm. "Oh," she gasped as he pulled her close with his other hand, keeping his lips on her skin. "Ross," she sighed as she molded herself against him, sensing the massive press of his erection against her stomach. She wanted him so badly it was a physical ache, centered between her legs. But it was more than sexual, somehow. She'd had plenty of orgasms in her early days with The Monster. This, however, was something else entirely.

"What are these?" he whispered as he kissed the last star, the one on the inside of her upper bicep. "Tell me what they mean?"

She reached down and slid her hand into his shorts, smiling when he hissed an exhale at her touch. "There is one star for every year I've been free of Him." The tip of his cock was wet and as she slid her hand down, then back up, he groaned and thrust his hips against her.

"Oh," he said, pulling her hand off him. "I see. So, let me

suggest one for this year." He eased her down onto the bed, spreading her dreadlocks out in a fan around her head.

"Okay," she said, unhappy to no longer be touching him, but figuring there'd be time enough for that later. "Suggestions are welcome."

"I think," he said with a smile as his large, warm hand slid up her legs to her hips, her waist and finally to her breasts. She gasped and arched her back as he teased her nipples with his thumbs. She had her arms up over her head, eager for more, aggravated and hornier than she'd ever been.

His lips found the spot where'd she'd planned the eleventh star, almost into her armpit. He pressed his nose there, then his tongue, making her groan with pleasure and wrap her arms around his hips, eager for friction, for a release. "I picture a heart here." He kissed that spot again, leaving her gasping and squirming. "I heart with a big..." He kissed her neck. "Fat..." He slanted his lips over hers, staying somewhat detached from her, propped up on his strong arms, probing and teasing her mouth again. "R," he said after he broke away.

"A...what?" She was clutching at him, feeling like a stupid virgin, wanting something she didn't understand but something was urging her to do things that felt natural, not forced.

"An R. For Ross. Because these..." He trailed his fingertip up the line of stars. "These end now. No more gauging your life in terms of how many years you've been free of him."

His blue eyes were dark with lust as he stared at her. She let go of him and lay back, pondering this. "All right," she said, her voice cracking with emotion. "If you say so."

"No, God damn it." He rolled onto his back, one arm draped over his eyes. "I'm not that guy, Elisa. I'm not the guy who tells you what to do."

She propped herself up on her side, draping her leg over his thigh and pulling his arm off his face. "I'm sorry. I didn't mean it that way." But she had. It was pure reflex, of course. A sort of sick Pavlovian training she'd probably never be free of. When he turned his head to look at her, the anguish on his fact made her want to weep. "Maybe this is more than you want to get into, after all."

Resigned, she slid to the end of the bed. But he pulled her back, tugged her until she was on top of him, straddling his hips. That incredible cock was rock hard, now nestled against her pussy. But he didn't move. His hands rested on her thighs. "Do you mind?" she asked, as she did her own exploring, letting her fingers do the walking from his shoulders, down his arms, then across his chest. She flicked his nipples, smiling when his dick jerked beneath her. She lifted her hips so she could get at his shorts and slid them all the way down, while he lay there, quiet but for his rapid breathing.

"Ross," she whispered in his ear as she used her lips on his skin, tasting every inch of him, including the salty tip of his penis. As she attempted to slide her mouth down his shaft, he grunted, and eased her up. "What?" She swiped at her lips, more eager than ever to have him inside her. "You don't enjoy that?"

"Oh, I enjoy it all right. Too much so. I'm not skipping any steps tonight, Elisa. Now, lie back. It's my turn to taste you. And I can't wait to see what kind of jewel you put there for me to find."

Giggling, she scooched up until her head was on the pile of fluffy pillows while he watched. When she got her first glimpse of his cock, she couldn't help but gasp. "That is… one impressive piece of equipment, *Herr* Hoffman." She put her hands behind her head and bent one leg, loving it when he focused his gaze on her pussy and licked his lips. "Women must line up for miles for that thing."

He touched himself, his hand moving up and down its impressive length as he smiled. "Yeah, that's what they tell me. But the line stops here…even if you don't get to have it quite yet, *Fraulein* Nagel."

She pouted, then yelped in pleased surprise when he dropped over her, kissing her hard, shoving his tongue into her mouth as one hand roamed down to her breasts, then lower, cupping her entire pussy in his hot palm. "I can smell how much you want me, Elisa," he whispered, taking the ball in her lip into his mouth, then kissing his way down her neck and shoulder, pausing to suck each nipple gently, before placing a line of fluttery kisses down her belly. "I want to taste it so very badly." His voice was hoarse. She felt as if she could taste his lust, his need for her, as he draped her legs over his shoulders and cupped her ass in his hands. "*Ach*, my love," he sighed as he touched his tongue to her clit, teasing and nearly making her come before backing off and licking her lower lips slowly.

She felt his mouth on the curved bar that went through her hood. The pressure sensation that provided her clit as the tiny jewel pressed against it was, indeed, mind blowing.

"Oh…oh…God, yes," she sighed as she buried her hands in his hair and tilted her hips up, giving herself up completely to him. "Ross…I need…I must…"

He latched onto her clit again, sucking it hard as he slid fingers inside, stretching her, which hurt, since she'd gone a long time without a man inside her. She made low cooing noises and thrust her hips upward as the low-lying tingling that had been creeping up her spine hit brain with the force of a hammer blow.

She cried out, not even aware of what she was saying as she let go of his hair and grabbed the pillows behind her, while the blessed release of a massive orgasm transported her. He kept stroking inside her, but had let go of her clit, somehow knowing it would be sensitized by that point.

"Oh. Oh. Oh. Oh," she kept saying as her back arched. "My God in heaven," she groaned when her eyes opened again.

"That was lovely," he said, looking up from between her legs. "You are delicious."

She sighed and stretched, relishing this amazing freedom from fear. "I want you inside me, Hoffman," she managed. "I need it."

"That makes two of us," he said, but he backed away from her.

"Well, then where in the hell are you going?" She rolled to her belly, feeling sated, and revved up beyond belief. "Hoffman, come back here and bring that giant dick with you."

"It goes where I go, my love." But he remained on the other side of the room, staring out of the window.

She got up and went to him, wrapping her arms around him and laying her head against his strong, sweaty back. She touched her tongue to his skin, tasting salt, which made her want to taste more. Dying to get her hands on it again, she slid them down his torso, wrapped one hand around his thickness and cupped his heavy balls with the other. He grunted, and his hips started moving as she stroked him. Just when she thought he would blow, he pulled away, turned and stared down at her.

"I can't do this, Elisa," he said around clenched teeth.

"I don't understand," she said, pressing against his warm skin. He ran his hands down her back, cupped her ass, then let go with a loud curse.

"I…can't love you. And I do. I mean… I will. You know?" He raked his fingers through his hair.

She smiled and slid her hand around the back of his neck before pressing her lips to his. He groaned into her mouth, picked her up and sat on the edge of the bed with her on his lap. "I need to be inside you, Elisa. But I can't promise what will happen after that."

He reached into a drawer for a condom. As she stood and watched, he opened the packet and slid the thing down his length, then pulled her back to the bed.

He lay back slowly, never taking his eyes from hers as she straddled his hips, put her hands on his incredible shoulders and rested her eager pussy against the top of his dick. They both sucked in a breath at the contact. He pressed his fingertips into her thighs. "Do you understand me? Elisa? I want this as much as you do but it changes everything. Absolutely…everything."

Nodding, she slid down, taking him inside her, feeling her delicate tissues stretching to accommodate him. They stared at each other as she moved down, inch by exquisite inch. "Everything?" she asked, loving the sound of that word almost as much as she loved the feel of his massive cock.

"Everything," he said, before he sucked her nipple into his mouth, flicking it with his tongue. He was barely holding back, she could tell. Their combined sweat slickened their skin as she took the last bit of him, crying out in pain and pleasure. She felt impaled on him but in a way she wanted, a way that she craved.

"I'm not going to last, my love," he gasped against her breasts. "But I want you to come again. I want to feel you grip me so hard it makes me come." He leaned back, his dark blue gaze meeting hers. She pressed her hands against his chest and ground against him, getting the combination inner and outer contact as he palmed her breasts and flicked both her nipples. Feeling it coming at her, bearing down in a way that made her move faster, she leaned her head back, keeping her hands on his shoulders and let it happen.

It did hurt a little, but the sensation of his thick girth spreading her, of his length reaching places inside her she'd never felt before as he teased both her nipples at once and begged her to come, to make him come with her pussy, she yelped and shuddered from head to toe gasping for breath as the orgasm spun her around and bowled her under.

Ross cried out with her, his hips moving fast beneath her. "*Küss mich*," he demanded. She did and they rocked, riding out their respective climaxes together. "Fucking hell." He broke from her lips, his sweaty face pressed into her neck. "I don't think…I've ever felt anything like that." He leaned away from her, but didn't push her off him. She liked staying connected with him, in the most intimate way possible. "Are you a witch?"

She giggled and pushed him back. He flopped onto the

pile of pillows, pulling her with him, kissing her with a ferocity that she matched with equal fervor. Her mind was a near blank, her body tingling and sated. The sensation of his beard rasping her raw cheeks was something she was already addicted to. She pulled away and stared down at him. "I could kiss you forever," she said.

"Sign me up." He grinned, cradling her face between his hands. "You're amazing. And I wasn't kidding earlier. It's all changed now."

She sat up. He was still as hard as a rock inside her. She rolled her hips, propping one hand on his chest and the other on his thigh behind her. "I want to come again. I think I am addicted to it."

"Allow me to assist." His full lips twitched into a smile as he reached up and tweaked her nipples, accommodating her and pulling her straight into a strong, aftershock climax. Shivering, she dropped over his chest, loving his arms around her, his lips on her hair. Her eyes closed and she slept that way, her nose full of his smell, his taste of his sweat in her mouth, his cock still inside her. For the first time in almost eleven years, she slept without a single nightmare invading her peace.

Chapter Twenty-Six

When Ross' inner alarm brought him to wide awake at five-forty-five a.m. he'd been confused at first, finding the small form tucked against his side, the wild tangle of blonde dreadlocks half on his chest, half draped over his face.

But within seconds, a satisfied contentment had suffused his entire being, reminding him of how the night had ended. He pulled her closer, burying his nose in her hair and getting a whiff of her shampoo. The subtle floral-like lavender with a slight tinge of sweat reminded him of home, his *real* home, where women always did go a bit more *au naturel* than they did here in the good ol' US of A. She mumbled something, threw her arm over his chest and hiked her knee higher on his thigh.

He hadn't willingly slept with a woman post-sex since Evelyn. As he stroked her arm absently, he mused on this fact and how great it felt right now, waking this way, piled together like puppies. The sun was already lightening the edges of the sky, promising another lovely Michigan early summer day.

Perfect.

That was a good word for how he felt right now. As he poked around that emotion, searching for its edges, its limitations, as was his tendency, he found none. It was Sunday and she'd not scheduled either of them for time at the brewery, although, knowing them both they'd end up there at some point. But for now, he was here, his body and heart fully sated after a night of love with this exotic, beautiful creature. She still lay in his arms and that sensation had to be one of the most satisfying ones he'd ever experienced.

Love?

Possibly.

The fact that she'd shown up, eager for him, willing to set aside her earlier tantrum over his nosiness was, to say the least, a good sign. Ross shook his head at himself. Feelings. Since when did he give two shits about how a woman *felt* about him? Only once, he thought. And he'd known Evelyn's complex emotions over him and Austin could and would only end one way. A way he'd machinated himself, even though it cost him months of anguish.

Elisa's fingers twitched on his chest. She muttered against his skin. He kissed her hair again, and placed his hand on her arm—the one he'd bestowed so much attention to last night, driving her crazy with his kisses and teasing up that long line of admittedly attractive ink.

The line of stars he would stop, by God. No more running was necessary. He was here. And he would protect her.

That thought brought it all back—all the confessions and his first glimpse at her sweet body. Frankly, he'd barely paid attention to her litany of abuse, he'd been so utterly fascinated by her naked torso. She was petite—more so than any woman he'd been with. But her physical strength was obvious in the lean musculature of her arms, her back, her legs and ass. Her figure was not at all boyish, once he got a good look at her. Her waist was tiny, and her hips flared out from there, balanced by her breasts which, while more than a mouthful were not much more so. And to him, they were amazing. Him, a long-avowed tits man who'd claimed to like them C-cup or higher, or not worth bothering with.

She quivered against him and made a funny yelping noise, obviously in the throes of a dream. He stroked her arm and made shushing noises, loving the softness of her skin under his palm. Everything about her, up to and including her smart mouth with its snooty Berlin city accent pleased him. Even all the bizarre ways she'd hurt herself repeatedly— the complex tattoos and the many piercings. Even that protective shell she'd thrown up at the last minute when he'd more or less ruined their nice dinner with his questions made him smile.

My Elisa, he thought as she continued to tremble, then calm, as he drifted, allowing himself a rare sleeping-in morning. He wanted all his energy so they could spend the day learning each other's bodies, eating great food, then diving back into the sheets. His dick had hardened while he'd been recalling her, ripping off that scrap of dress and standing there, in nothing but that pair of hot pink panties, glaring at him. He put a hand on his erection and stroked as his nose and brain filled with her scent—the lavender mixed with sweat, mixed with the tang of sex that hovered over the room.

His finger must have grazed the leg she had draped over him, which, he noted, positioned her pussy nicely against his upper thigh. He felt its warmth, smelled her spiciness, which made him get serious with the stroking, figuring he might as well rub one out, which would leave him less inclined to blow like a rookie within seconds of getting inside her again.

He focused on the ultra-sensitive area around the head of his cock and made short, tugging motions. Plenty of practice in this area had proven him an expert at the fast and silent jerk off. His familiar friction caused the orgasm to roll up his spine, landing in his brain, which yelped *ships ahoy!* and allowed him to release with a quick exhale and loud sigh, coating his fingers with cum. At the split second that his brain shut down and with his hand still around his pulsing dick, Elisa cried out, pulled away from him and scrambled to the far side of the king-sized bed.

Gasping in the aftermath of his quickie climax, Ross propped on his elbows, trying to wrap his befuddled mind around what he saw. She dragged the sheet with both hands to cover her nakedness. Then she balled herself up as she'd done the night before on the futon, wrapping both arms around her legs that were bent against her torso. She wouldn't meet his eyes and her teeth chattered as if she were freezing.

A small pinprick of anxiety hit his brain. What would trigger this, he wondered as he got up, grabbed a towel to wipe his belly, washed his hands then pulled on his shorts before approaching her. She was like that rabbit he'd first thought of when pondering her body language—cowering, frozen in place, waiting for the killing blow from the hawk above her.

He sat facing her, one hand on resting on her knees. Instinct told him not to move too fast, or do anything rash, but to wait and let her come fully awake. She kept her face pressed to his hand, but didn't try to move further away from him. He waited, remaining patient, as those odd protective hackles he'd developed rose, making his pulse race and his hands itch to wrap around the neck of the asshole who'd done anything to her, much less the level of abuse she'd sustained.

She raised her face. Her eyes were dry, her jaw clenched. He stroked her cheek with a fingertip until she relaxed. But her arms stayed tight around her, protecting herself, he understood, from whatever threat she'd imagined. He waited a few more minutes until she let go of herself and crawled into his lap where she belonged.

He held her close, rocking her like a child, making the crooning noises that one of his many nannies used to make when he'd awake from some night terror or another. He held her until she stopped shaking. "What happened?" he asked, resting his chin on the top of her head.

"You startled me when you…um…" She pulled back and gazed at him in the early morning light. "The smell of your spunk," she said, matter-of-factly. "It woke me and scared me."

"Scared you," he said, unable to resist the urge to kiss her flushed cheeks, her forehead, then her pursed lips. She allowed it, opening her mouth to him in a way that caused an odd, gooey feeling in his chest.

Love?

Probably.

Worth it?

That remained to be seen.

This woman was a bundle of nerves, anxieties and phobias, and while he wanted it all—the full package of her—he knew he wouldn't be able to handle it without some help. She wrapped her arms around his neck and shifted so she was straddling him again. Ross' cock, so recently active, surprised him by hardening the second that cold metal bar in her hood touched it. In silence, he slid his hands up her back, then leaned forward and licked her nipple, the deformed one, with the scar where some freak show of an excuse for a man had bitten her, on purpose. He licked and teased it to a lovely, firm peak, then did the same with the other.

She made that soft, repetitive noise she'd made the night before, deep in her throat and breathy, as he sensed her lust increase, curling around them like the world's sexiest fog cover. Keeping his attention focused on her breasts, as she was obviously highly sensitive there, he forced all misgivings and thoughts of her crouching like a doomed rodent out of his head.

He would drive that from her with his love and attention. He would gain her trust back, prove to her that he was worth it. Slowly but surely.

"*Slowly,*" his inner smart ass intoned, distracting him for a moment. "*Since when do you go slowly? Even Evelyn wanted you fast and hard, then faster and harder and you loved that about her. This chick...*" The smart ass that passed for his better self made a tsk-tsking sound in his head. Ross responded by shifting his hips so the length of his dick was pressed fully against her warm and now wet, pussy. He kept up his attention to her nipples as she ground down on him, using the head of his dick to gain friction. "*This chick is trouble, Hoffman. The capital-T kind of trouble.*"

"*I don't care,*" he responded in his head, frowning against the soft skin of Elisa's neck as she moved faster against him, making him ache to be inside her but knowing this was what she needed right now. The hard bite of the curved bar even felt good to him, in a painful sort of way.

"Oh you will care, Mister," the jerk in his head intoned. *"Mark my words. She's gonna fuck you up six ways to Sunday. Worse than Evelyn ever did."*

"Shut up," he muttered, making her pause and look down at him. Her cheeks were flushed, her eyes bright, her hair a crazy halo around her face.

"Good to know someone else has to put their conscience in its place every now and then," she said, before pressing her lips to his. Groaning, he dropped back to the bed and let her do whatever she wanted to him, biting his lower lip, his nipple, lifting his arms up and over his head as she kissed and licked her way down his neck and shoulders.

He felt like one giant, exposed nerve, centered deep in his gut, and at the tip of his cock. She roamed down his body, lapping around the edges of his head in a way that made him thrust up, needing more. He closed his eyes and let her set the pace, dipping her tongue in and out of the slit, before sliding her lips down over him, going as far as she could, before releasing him, and doing it again.

The white noise descended, his preface to a monster climax. He wrapped some of the ropes of her hair around his fists, not pulling, just wanting that connection as she drew him closer and closer to the edge. She cupped his balls then used her finger to stroke beneath, making him shudder in anticipation.

He grabbed a pillow so he could prop his head up, wanting to watch her working him over. She was looking up at him, her lips spread wide around his glistening dick, her hand clutching the base, her other hand tickling the smooth skin between his balls and ass. His hips jerked up, he closed his eyes and shot down her throat, coming so much he thought he might pass out from it, gripping her hair and shoving further into her mouth with every spasm.

As he lay gasping and spent, staring at the bland hotel ceiling, that warm, happy feeling he'd woken with filled him once again. He tugged her up and against him, kissing her and tasting himself on her lips.

He was still hard as a rock, against all laws of biology, and he wanted to taste her again. Ross had always been a huge fan of providing pleasure with his lips and tongue. His first instructor in this had been insistent that even women who claimed not to like it would fall at his feet and beg for it as long as he did it the correct way — focusing on the clit, and nothing else, until it plumped up, went erect in his mouth, at which time, he was to use two, or maybe three, fingers and slide them inside, angle up and toward her pubic bone.

Sometimes he felt something there. Sometimes not. But regardless, it was, truly the elusive G-spot for most women that he'd stroke, along with sucking her clit which would always provide the sort of mind-shattering orgasm most women had never experienced.

He tugged her around so she was on top of him, barely a weight he registered. "My turn," he said, his voice croaky. "Or, better yet, yours." He pushed her back so she was sitting, then pulled her hips forward. "Grab the headboard, *Mein Shatz*," he crooned as the smell of her, and of him, and of them, roiled around in his head, driving him mad with need. "Hold on tight."

He got to work. When she came it was with a surprising gush of fluid that coated his lips and filled his mouth with a strange but entirely pleasant taste. She was gasping and moaning and moving her lips as she came down from the climax. He looked up at her from between her legs. Her face was coated in a sheen of sweat, her eyes closed. He waited, content to watch her and smell her and still taste her until she calmed and opened those incredible, somehow fairy-like eyes.

"A unicorn," he said, as he moved up her body and flopped bedside her with a contented sigh.

"A what?" She stroked his beard with one hand and

pressed her lips to his chest.

"Unicorn." He took her hand and kissed her palm, then her wrist, wondering if he would or could ever get enough of her.

"What is that supposed to mean? Should I be insulted?"

He held her close with both arms and began to drift. It was so completely unlike him to be sleeping at this hour, it felt almost as sexy as giving her head in return for his. "No, my darling. You're the thing everyone looks for but never finds. The woman who will ejaculate."

She raised her head and stared at him. "I did no such thing."

He grinned and touched her nose, amused at her alarm. "You did. You came in my mouth and it was delicious. From what I understand, it's something very few women do and they don't always. Only when aroused to their full potential."

"Well." She snuggled into his side again, bringing on that warm covering of unfamiliar happiness once more. "You did that to be sure. Arousing me to my full potential, and then some."

"No more mouth-breather insults, then, eh?"

She looked up at him again, frowning. "Hmm. No promises there, sorry. You turn into a bit of a bossy caveman in the brewery, you know."

"Well, I am the boss caveman there."

"Can we sleep some more? I feel so...so very right here, in your arms. And I never thought I'd feel that, much less say it, ever again."

"Sleep, my darling," he said softly. "I will watch over you." But before she could make fun of this particularly alarming and sappy comment of his, she was dozing. Ross smiled, and drifted to sleep again, his mind blessedly blank, his body—pent up even after Holly's little stunt—completely sated for the first time in months.

Chapter Twenty-Seven

The weeks that followed made Elle feel in turns happy and content, then anxious and jumpy. Ross wouldn't keep his damn hands off her, no matter where they were, which wasn't exactly unpleasant, but made her worry about appearances and propriety. The ease with which he'd guided her out of the gloom of a decade's worth of man-draught into the light of pure erotic pleasure shocked her if she gave it any serious thought.

Considering that her first and only sexual experience had been with an older man who'd deflowered her in the most perfunctory, mechanical way possible, then had taught her every trick in the book — like how to give the right blow job, how to relax into an orgasm herself. How to be at home with her own body, exploring it with Him for the first year and a half, using soft handcuffs, blindfolds, mild pain as pleasure.

But after that, when He'd convinced her to leave with him for the jobs in Chicago, once they'd moved into the too-expensive flat and they'd begun working side by side, all of that had changed in a brutal blink of an eye. She shook her head to dispel the evil, something she was having better luck with lately and no wonder, considering Ross kept her either on the knife edge of an orgasm or spilling over into it, rolling around in it, reveling in it with him in a way that surprised and thrilled her.

Working with him — something she'd dreaded since that was what had seemingly spoiled things for her once before — was even an erotic experience. He'd tease her, brush her neck or arm or ass with his fingertips. He'd send overtly dirty text messages out of the clear blue sky, with her sitting on one side of the table at lunch, Austin or Evelyn, or some other brewery employee between them and carrying on a conversation as if he had not just described how he'd make her come so hard she'd squirt. Something that still made her slightly uncomfortable in its description but certainly not in its actuality.

She'd never come so many times or in so many ways. She had no idea it was even possible. And his body was her playground. His massive dick was no less impressive and stunning than the first time she'd laid eyes on it. It still hurt when he was fully inside her but she didn't care. Because it was his favorite way to come — buried deep inside her, as she rubbed her piercing against his pubic bone. He would cry out so loudly she had to slap a hand over his lips, worried the thin walls of the hotel would betray them.

She'd even convinced him to forgo the condoms. He'd balked, saying he'd had too much unprotected sex and didn't want to do anything that might harm her. So, she'd dragged him to a doctor's office and ordered the barrage of tests to ensure them both that he was, in fact, completely clean. When he'd looked into her eyes and asked, innocently and with some earnestness, if she worried about getting pregnant, she'd said no. That the Monster had taken care of that and they'd have to talk about that more later.

He'd dropped the subject. And thrown out his stash of Magnum-sized condoms.

She'd slept every night since their first one together wrapped up in his arms, in his hotel bed. While the practical side of her realized that arrangement wasn't sustainable, for the moment, she was content to let it sustain her as her new reality.

Three weeks after their first date, they'd finally caught up to the aggressive production targets. To celebrate, Evelyn and Austin threw a company-wide party, going so far as to close down the pub on a Tuesday night and catering in food so Melody and her staff could relax and enjoy.

"Wear the black dress," Ross insisted as they got ready after a long, hot, sexy shower together.

"Don't be ridiculous. It's not that kind of a party."

"It's whatever kind of a party we want to make, dear heart. And I think you look like a knockout in that thing. I want to show you off."

"Show me off, eh? Don't you think everyone pretty much already knows we're together? Evelyn's assistant did catch us screwing in the women's locker room and you don't make any effort to curb yourself at work, *Herr* Grabby Hands."

He reached for her and dragged her onto his lap, lifting up her hair and kissing that spot he'd found at the nape of her neck that drove her up the wall. She squealed and slapped his shoulders, before giving up and kissing him—hands down, one of her top two favorite things to do with him—her man.

"You are so naïve. This man belongs to no one. He's amused by you, that's all. And soon enough, he'll be over you and your incessant anxiety attacks and lame emotional outbursts," her inner nag reminded her. But both the inner nag voice and The Monster's had faded so much in the face of Ross' onslaught, she barely heard it.

"Aus! Lustmolch! We have to go," she gasped, pulling away from him and standing up. Her towel had ended up on the floor so she grabbed it and headed for the closet, where she'd been keeping a lot of her things lately.

"Oh, all right. Buzz kill." He smacked her ass lightly on his way past, whistling as he brushed his wet hair and tied it back.

"Tell you what," she said, pulling the dress off a hanger. "I'll wear this, if you'll keep your hair down."

"Like this?" he asked, yanking out the leather tie and doing a model-worthy head swing.

"Yes. Like that." She stepped into the dress, then reached for a pair of panties in the drawer she'd appropriated. But he grabbed the small scrap of silk from her, tossed them to the floor and stood over her, grinning that grin that made her knees melty. "Excuse me, but I needed those."

"No. You won't be needing those at all." He pulled up a pair of black jeans, then stuck his arms into a neatly pressed, soft blue button-down collar shirt. "I want access, just in case I get an urge…you know." He waggled his eyebrows at her like a fool, but she laughed and rolled her eyes at him, feeling happiness seep through her again, against her own better judgment.

They arrived as the party was headed into full swing. The music was blaring and the place packed with their brewing personnel, office staff, cleaning crew, kitchen and wait staff. Austin, Brock and Evelyn were acting as bartenders for the night. They'd set out a huge jar for tips, all of which would go to the Fitzgerald Charitable Trust, a non-profit that Austin had set up and put Brock in charge of managing.

As they stood in the door, initially unnoticed, Elle held back, pressing herself against Ross' side. He kissed her hair then raised his arm and hollered to the room, "The superstar has arrived. Please make way!"

The room turned with a collective cheer that died on their lips. It was an odd, seemingly scripted moment that sent a jolt of anxiety all the way through Elle.

"I need a god damned beer. Somebody get me a good one?" Ross tugged at her, but her feet felt mired in concrete as the eyes of everyone in the room—people she knew, had worked with, liked and even considered close friends—locked onto her. Many mouths were agape. Hands with glasses in them were paused, mid lift to mouths. "What's the matter with you idiots?" Ross bellowed good-naturedly. "Never seen a beautiful woman before? Jesus. Close your mouths. You're depleting my oxygen. Come along, my love, ignore these peasants."

He held out his hand. She stared at it, then put her palm in it. That seemed to break the collective trance. Both Melody and Evelyn ran up to her, chirruping and otherwise making admiring noises. But her ears were buzzy. Her head spun.

She never should have worn this damn thing. It was too showy. She shouldn't parade her happiness with Ross around either. It was bad luck.

As if sensing her panic, Ross tugged her to him as he stood in the middle of a circle of fellow brewers and others. Someone pressed a glass of stout in her hand. Austin was standing up on the bar, swaying more than a little. "Here is to you all," he yelled, quieting the din. "All you amazing assholes. Without every single one of you we would not be celebrating selling over a million god damned dollars' worth of Fitzgerald Brewing Company liquid today." He raised his glass. The room parroted him.

"But of course, mostly to me," Ross declared, holding up his beer and letting go of Elle long enough to run a hand down his chest.

"Nah, I'd say mostly to the woman to your immediate right," Austin claimed, winking at Elle. Her face flushed hot but she held her glass higher.

"Who? Oh, yes, her," Ross said, eyeing her in an odd way. He held his glass out to her for a private toast. "I'll drink to her any day of the week." The room let out a sigh and several sarcastic "Aw, isn't Ross cutes?" but Elle had ears and eyes for one man. Her man.

"I love you," he mouthed to her. She flinched, sucked in a breath, and sipped her beer.

"As you well should, my friend." Austin had materialized next to them. His dark green eyes were shiny and his words ever so slightly slurred. "You need to catch up," he said, poking Ross in the chest. "Somebody get me some shot glasses."

He brandished a bottle of bourbon, something expensive, Elle had no doubt. But bourbon wasn't her thing. If she weren't drinking beer, she preferred wine. Hard liquor did nothing but give her an ugly headache.

"Fuck that, ya pussy," Ross hollered, wrenching the cork from the bottle and knocking back a huge slug before passing it back to his friend. Austin did the same. Evelyn tugged her arm. As she moved away from him, Ross turned, concern in his blue gaze. "You all right?" he yelled over the increasingly loud party.

She nodded, lifted her glass, winked and followed Evelyn toward the bar. She didn't really want to *not* be standing with Ross but she knew they were grown-ups and expected to behave that way at a social gathering. She kept her eyes on him as he was approached by brewers, kitchen staff, the night cleaning crew, and slapped on the back, hugged, or kissed.

A warm feeling was spreading through her, starting in her chest. Partly the second beer she was drinking, she knew, but also in large part due to the fact that for the first time in her life she felt a part of something, surrounded by people who loved and cared about her.

"They're gonna get shit-faced, fair warning. Austin already told me that was his goal tonight." Evelyn was leaning opposite her, letting Brock handle the beer pouring. They'd set up a self-serve liquor bar, confiscated everyone's car keys at the door, and arranged for a phalanx of taxis and ride share cars to be ready at a moment's notice should anyone want to leave.

"Yes, I can see that," she said, sipping and watching him, her man, her Viking hero, her lover, work the room like a pro.

"So, Trent and Melody have invited us all up to his cabin, in Petoskey."

Startled, Elle faced her friend. "Us?"

Evelyn smiled. "Yes. Us. You, me, Austin, Ross, Brock and his...current squeeze."

"Oh." Elle covered her discomfort by draining her beer. Brock immediately snatched up the empty.

"You look amazing, lovely Elisa," he said with a wink before fetching her another. When he returned, Elle grabbed his arm.

"You have a squeeze?"

He blushed adorably. "Yeah, well, she's a bit of a blast

from my past. But…hang on, duty calls." He ran down to refill more beers, bantering easily with the staff and pouring like a pro.

"Did you try these?" Melody walked up holding a clear plate piled high with what looked like coconut encrusted shrimp. "*Mi Dios*, they are like heaven." She dipped one in an orange sauce and ate it, then put the plate on the bar between Elle and Evelyn. "So, did you ask her?"

Evelyn nodded and ate one of the shrimp. Elle sipped, not hungry, suddenly nervous, as if a door had opened somewhere and a cold wind had blown across the back of her neck. She reached into her small bag for her phone for some reason, and gazed at the screen, as the words there registered.

The room narrowed to the smallest pinprick of light. All the rowdy party sounds faded, leaving nothing but the rapid, echoing beat of her heart. The words seared her retinas, branded onto the front of her brain, and sent a rush of bitter bile into her throat.

Showing off, Elisa. Pretending everything was okay. That's what you get, silly cow.

"Um, excuse me?" She hopped off the barstool and pushed her way through the crowd. Plenty of people tried to stop her, to compliment her brewing abilities, her dress choice. But she pressed on, apologizing randomly as she went. Finally, she reached the back hall connecting the pub with the original brewery. She paused, hand to her throat, trying to calm her breathing.

"Elle?" Evelyn's voice carried down the hall from the kitchen. "You all right?"

God, she was such a mess. Everyone always had to be looking out for her. She hated it.

Without answering, she ran for the brewery, the place she felt happiest—well, the second place she felt the happiest lately. After a month of running twenty-four seven, the space was oddly dark and quiet. But the residual odors soothed her. She leaned against the huge kettle, currently empty and sparkling clean, ready for the next day's normal level of production, still clutching her phone in one hand.

"You knew He'd do this, eventually. He probably followed your progress to Germany and back, to brewing school, then as you hopped around trying to find somewhere to land. Silly bitch. He will always find you."

She slid to the floor, arms around her legs, face pressed to her knees, trying, and failing, not to cry.

"Elisa!" Ross' voice boomed through the empty space, bouncing off all the stainless surfaces and echoing in her ears. "Where are you?"

"Here," she said, before clearing her throat and getting to her feet. She had to leave. The Monster would come and He would take her away, and He would kill any man who'd touched her — much less touched her the way Ross had been for the last few weeks. "I'm here."

He emerged from behind the line of fermenters. "What happened?" He held out his arms. But she stayed put. She couldn't do this to him. It wasn't fair.

"Nothing," she said, swiping at her eyes.

"Bullshit," he spat out. "Sorry, I've had too much to drink already. Ugh." He leaned against the kettle next to her.

"Don't be sorry. I am ruining your party. I'm the one who's sorry."

The German flowed between them, allowing her to rest her brain from non-stop translation. "It's all right." He draped an arm around her shoulders. She let him, but steeled herself against anything else. "Want to go home?"

She snorted at the concept of that silly hotel suite being their 'home'. She truly was a naïve fool. At that moment, what she wanted was space. She'd been with Ross almost non-stop since their first night. And while she relished all of it — the meals, the working together, the arguments over brewing issues, sitting and watching movies late at night, and most of all the wild, amazing sex — she suddenly desired a night alone, to think and plan her next move.

"Your escape, you mean," the inner nag said, sounding smug. She nodded, as if agreeing with it.

"You go back to the party." She stepped out from under his arm, already feeling bereft but knowing it for the right thing to do, the only thing she could do. "I mean it." She put her palm alongside his newly trimmed beard. Dear God, she loved this man. It really was too bad that reality had reared its ugly head and she wouldn't be allowed any more of him than these past few weeks. He kissed her palm, then her wrist, making his way up her inner arm. She let him, shivering, but blocking the impulse to respond. "I will stay a bit longer," she said, pulling him toward the door. "Then I'll get a ride home."

"You are so fucking gorgeous," he said, grabbing her as they circled behind the row of fermenters and backing her up against one. "So bloody amazing." He propped his hands over her head and laid a Ross-patented toe-curling kiss on her, making her rise on her tiptoes and wrap her arms around his neck. One of his hands was between her legs, as he held their lip-lock. His finger found its target and he teased her piercing, rubbing it until she came with a squeak and a full-body shiver. He grinned and pulled his hand from under her skirt. Putting the finger he'd used on her in his mouth, he winked at her. "I told you going commando was for the best."

"Going...where?" She fumbled with his belt buckle, his zipper, needing all of him so badly she tasted it on the back of her tongue. He hissed and put his hand on the fermentation vessel behind her as she released his erection from his jeans and boxers. Her ears rang, her heart pounded as she gripped his newly familiar dick in one hand and slanted her lips over his, gripping his shoulder with her other hand. "I want you, Ross," she whispered into his mouth. "I need you inside me. Now."

"That would be a serious health code violation," he whispered back, lifting her hips so she could wrap her legs around his waist. "You minx," he said, exhaling as she shifted so she could take him inside her. Pressing her up against the tank, using his strong legs to hold her up, he leaned into neck. "Come on me, my darling. My Elisa. I want to feel you come on my cock."

He slid the strap of her dress aside and sucked her nipple into his mouth as she rolled her hips, gripping and releasing, while rubbing the tiny jewel against him. The amazing sensation of being so completely filled by this man forced tears down her face. He groaned and sucked harder, pressing the small of her back into the cool stainless steel. He released her, looked into her eyes and said it again, sending a shiver down her spine and a spike of agony through her brain. "I love you, Elisa. I love you. I... Oh, shit..." He groaned into her neck, thrust hard and she felt his warmth spill into her even as she was pulsing from the strength of her own climax. "I love you," he whispered, kissing her all over her face before finding her lips.

"I... I..."

He lifted her off his cock and set her on the floor before reassembling his jeans and smoothing his shirt tail over his zipper. She stood, shaking and sated and horrified at this whole fucked-up situation. "I know you'll say it when you're ready," he said, stroking her cheek with the back of his knuckles, then taking her hand, kissing it and tucking it into his elbow. "Need a tissue?"

She nodded, waiting while he grabbed some from the locker room, then pressing them between her legs, helping her, babying her as he always did. The way she absolutely adored. The way she would have to leave behind.

"Back to the party?" He held out his elbow after tossing the tissues into the trash.

She nodded, stuck her hand into his arm, and accompanied him into the clamor once more.

After about an hour of agonized observation of all this glorious normality, relishing the stinging soreness between her legs she always got when she took him all the way inside her, she whispered apologies to Evelyn and slipped out of the door, managing to avoid Ross — who was engaged in a shot drinking contest — on the way.

She took the ride share to her own place, unlocked the door and stood inside, smelling the emptiness, old carpet, and stale cooking from her neighbors. She lit a candle to dispel the worst of the stink, found a half empty bottle of cheap red wine, and drank it, not bothering with the nicety of a glass.

Eventually, she felt propped up enough to pull her phone from her bag. She had a Google search set up for The Monster's name. Given His celebrity status in the restaurant world, she got occasional notices when He was opening a new place — most recently in a ritzy Las Vegas casino — or when He had stepped onto the red carpet with some has-been celebrity or another. He loved the limelight. He'd claimed to love coming home to her, though. Which made sense, as no self-respecting celebrity would let Him to do the things she allowed.

Today's announcement — via the local, daily paper of all things — declared that He would be here, in this town, in Grand Rapids Bloody Michigan, of all places. He'd apparently franchised His name for other, more lowly casino restaurants and the Native American casino here had landed one. His brutally handsome face was at the top of the news article. He was in a tux, smiling and waving at someone. His dark eyes gleamed. His teeth shone, like fangs, she thought, almost objectively.

He would be here, in her town, in two weeks.

She had to leave.

Chapter Twenty-Eight

The next morning at Fitzgerald Brewing was quiet, as those who had to come in walked around groaning and drinking water, looking much the worse for wear. Elle figured she did too, but for a different reason. She went about the usual tasks, checking the brew schedule — now back to its usual busy, but not utterly frantic, level — before she began measuring out the ingredients for the Czech Pilsner, one of her favorite summer brews.

Ross wandered onto the brewery floor around noon. He found her in the lab, checking the specific gravity of the Pils before moving it into fermentation. She ignored him, content to let him watch her move around the room, doing her job, as her brain fumbled for something to say. She wanted so badly to confide in him, to lay the whole thing at his feet and ask him to help her through it. But years of training and even more years of avoidance had taken their toll. She kept her lips zipped.

When he reached for her arm at one point, she ducked out his reach, claiming she didn't have time for nonsense. "Elisa, every tooth in my head aches, each in its own special way I am so hung over. Be nice to me? I hear kissing would help."

"Not now, Ross. Okay?" She ran out of the lab, gnawing at her lower lip, finding make-work jobs to do to keep from having to see him for a few more hours.

By four-thirty, she and the silent, slow-moving cleaning crew had the brew house ready for the next batch. She sat, wiping her face with a towel, exhausted and drained from avoiding Ross all day. Groaning at the ache in her lower back, she pushed away from the edge of the mash tun, needing to write up the brew's progression in the log, then get the second shift going before she headed home.

Rounding the corner, doing a mental check of her meager pantry and wishing she could go to Ross' hotel for dinner and more, she ran straight into his chest. "Watch where you're going," she spat out, backing away from him. Nerves jangling, she found herself staring at the floor, hand to her neck when she registered the fury in his expression.

"Elisa," he said, keeping his voice steady. "Look at me."

She did, setting her jaw against the compulsion to throw herself into his arms. "When were you going to share this with me?" He held up a phone—her phone—face out so she could see the screen, filled with the last thing she'd been reading, for the millionth time. The Monster's face filled her brain, making her blink and take a few steps back.

"What do you mean?" she asked, her voice low and wimpy.

"I mean, this asshole is going to be here, in this town, and you've obviously been obsessing over this article. This was what was wrong with you yesterday. So, I'll ask again. When were you going to tell me?"

"Never," she said, blinking back tears. "I wasn't going to tell you at all."

"Well, at least I got an honest answer out of you."

She grabbed her phone and tucked it into her jeans pocket. "That is a violation of my privacy. What gave you the right to open my phone, anyway?"

"That is completely beside the point," he insisted, crossing his arms and letting the line of stubborn between his eyes deepen.

"No, actually, it's part of the point. I'm entitled to my own life, you know. Just because you…we…I… Oh never mind." She tried to stomp past him, but he held out an arm, nearly clothesline choking her in the process. "Move your stupid arm," she hissed under her breath.

"Talk to me, Elisa," he said, griping her shoulders and

pulling her so she stood in front of him again.

"Go to hell, Hoffman," she said, keeping her voice and expression as neutral as she could manage.

"At the moment, I'd consider myself already there."

They stood, glaring at each other for a few seconds. She could smell the booze wafting from his pores, but instead of making her angry, it made her feel terrible for ruining this triumphant week. She slumped back against the wall.

He stepped forward and gathered her close, murmuring into her hair. "Let me help you. I know it's a new thing for you, but I want to. I love you, remember? Stop making that so fucking hard, why don't you?"

"I never told you I'd be easy to love." She had her face pressed against his chest and could smell his clean-showered skin under his shirt.

"Okay, fair enough." He leaned away and lifted her chin. "Talk to me. Tell me what we can do to keep you safe. Do you want to go away? Now that this place is back on track, I don't have a damn thing to do, nor a job to go to out west. Let's take a vacation. Maybe head to someplace with a beach, a private hut, room service and lots of…"

"Stop it," she said, shaking her head. "I can't just go on vacation to avoid him. He found me. And I guarantee the reason He's here is to…to…" She buried her face in his chest again, relief at having told him this making her dizzy.

He frowned. "Do me a favor?"

"What?" she muttered, still pressing her face into his chest.

"Stop using capital letters in your voice when you refer to that asswipe. I can hear it, you know. I can tell you're doing it."

"I…don't know what you mean."

"Yes, you do."

They stood staring at each other a few seconds, seemingly sunk deep in their own thoughts.

"I know," he said, gathering her in his arms again. "Let's take Trent up on his invite to Petoskey. That's not running away. It's right here in Michigan and you'll be surrounded by friends. The weekend he does whatever the fuck he's doing at the casino, you won't be anywhere he can reach, or even know about."

She sniffled and disentangled herself, pondering this, trying not to reject it outright.

"Maybe," she said, swiping at her streaming eyes. "I don't know." She looked up at him. "I do know one thing—I'm starving. And you could probably use some food to soak up the booze, no?"

"Yes, I absolutely could. Let's head into the pub. I want one of Melody's bloody burgers. She'll burn one for you, I'm sure." He kissed her forehead, cupping her chin in one warm hand. "And we can talk about the weekend with her." He raised an eyebrow.

She nodded, and let him lead her across the back hall into the kitchen, then into the early evening business of the Fitz Pub.

* * * *

By the time she was draped over Ross' inert body as he snored softly, the weekend had all been arranged. She and Ross were even going to stay another week after everyone else left, to ensure that The Monster had left town without His—his—prey.

As she drifted, something prodded her wide awake. She rose, careful not to disturb Ross too much, but he was way gone, having eaten a huge meal, drunk about a gallon of water, and fallen sound asleep in front of mid-season baseball game on the telly. After pulling her phone from the heap of clothes she'd left on the floor, she opened the calendar and stared at the date, exactly four weeks from today when her preliminary hearing was scheduled.

Sighing, she leaned back against the foot of the bed, staring the ceiling as Ross' soft breathing sounds floated into the air. That's right. She had a damn manslaughter charge still hanging over her head.

"You're quite the little troublemaker, aren't you?" the inner nag piped up, as clear as day. *"Not on the job a month before you're blowing some hapless asshole's brains across your boss's office."*

Of course, both Austin and Ross had done nothing but sing her praises for that act. And the crack team of public relations pros in the Fitzgerald marketing department had done their job, keeping the gritty details from the press. But once she was in court, the whole thing would spill out, tarnishing her as a crazy, gun-toting, German whack job.

What she would not give for something resembling a normal life, she thought. What would that be?

She woke to the sensation of being lifted up into a set of strong arms. Of familiar lips on hers, of warm hands stroking her, caressing her, loving her. They made love in utter silence, slowly, and yet with an urgency that made her breathless by the time he pulled her on top him, once he'd licked and sucked her to a beautiful climax. The hot length of his dick along her eager pussy made her gasp. As she stared down at him, the ropes of her dreadlocks blocked out the world, leaving just the two of them, two lost souls who found each other in a foreign land.

"I love you, Hoffman," she whispered at the same time she shifted her hips and took him fast and deep—so deep all at once she cried out into the cool, dark air.

"Shh," he said, stroking her breasts, her stomach, her hips and thigh with a sort of reverence that thrilled her. "Just be still. Feel me inside you."

She nodded, sitting up straight and relishing that angle as he continued to lightly stroke her shoulders, her arms, returning to her breasts and tweaking both her nipples at once. She gasped as her hips began to move.

He rose on his elbows, then sat all the way up, keeping their bodies intimately connected as he pulled her legs to either side of his hips so they were rocking together on the bed. "Ah...God, yes." She sighed into his chest, feeling him deep, the angle of his dick mirroring the way he'd use his fingers. "Yes." She exhaled as the orgasm hovered, teasing her. He was close too. She'd gotten so that she could sense his triggers and signs. His breathing was quick. His fingers flexing on the small of her back.

"Now, lie back, my love," he said, pulling her arms from around his neck and pushing her slowly away from him. "Lie back…like that."

She propped on her elbows, keeping her legs draped over his hips. His jaw clenched as he kept a tight grip on her. This even better angle, combined with the way he stroked her clit with his thumb, brought on the fireworks. She pressed against him, matching his rolling thrusts into her, knowing that her pussy tightening and pulsing around him from the climax would make him come.

He groaned, his hands dug into her upper thighs and his head tilted back, matching her stance. He came hard, continuing to thrust against her in rough spasms. When he opened his eyes, they were bright, lit from the moonlight streaming through a break in the blinds behind her. "I adore you, Elisa. Marry me."

"Don't ask me that right now, please. Just let me enjoy this feeling." She lay all the way back, forcing him to lean forward. When he did slide out of her, she winced, but didn't mind the pain. He headed for the bathroom, returning with a warm, wet cloth he used between her legs, always muttering intimacies in German as she drifted, stretched out with her head to the foot of the bed and her feet on a pillow.

"Marry me, Elisa," he insisted, dropping down next to her, propped on one elbow.

She turned to him, touched his jaw, and smiled. "All right," she agreed. "But let's keep it to ourselves a while, at least until I can get past that…that weekend, okay?"

"Yes. Anything you want, darling Elisa. My love." He gathered her close, flipped her onto her side and they slept pressed together like spoons, upside down on the bed, through the rest of the night.

Chapter Twenty-Nine

Ross wasn't quite sure what to expect from the weekend away with the two richest men he knew and their women, plus — bonus — baby Rose Hoffman Fitzgerald along for fun. When he and Elisa arrived at Trent's cabin on Lake Michigan in the quaint, picturesque, very moneyed town of Petoskey, they sat for a moment, staring up at the clapboarded, arts and crafts-style mansion, with the glittering blue of Lake Michigan as its beautiful backdrop.

"If that's his cabin I'd sure like to see his regular house," Elisa said.

"No shit," Ross agreed, before climbing out of the rental. He'd upgraded to an SUV so they could pack in supplies, since he and Elisa had been responsible for choosing the beer and wine for the long weekend. People with money didn't faze him. He'd grown up around it, but had never been one of those guys who thought it was the be-all, end-all of his existence. Give him a comfy place to live, some great beer and food, good friends, and a hot woman in his bed and he'd be satisfied.

He glanced at Elisa, who was still peering through the windshield in awe. "Great to have friends with plenty of dough, and the willingness to share the wealth, eh *Fraulein* Nagel?" She turned to him, her gray-blue eyes wide with admiration. "Trent's a good guy. I've met him a few times. You should know something about him though. About him and Melody's relationship."

"I already know," she said, unhooking her seatbelt. "Silly man. We ladies are on top of all the relationship gossip."

"That a fact? And what do you tell your lady friends

about me?" He cocked an eyebrow at her.

She grinned. "Enough…but not too much."

He popped open the hatch, admiring the range of beers—some Fitzgerald products, many not—and wine they'd chosen. Elisa had been in hog heaven planning menus, while Evelyn and Melody had been, as well—not having to do that chore. She'd made a million different lists, asked his opinion, then done more or less the exact opposite of what he'd suggested. Finally, she'd handed the meticulously organized list over to the ladies and turned her attention to the booze choices with him.

Trent trotted down the drive. "Welcome to the Hettinger Cabin," he said.

Ross handed him some cases of West Coast IPAs. "Some cabin, dude."

"Thank you for having us," Elisa said, as she hauled two bags of wine from the back of the SUV. Ross watched him watching her. He could see the man's eyes narrow when he caught sight of the ugly, inked choker around her neck. Something about his body language made Ross feel instantly comfortable. As if he had Trent solidly in his corner when it came to protecting Elisa.

"Give me one more," Trent said, jerking his chin at the rest of the beer. "I can take it."

"You got it," Ross said, stacking another case on top, then piling his own arms high. They made their way up the long drive, following Trent around to a side entrance that opened into a mud room cluttered with drying towels, canvas bags, flip flops, sunscreen and bug spray.

"Sorry in advance but you're getting the full Hettinger immersion this weekend, guys." He set the beer on a long, granite countertop in a hall between the mud room and kitchen. "Here, let me take those," he said to Elisa. She visibly flinched when she met his eyes. Ross set his cases down, tucked his hands in his jeans pockets and watched her gaze hit floor with a near audible slam.

There was certainly something about Trent—a kind of

power that might intimidate some men or women—that Ross could sense as well. But underneath that strength lay a man hopelessly in love with the feisty Melody Rodriquez. And Ross auto-respected the hell out of any man who'd take that on and tame it—or whatever it was he did with her.

"Daaaaaaaa—aaaad," a loud, female voice called from somewhere inside the house. "Can I drive the boat?"

"No," Trent said, without taking his eyes off Elisa, who was still staring fixedly at the floor. "It's getting late," he amended when a pretty teenaged girl stuck her head around the corner. "You can take it out tomorrow morning. Taylor, please meet our guests. This is Ross Hoffman and Elisa Nagel."

The girl stuck out her hand and smiled at them both. She looked nothing like her father but for a little something around her eyes and her height. Her nose was aquiline, patrician even. Dark, chestnut-brown hair was tugged back into a ponytail. Her eyes almost matched her hair color and were large, like Trent's and as expressive as any teenager's, Ross supposed.

What shocked him was her miniscule black bikini. He averted his gaze when she flounced into the hallway and stood in front of her father, hip cocked.

"Uh, excuse me," he said, heading back outside for the rest of the booze, leaving Trent to handle the girl. Elisa followed him. They loaded up in silence, and headed back to the house. Austin and Evelyn pulled in as they were opening the side door. Ross put the beer down and headed for their car, knowing they had half the massive amount of groceries Elisa would require to make this weekend a gourmet experience.

"Here," Evelyn said, thrusting the baby carrier into his hands. "So help me that kid has been squalling for the last twenty miles, and I'm going insane." She hooked her thumb at her husband, standing on the other side of the car, stretching his back. "Sleeping Beauty here snoozed the whole damn time." But her gaze was soft and affectionate as Austin made his way around to the back of their SUV and lifted the gate.

"Give her to me," Elisa insisted, poking his shoulder and holding out her arms for the baby. He hesitated, recalling their first date night conversation on this topic. She stamped her foot in mock temper. "I want to hold the child, mouth-breather. Give her up and help our friends carry in the food."

Gratefully, he handed over the seat. Elisa began crooning to Rose in German and carried her up to the house.

"So," Evelyn said, as she piled his arms full of bags from two different groceries. "You'd better not fuck this up, Hoffman."

"I'm capable of carrying these up to the house without dropping anything or tripping over my own feet," he huffed.

She glowered at him. "You know what I mean."

He leaned over and pecked her cheek, more ecstatic than he could ever express that he could do that and not want to jump off a cliff in despair. "I love her, Evelyn. It's as simple as that. And you, more than anyone, know how I am when I'm in love."

She paused, tilted her head and gave him one of her patented Evelyn-soul-searching stares. "I do know," she finally said, reaching for Austin and snaking her arm around his waist. "And I couldn't be happier for you."

"Yeah, well, since you had to settle for this poor substitute," he said, nodding Austin's way. "I guess you might as well be happy for me."

She smacked his shoulder. Austin chuckled and put him in a headlock. "Dude, you should check the entry for 'poor substitute' in your German to English translation dictionary. Your photo needs updating."

"*Ach. Touché*, my friend. *Touché*. Come on, hurry up with that grub. My woman has a killer meal planned for us."

He saw his two friends exchange a look that was equal

parts amusement and relief. He smiled at them both and whistled his way up the drive to the house. Once all the food was delivered and spread out, Melody jumped in to help organize it all, encouraging everyone else to head outside to get the last of the afternoon sun.

"You should go too, Elle," she said as Ross sipped a beer and watched the women maneuver around the biggest kitchen he'd ever encountered.

"No, it's okay. My skin and the sun are not the best of friends. I'd rather stay here and get things going for dinner. But thank you." She glanced over at him. "You go on, Hoffman," she said, switching to German. "I'm sure you're itching to be on a boat or someplace equally awful. I'll stay to listen for the child if she wakes so grab Evelyn and Austin on your way out."

Trent hollered in from the deck that spanned the entire back of the house that he was taking the pontoon out for a late afternoon spin and anyone interested should report down to the dock in thirty minutes. Ross finished the beer and set the empty in the case he'd opened inside the garage then came back to the kitchen, swept Elisa up in his arms and kissed her until he saw stars.

"All right, enough," Melody said, smacking the back of his head with a spatula. "Don't make me get out the water hose."

When he set her down and cupped her chin, her eyes seemed more gray than blue in the ambient light. "You sure you want to stick around here? This bitch can be hard to handle." He grabbed a bundled bunch of cilantro and flung it at Melody's head. She ducked, flipped him off, and returned to the pile of groceries on the granite topped island.

"I'm sure," she said, going up on her tiptoes to kiss him again. "Go on. You're in my way."

He found Austin, Evelyn, Brock, and a very attractive redhead lazing on lounge chairs, holding beers and wearing identical sunglasses. "You guys look weird," Ross said,

213

saluting them and holding out his hand to the newcomer. "I'm Ross. I'm better than either of these two assholes at pretty much anything. And you are?"

She slid the shades down her nose and gave him a blatant checking out, from his head to his toes. "Hmm…maybe." She held out her bottle. "I'm Caroline. Did you make this?" Ross squinted at the label.

"I did, indeed, fair lady."

"Okay, then you can stay."

He grinned at her, then slapped Brock on his bare calf. "I like her. You can keep her."

"That remains to be seen," Brock said, sipping and not looking at her.

"I've known Brock and Austin since forever," the woman said, as she lay back on the lounge again. "Our parents were friends."

"Ah, another trust fund baby. Cool."

Evelyn flipped him off, but her eyes remained hidden behind her dark lenses so he couldn't gauge what she really thought.

"Are all you layabouts coming on the fucking boat, or what?" Trent hollered from the steps. Ross looked over the deck railing and saw an elaborate set of steps leading down a brick paver patio with a fire pit in the middle. A vast stretch of green grass lay between that and the sandy beach.

"Come on, I haven't ever been *on* a Great Lake before," he said, jumping up and running down the steps and across the grass. The sun on his shoulders and face had never felt better. The boat ride took an hour and by the time Ross and Brock had tied the thing to the dock, several teenaged girls were gathered around the fire pit.

"Come on up to the house, Tay," Trent called on his way past her and two of her friends. They were all staring at their phones, ignoring the beauty all around them, as well as Trent, Ross noted.

Trent stopped, turned around and went back to the pit. "Taylor, I said come up the house. One of our guests is a chef and is taking care of dinner but I want you and your friends to set the table."

She rolled her eyes, sighed and got up as slowly as possible. Her friends followed suit. Brock and Caroline were sitting side by side on the dock with their feet in the water. Austin and Evelyn were still on the boat, enjoying a few more moments of quiet before the kid woke up and demanded their attention. Ross looked out over the expanse of water, then up at the back of Trent's lake house, and acknowledged that he'd never felt more content.

"Hoffman!" He spotted Elisa's head sticking out of one of the glass doors along the back of the house. "Get your ass up here. Please." She smiled, then disappeared. As he ran up the steps to the upper deck, he could hear the robust wail that could only mean Miss Rose was up and at 'em.

Melody was jiggling the unhappy child while Elisa warmed a bottle of breastmilk. "Here," Elisa said, putting the thing in his hand, then taking the now-screaming kid from Melody and handing her to him. She smiled and patted his cheek, the turned back to the dinner prep.

"Wait a second. I'll go get Ev—"

"Oh no, you will not," Elisa said, whirling on him, her hand on her hips. "Sit down and feed her. Surely, you are capable of that simple act?" She raised an eyebrow. Rose was snuffling into his neck, which felt disgustingly wet and warm.

"I am, thank you very much. Aren't I, *Liebling*? I am more than capable." He sat in a leather recliner, leaned back so the footrest popped up and attempted to figure out the best way to hold the kid. She was reaching for the bottle, so that was good. He popped the nipple into her mouth and she gripped the thing with both hands, closing her eyes with the effort of pulling the nutrition from it.

He watched her, fascinated with her miniature features. When he touched her cheek with his fingertip her eyes flew open and she let go of the bottle. She shot him an irritated look that made him laugh out loud, it was so very much like her mother's. After glancing around to make sure no one was watching, he pressed his lips to her forehead, sucking in that distinct baby smell he'd discovered the last time he'd held her.

She resumed her meal and they both dozed, once he'd propped the arm holding her on a folded blanket. When he realized she'd maneuvered herself around and was now sitting on his chest and had her small hands on his beard, he grinned, and rubbed her soft cheek with it, making her giggle.

"Da," she declared, keeping one hand on the soft curls along his jaw.

"No, kid. It's complicated. But no."

"She's talking to me, *dummkopf*," Austin said from behind him before plucking the girl up and making her squeal

"Da! Da! Da!"

"Bona fide daddy's girl," Evelyn said. She pressed her lips to Austin's cheek, then Ross' before heading into the kitchen.

"Don't confuse her," Austin said, as he sat on the couch, the baby on his knee before she wiggled her way down to the floor. She crawled straight over to Ross' chair and pulled herself up to standing.

Waving one hand at him, she yelped "Da!" again.

Austin and Ross both laughed, which made her laugh — the most beautiful sound Ross thought he'd ever heard. He put a hand on her strawberry blond curls. "Lucky girl, gets to call us both that, I guess." She grabbed his hand and jammed one of his fingers into her mouth. "Holy shit, ow! Dude, she's a biter. Better nip that in the bud."

"She's getting her molars, you giant fool." Elisa perched on the arm of his chair, holding out her hands so the baby trundled over to her from where she'd been gripping Ross' knee. When Elisa picked the girl all the way up, saying she had a special treat for her in the kitchen, Ross stretched out in both directions, then put his hand behind his head.

When he registered the odd silence around him, devoid of

the various conversations that had been going on earlier, he saw Brock and Caroline standing in the doorway. Taylor, Trent's surly teenager and her friends paused in their table-setting task. Austin frowned at him, then shrugged and got up. "I need a beer."

"Grab me a pils, will you?" He rose and glared at the small, gawking crowd in the living room. "Okay, so who in here doesn't know that Rose my biological daughter. Go on, raise your hand." None of the adults raised theirs. He nodded. "What I thought."

"Um, I didn't know that," Taylor said, looking from him to Austin and back to him. Ross' face got hot. Trent shrugged and draped an arm around his daughter's shoulders.

"Full immersion, like you said, my friend," Ross said, giving Trent a little salute. "Ask your dad to explain, kid. I'm gonna go check on dinner." He took the beer from Austin and got the hell out of that awkwardness, fast.

Chapter Thirty

Dinner the first night was simple—grilled lamb chops dusted with a special Moroccan seasoning mix she'd concocted, along with a fresh spinach dotted with dried cherries, pecans and goat cheese, plus two loaves of crusty bread. For dessert, she'd made a batch of double chocolate brownies. Everyone raved about all of it, even the teenagers who were at first appalled that Mary's Little Lamb was being served to them to eat.

She and Ross had chosen a rich Zinfandel to complement the food and three bottles had quickly disappeared. Afterward, she supervised the teenagers as they loaded the dishwasher and wiped down the table. She'd already cleaned the counters and there hadn't been any pots or pans so the tidy-up was easy.

"I love your hair, Elle," Taylor had said. "How long did it take you to grow like that?"

She touched her dreads, which were hanging down past her shoulders. "Almost eleven years," she admitted, sipping the last of her wine.

"I love your tatts," one of the other girls chimed in. "What is that for?" She pointed to Elle's neck. Elle put her fingers on it, pondering her answer, and noting that she didn't feel self-conscious about it for a change.

"This was a mistake." She smiled as the girls clustered around her on the barstool she had pulled up to the island. Breakfast was to include a massive fruit salad so she'd decided to cut the mangos and kiwis tonight, and sleep in…or something…in the morning.

"What about those?" Taylor asked, leaning across the

island and pointing to the line of stars up the inside of her arm. She had on a utilitarian sleeveless T-shirt, which exposed all her ink.

"These are not a mistake," she said, holding her arm. "There is one star for each year I was…here, in the US."

"Cool." Taylor's eyes shone. "When I got this," she said, pointing to the small jewel in the side of her nose, "my dad almost had kittens. But I want more. I love that one." She pointed to Elle's lower lip.

Melody came in bearing the decimated platter of brownies. "Leave Elle alone, girls. Go on. Shoo."

"No, it's all right. I enjoy their energy." Elle turned to the cutting board again.

"What's for dinner tomorrow?" Taylor was still staring at her. "How'd you learn to cook like that? I thought you brewed beer, like Ross."

"I do brew beer." She held up a bite of mango. Taylor smiled and ate it. Melody was standing behind the line of teens, tying an imaginary rope around her neck and sticking her tongue out in a parody of suicide. Elle could only imagine how hard it must be to be in love with a man with a nearly grown daughter. She waved Melody away, determined to make the most of this, and put in a good word for Taylor's no-doubt future step-mother.

"I went to the most famous cooking school in France. *L'ecole Cordon Bleu*, in Paris. After I graduated there, I moved to Chicago and worked at a famous restaurant. But…I got tired of that life. It's full of prima donnas and assholes. Whoops," she said, putting her hand over her mouth. "I'm sorry."

The girls fell all over themselves laughing. Taylor extracted herself and propped her elbows on the granite top while Elle continued cutting the fruit, putting it in separate plastic containers. "So you learned how to brew beer from Ross?" One of the other girls asked with a dreamy look in her eyes. Elle sympathized with her. Ross Hoffman would qualify as any girl's dreamboat.

"No. When I left Chicago I went back home, to Germany. My *Oma*—grandma—had died and I needed to take care of some things. Then, with extra money thanks to her will, I came back to the US, all the way to Oregon and enrolled myself in their brewing science program. Took me two years to get it but I never thought I'd make it. So many men in the program being...you know..."

"Assholes," the girls intoned in unison.

"Exactly. And I was...well...anyway, I got my degree and my first job on the west coast. I bounced around for some years after that and found myself here, at Fitzgerald."

"Where you met Ross," the dreamy-eyed girl said.

"Indeed. I did."

"All right, it's poker time," Trent called from the living room. "Who's in?"

Taylor retreated, rolling her eyes at the annoying fact of her father's existence. "Do you play poker, Elle?"

"I do. I learned it while in cooking school. I'm told I have a great poker face."

The girls chuckled and elbowed each other. "You know," Elle said, handing the sealed containers to Taylor's friends to put in the huge double-doored fridge. "Melody is pretty cool. She taught me to swear in Spanish."

"Whatever." Taylor officially disengaged from the conversation.

"Give her a shot, Taylor," Elle said. "I think you won't be disappointed."

The girls all looked at each other a minute. "Can we help you tomorrow?"

"Of course you can. We're making lasagna so it has a lot of steps. I make the sauce from scratch."

"Cool. Thanks, Elle."

Trent poked his head in the kitchen. "Who in here is ready for me to beat them at Texas Hold 'em?"

"Can I play?" Taylor wandered over and hip-bumped him. He bumped her back.

"Of course. I taught you how to play myself. How about

you, Elle?"

"Sure. Give me a few more minutes to put some things away."

"Sounds like a plan. Ladies, I need your help to uncover the poker table, and get it set up." They followed him out, leaving Elle to contemplate the day, the meal, her new friends, and Ross.

* * * *

Within two hours, it became clear the Elle was a total ringer. More wine had been opened while she'd tripled her stack of chips and eliminated almost everyone from every single round. Ross sulked, while Evelyn and Melody picked up her chair and paraded her around the room singing *We Are the Champions*.

The teenagers had given up after the first hour in favor of draping themselves on the couch and texting boys. Rose had been asleep, but a loud bleat from the baby monitor indicated she wanted to join the party. With a soft, summer breeze blowing the gauzy curtains along the wall of glass to the deck, the teens led half of them in a video game dance contest, leaving everyone but Melody gasping for breath.

"You're pretty good at that," Taylor said to her, reluctant admiration clear on her face.

"*Si, chica*," the woman snapped her fingers. "Stick with me and I will teach you to samba and tango."

"Oh, I don't know if that's a good idea," Trent said from his perch on one of the recliners, gasping for breath.

Evelyn was tucked into a bay window, nursing Rose. Austin, Ross, Trent and Brock returned to the card table, leaving the women sitting on the couch, scrolling through the movie options. Elle headed into her haven, the kitchen. She ran her hands along the expanses of cream and brown granite, the top-of-the-line appliances, the under counter wine cooler, the natural cherry cabinets.

Someday, she thought. *Someday I'll have a kitchen like this again.*

"Hey," a male voice said, interrupting her daydream. She jumped and turned, a hand to her neck to find Trent pulling a bottle of water from the fridge. "I'm so glad you and Ross came up."

"Me too. Thank you for including us. And for letting us hang around a few more days."

"No problem." He waved a hand, drank half the water, then leaned against the counter opposite her, much to her dismay. Trent was an Alpha Dom. She'd been trained to know one when she saw him. Plus, Melody had filled her in on how their relationship had begun, then ended, then picked back up again. She'd hinted at the D/s nature of it, but never given much detail. Which was fine with Elle.

Trent Hettinger oozed confidence. His body language — a languid, sexy comfort in his own skin — combined with the super deep timbre of his voice and with his shocking, unconventional handsomeness made for quite a man. She studied him in the gloom of the kitchen. Her first reaction to him had been to drop to her knees. But she'd settled for not looking at him. Then, they'd gotten busy with dinner and the cards, and everything else and she now realized she'd become comfortable in his presence without even realizing it.

Her hand went to her neck on reflex. His gaze rested on her hand, then on her face. She flushed hot and directed her gaze downward. "Sorry," she muttered, trying to figure out how she could get out of here and over to Ross. She was tired. She wanted to go to bed and have him hold her as she fell asleep.

"I'm sorry that you were so badly treated, Elle," Trent said, shocking her to her toes. "That never should have happened to you. And I want you to know that I think you're braver than any woman I've ever met — well, almost any woman." His eyes flickered to the doorway where Melody's raucous laughter could be heard coming from the living room. He sighed and rubbed a hand around the back of his neck. Trent was completely bald but he rocked it better than that famous, sexy, bulked-up movie star whose name she could never recall. He was even taller than Ross, tanned from his time in the sun, with a lean strength to him that she admired. But right now, all she knew was mortified horror.

"I didn't know…that you knew…about it."

He smiled at her. "Melody thought I should know, before we met." He put a hand on her shoulder. Instead of making her want to drop to her knees again, she felt comforted by it. Safe. Protected.

But yet…

"I guess I didn't realize that Melody knew either." She'd told Evelyn some things but not all. Ross was the only other human on the planet who knew about the worst of the abuse. Well, she guessed now that number included her host and hostess for this weekend. She ground her teeth together, trying not to blurt out something rude. It wasn't Trent's fault that Hoffman couldn't keep his stupid mouth shut.

"Oh. Well, um…" Trent seemed rattled, which on some level amused her. He was, after all, only a man, with a man's weaknesses, needs and emotions. And he was so head over heels for Melody, she couldn't wait for him to pop the question. Elle and Evelyn had a feeling he'd be doing it this weekend since they knew Trent and Melody enjoyed playing to an audience.

"So, maybe we should shut it down for the night. I hear you have a delicious breakfast planned." He backed away. "Thanks for cooking, Elle. I hope we didn't make you feel like you had to."

"No, I like doing it. If you'll excuse me, though, I need to have a word with Ross."

She marched over to him. He was laughing with Austin and Brock over something, sipping amber liquor from Trent's cabinet. "Come over here, sexy lady," he said, reaching for her. She stayed just outside of his range. He stopped, reading her expression. After knocking back his whiskey, he rose, shot a salute to the men and took her hand. "Let's go for a walk," he said, grabbing a sweatshirt, then leading her to the open door onto the deck.

Silently, she followed him down the flight of steps to where the fire still spluttered in the pit. He drew two chairs closer to it, and handed her the sweatshirt. She tugged it down over her head, relishing the Ross-ness of it—the malt, hops, leather, and outdoors smell that suffused the fabric. Before he had a chance to get situated, she spoke. "Why did you tell Melody about…what happened to me?"

"I…um…"

"That was not anyone's business but mine, and I made it yours, thinking you'd keep it private."

"You told Evelyn," he began. She held up a hand.

"I didn't tell her even half of it. Just enough so she'd know I had…issues." She pulled her legs up to the large wooden Adirondack-style chair and wrapped her arms around herself.

"I'm sorry," he said, softly. "I wasn't doing it to betray your confidence. I'd talked with her before our first date, you know? To ask about this lifestyle thing she and Trent are into, so I could understand you better. Then, after I got the whole story, we talked again. It's all out of concern for y—"

"Stop it," she said, jumping up and pacing around the fire. "Stop trying to justify it." Her voice rose. "I trusted you with the most intimate details of my life. And you… you blabbed them around like some kind of a cheap gossip rag reporter."

"Elisa," he said, trying to grab her wrist. She jerked away from him, shaking her head.

"I'm going to bed. I suggest you find a couch for tonight."

"But…"

She ran up the steps, tears burning her eyes before he could finish. Austin and Brock were at the poker table with Trent. They all studiously ignored her as she walked past them.

Without speaking to anyone, she headed for the kitchen, drank down an entire bottle of chilled water, then let the empty bottle drop into the deep sink. Her heart ached, and her skin itched all over. She already missed him. But he had to know that this wouldn't fly. He couldn't spread her story around as if she were the sad sack heroine of some romance novel.

"You all right, *chica*?" Melody asked as she grabbed her own water bottle.

"I'll be fine, thank you. I need some sleep. Good night, and thank you again for inviting me to your lovely home."

Melody waved a be-ringed hand around. "It isn't my home, trust me. Taylor reminds me of that every chance she gets."

Elle sighed and slumped against the counter. All these lovely people and their ideal lives she'd admired — not so ideal after all, she supposed.

"Anyway, go easy on the Kraut, all right? He didn't mean anything by telling me."

Elle closed her eyes, her innate sense of privacy violated yet again.

"Don't be mad, Elle. That damn sap is so in love with you, it's downright sickening."

"If you'll excuse me? I'm nearly asleep on my feet."

Melody grabbed her and squeezed her tightly, putting her on edge again with the unexpected intimacy. "Relax, Elisa. We all love you here." She let her go, kissed both her cheeks, then left the kitchen, calling for her *amour* and telling him it was time to take her off to bed.

Without saying anything to anyone else, which made her anxious for being rude, she ran up the wide wooden stairway and found the room that contained hers and Ross' luggage. Each room had its own private bath so she turned on the hot water and filled the tub, dumped in some kind of flower-scented bath beads, shed her clothes and slid into the water with a satisfied sigh.

She was mad. But it felt blunted, its edges rounded — not

her usual type of anger at all. Likely because she knew Melody was right. She'd flown off the handle at Ross and owed him an apology. But only if he apologized first, she decided, as she slid farther down.

Underwater, she studied her body for the first time in years. It had been something worshipped by The Monster — by Nolan — for several months. He'd really bamboozled her into thinking that all that build-up, all those sexy times in his 'Playroom' would continue. Obviously, she'd been a good target. Young, even younger looking than she was, and a virgin. He'd probably sniffed that out the first time he'd seen her in class. She'd been eager for friendship, attachment of any kind. And he'd pounced.

She let her fingertips wander across her breasts. Ross liked to pay special attention to her one poor mangled nipple, giving it as much love and caresses and kisses as he did anywhere else on her body. He totally ignored the ugly scar on her ass, not that she blamed him. And his favorite place on her entire body was the spot he'd claimed for himself — right above the tenth small star on the inside of her upper arm. She touched that spot, making herself shiver.

It made her horny is what it did. And she had no idea how he'd managed that, other than with his constant, loving care.

Love?

Without a doubt.

Did she love him?

With everything in her.

"*You're a silly bitch,*" the nag said, as loudly as if she were under the water with Elle.

"*I'm going to find you,*" The Monster insisted, just as stridently. "*And when I do, you are going to wish you'd never been born. But first, I'm going to gut that fucking Viking with my filet knife and make you watch.*"

With a loud gasp, she jerked upright, spilling water all over the floor. "No," she said, slapping her hands over her ears and curling into a ball in the cooling tub. "No, no, no!"

But the words kept rolling around in her head, which had turned into a giant echo chamber. Nolan was more than capable of that and it would just like him to wait almost eleven years to exact his revenge.

Shivering, she got out of the tub and wrapped up in a towel that was so big it went around her twice. Her knees wobbled so she sat on the closed toilet seat clutching her arms.

He. Him. Sir.

That Monster had her so well-conditioned she kept using the capital letters in her own damn head. But He was right. She'd never be normal. Never be allowed to live a normal life. She was shit. But she was His shit. His to do whatever he wished. She was kidding herself that any other ending would come for her life.

"Elisa...?" Ross' voice floated through the closed door, breaking through her semi-trance. He knocked. "You all right in there?"

"I'm fine. I just need...a little time alone. Go to bed. I'll be there soon."

"I am truly sorry, my love," he said, using the sweetest possible German word for the endearment. "Please forgive me? I'm an idiot for telling anyone."

She sighed and pressed her forehead to her knees as His voice filled her head, drowning out anything good. Scrambling off the toilet in a vain attempt to escape it, she crawled to the corner behind the claw foot tub, grabbed her knees and began to rock back and forth. The self-soothing action had seen her through many a long day or night, alone, in pain both physical and emotional. She slipped back into her safe space, even with the man who promised to save her from it asleep on the other side of the bathroom door.

Chapter Thirty-One

Ross stood outside of the bathroom for a solid ten minutes, listening, waiting, willing her to unlock it. After that, he turned and slid to the floor, his back to the still closed door, elbows on his knees, his mind awash with anger, frustration and worry. Finally, when she'd been silent for over half an hour, he rose and headed back downstairs, seeking water — or another shot of Trent's good booze.

The glass doors were all open and the breeze had picked up. The filmy curtains billowed and flowed, giving the great room a surreal tint. He could hear random thumps and murmured words above. A baby noise here, a bit of music from the teenagers' room there. All normal, house-settling-in-for-the-night noises. Normal being the key word.

He wandered out to the deck and flopped onto one of the cushy lounge chairs. Propping his hands behind his head, he stared at a sky so vividly black and pinpricked with stars it could've been fake.

He'd had a normal-enough growing up life. An only child of a German banker and his American teacher wife who hated life in 'the sticks' of Bavaria, he'd had everything he'd ever wanted but, perhaps, anything resembling the unconditional love only parents can supply. They'd mostly ignored him, leaving him to be raised by a succession of paid staff.

He'd done well enough in school and in sports to remain under the parental radar his entire life. And when his mother's fellow university teacher had scooped him up as a teenager to teach him a thing or three about how to please a woman, he'd latched on to her like a duckling imprinting on a stranger. After that, women were nothing to him but objects — soft, pleasant ones to be sure, and ones he'd go out of his way to please, but only for a short while.

Evelyn had been different. And that had wrecked him for women for good. Or so he'd believed.

Elisa Nagel was something new, something exotic, both awful and wonderful. Figures he'd end up wanting to spend the rest of his life with a chick who was a foot shorter and fifteen kilos lighter than what he thought he preferred. And that hair… He chuckled and held up his hands, able to feel the silky ropes of her crazy dreadlocks between his fingers.

He dropped his arms to his sides and sat up, cursing himself for being such an inconsiderate jackass, telling her whole story to Melody, then letting her tell Trent. While he'd believed he was doing the right thing, confiding in someone who might understand the basics of her psychology at this stage, it was, hands down, the dumbest possible thing he could have done.

When he held up his hands again he curled his fingers into tight fists. He wanted nothing more than to pound that frog piece of shit Nolan Blanchard into a bloody pulp, then burn the pulp to ashes, then piss on the ashes. Once he'd figured out that the famous, celebrity chef was indeed the man who had tortured his beloved for years, had taken her baby from her and given it away without warning and still haunted her every waking and sleeping moment, Ross had gone on a serious internet manhunt. He had names and numbers of personal assistants, schedulers and knew every move the asshole would be making while in Grand Rapids.

He'd tracked the little shit's every move from the moment he figured Elisa had escaped him until this past week, when the news flash that he was, right now, in Grand Rapids likely trying to find her under the guise of opening some crappy second-rate casino restaurant. He sat up fast, clenching and unclenching his fists, fury coloring the edges of his vision.

Action. That was what he required. And he'd get it, too.

He'd managed to sweet talk the asshole's personal assistant into telling him where he'd be staying. He even had a room number, and the chick's room number too, should he 'want to stop by for a drink'.

He'd be stopping by all right, but not for a drink.

As he rose to his feet, he felt lighter, as if yet another stone had been removed from his shoulders. *Forward motion. Get your keys, drive back to Grand Rapids, beat the living shit out of the monster who'd ruined his Elisa, drive back. Done and done.*

As he headed for the door, he spotted Austin reading a book in the leather recliner. "What're you doing down here?" he asked, not kindly.

"Reading," the man said, ignoring Ross' tone. "I sincerely hope that you aren't thinking of going back to Grand Rapids tonight."

Ross stopped in the kitchen doorway. He turned and glared at his old friend. "None of your fucking business."

"Yes, it is, actually. You are first and foremost my friend. But you are much more than that to my family, and you damn well know it." He put the book aside and rose to his feet. "Ross, I get it. I know you want to do something, anything, right now."

"You don't get it. You'll never get it. Go upstairs to your wife and kid and leave me alone."

"Don't do it, Ross. You'll regret it for the rest of your life. You won't be helping her. The only thing you can do to help her is to be here with her, not out doing something stupid that gets you thrown in jail. It's bad enough we have to face her hearing this month. I don't want to have to deal with—"

"This isn't about you," Ross spat out, turning fully to face Austin. "Not everything is, you fucking spoiled brat."

Austin's jaw clenched and his nostrils flared. Ross clenched his fists, realizing at that moment he required contact, any contact, to dispel the whirling dervish of anguish in his chest. He also realized that Austin was right. He slumped in the doorway as the adrenaline rushed out of him, leaving behind nothing but the empty ache of frustration.

"Want a drink?" Austin asked, holding up the bottle of bourbon.

"Yeah," Ross grunted before he sat on the couch near the recliner. Austin poured them both one and they held up their glasses. "I'm going to ask her to marry me next week when we're here alone. Officially, this time."

Austin smiled. "Great. Cheers to that, then."

Grateful that his friend kept lectures about 'rushing into things' to himself, Ross clinked, tossed back the booze, then got up. He needed to see her, to hold her, to assure her everything was fine. And would be fine, if he had anything to say about it.

"Go on," Austin said, resuming his seat. "I'm good. Evelyn and Rose are sound asleep. But I'm not tired so…" He held up his book. "Be there for her, Ross. It's all she requires of you. As fun as it might be to pound that French shithead into the dirt."

Ross ran up the stairs and only hesitated a half second before kicking the bathroom door open, shattering the wood around the doorknob and sending it crashing back against the wall. He couldn't see her at first. When he spotted something that looked like her hair in the far corner of the room behind the tub, he reached down and picked her all the way up, cradling her in his arms. She was ice-cold and shaking like a leaf, making strange, hitching noises as if she wanted to cry but all she could do was make the sound, as if all her tears were dried up.

"Shh, my love," he whispered to her in German. "Arms around me. That's it." He pressed his nose to her hair, relishing everything about her before walking out to the bedroom, then onto the small, private deck after snagging a blanket off one of the chairs by the window. As he wrapped the soft fabric around her, she held tightly to his neck. The sensation of having found his mission in life—his soul mate and his mission—was an odd one. She was a bundle of contradictions all wrapped up in a psyche that had been forcibly warped by years of abuse.

But he wanted it. All of it.

He sat back in the chair, keeping his arms tight around her, making nonsense sounds, half-singing, half-whispering, until she stopped shaking. Her breathing evened out and they both dozed, wrapped together in the warm summer night air.

He woke to find her standing at the deck railing, utterly, gloriously naked. The wind blew the dreadlocks hanging by her face. As he watched, rendered immobile by the sight of her, she leaned forward, arched her back and grabbed one leg, lifting it back and up over her head. Then she did the same with the other leg. She was like a dancer, lithe and graceful in her movements.

His mouth was watering by the time she put her hands up over her head, clasped her fingers together and bent backward, pressing her thighs and stomach forward. She bent so far back, the long strands of her hair touched the deck.

The desire to keep watching her stretch in her yoga positions warred with the stronger desire to grab her and kiss her and make her come so loud the whole house would hear it. He gripped the arms of his chair, aware that his cock was making a serious tent out of his shorts. A tingling feeling raced through him, pebbling his skin and making his pulse race. All he heard as he kept watching her was the whoosh-whoosh of his heartbeat.

He rose and went to her, covering her hands with his, his arms alongside hers, raised over her head. She didn't move, or flinch, or speak. But as she bent forward, he went with her, his hands sliding down the inside of her arms to her breasts. They rose back up in unison and he did the opposite movement, running his palms up her arms to rest on either side of her clasped hands.

She bent backward, taking him with her. Together, they didn't go quite as far. They rose again. He turned her around slowly. "Leave your arms up," he whispered. He lowered his lips to hers, parted them with this tongue and met hers in a slow, sexy tangle. She kept her arms up as he kissed her, roaming all over her back with his eager hands.

When he dropped to his knees, she gasped. He looked up at her exquisite face. "I love you," he whispered, before pressing his lips to her stomach, then kissing his way along her ribs, then going lower. He moved his hands up the outside of her legs, to her hips, then around to her ass. She dropped her hands to his hair, tangling her fingers in it as he kept a grip on her butt with one hand, and spread her legs with the other, filling his nose with her distinctive scent. He teased her piercing, keeping his face pressed to her pubic bone. "Lean back again," he whispered into her skin.

She did, but this time with her legs spread so he could slide fingers inside her, feel her pussy hold him tight as her clit throbbed and pulsed under his thumb, the warm metal of her jewelry pressing against his fingertip. The moon lit one side of her face and body, giving her skin a strange, silvery glow. He rubbed fast, while reaching high inside her, knowing this for the gold medal move. Once he'd found her G-spot—a little higher and more forward than on most women—he'd memorized its location and could go there in a few seconds. But she required both exterior and interior contact so he gave it, gripping her ass with his other hand, and pressing soft kisses to the pebbled skin of her lower belly.

"Ach! Ross," she cried out in a whisper-scream. His cock jerked at the sound of his name coming from her lips and he sensed pre-cum coating his head, making him grunt into her stomach. "*Mein schatz*," she sighed as her pussy grabbed his fingers tight and a gush of liquid filled his hand.

He held on to her, riding out the orgasm, then pulled his hand free and licked his palm as she gasped and gripped the deck railing behind her. The wind picked up, blowing her hair around his face as he got slowly to his feet. She pulled his shirt up and over his head, then unzipped his shorts and dropped them to his feet. Without a word, she pushed him back so he dropped to the lounge chair, then fell to her knees in front of him, taking his cock in her mouth so fast he groaned and gripped the chair arms in an effort not blow in two seconds.

Her finger went straight for the soft space beneath his balls. He shifted forward in the chair, giving her more access. Head thrown back, he gave into it, into her, as his hips thrust up and she took him as far down his throat as she could manage. When he sensed the tightness there, her roaming finger found a target and slipped into his ass. She stroked his prostate gland, which made his vision blur and forced a loud cry from his lips. He came so hard the chair jerked backward on the deck. She sucked and swallowed everything, raising up to look at him after what felt like an hour-long orgasm, her smile sweet, her lips slick with his cum.

"Nasty," he said, his voice weak. "I like it."

She winked, headed inside to wash her hands then returned to his lap, curling into him the way he preferred. He wrapped his arms around her, lifting her hair to kiss the back of her neck – that spot he'd found within a week that made her shivery. As he grazed his teeth over that spot, she sighed. "I'm sorry," she said into his chest. "You were right."

"What's that?" he asked, pushing her away and giving her a fake smirk. "Might I record this, for our future children to hear someday?"

She smiled and stroked his bearded cheek. "I cannot have children, my love. I told you that." He sensed her tense up again, as if ready to bolt.

"I don't care, Elisa. I don't want a brood mare. I want you."

She tucked up under his chin, fitting into his arms in a way that seemed beyond perfect. But when he touched her face, his fingers came away wet. "I want to carry your child, Ross. But He... He... He made sure I'd never be able to do that. He had my tubes tied, after the baby was born, using his money and influence to convince the doctor that we both wanted it."

"But how…?" He tilted her chin up, his heart breaking all over again for this woman, his woman, and her anguish. "Never mind. It doesn't matter. None of it matters. We have each other. That's all I want."

She heaved a sigh and worried the ball in her lower lip. "I was so out of it. So heart-broken over the baby. And woozy from pain. I tore, you see. The baby…hurt me coming out. They had to use a lot of stitches and at some point while I was high on pain meds, they…took away my ability to be a mother. I'm…sorry."

"You have nothing to be sorry for. Nothing at all. Besides…having kids cramps your style. I know. I've seen it first-hand."

He got up, bringing her with him. She wrapped her legs around his waist and her arms around his neck. The tip of his cock rested against her warm pussy until she moved, taking him inside her and making them both exhale at the connection. "I don't know how you do this to me, my love, but I like it." He kissed her, shoving his tongue into her mouth, wanting her to feel how he felt, to know what he knew about the certainty of them together and trying to relay that with his body.

He sat, then lay back, letting her work him over, happier than he'd ever been in his whole, rather dull, life. She bit his nipples, kissed his neck, his lips, nipping his earlobe as her lower body gripped him, bringing him back from the edge of shut down. Marveling once more at how badly he wanted to be inside her, to come deep in her body, he hooked his leg around hers and rolled them, keeping their connection.

Speechless with lust, he bent one of her legs over his shoulder and moved faster, in and out, feeling the improbable second orgasm overtake his brain.

"Ross, my love," she said, pulling her other leg up and

235

making a yoga pretzel out of herself so he could go as deep as he'd ever gone inside her. She gasped in pain, so he stopped, mid-stroke.

"Look at me," he demanded. She opened her eyes, which were bright with unshed tears. "I will not make you cry, Elisa. Please don't cry."

She sighed and angled herself so he felt his cock bump up against something inside her. He backed off, alarmed but more turned on that ever. "I'm not crying over you, you fool. I'm crying because you're making me so happy."

He dropped his head and started rolling his hips again, the incredible sensation of her pussy stretching and tightening around him making his vision dim and his brain mushy. But his cock was rock hard as he pressed in, then pulled out, just for the pure pleasure of feeling that again and again. "I am…going to come, Elisa…I…oh…God!" He roared into the room and she put her hand over his mouth as he filled her, wanting this connection to mean more, to be the one she wanted it to be.

Then his entire body went limp. He felt as if he'd run back-to-back marathons as he pulled out of her and dropped onto his back. "Water," he croaked. She scrambled up and got a bottle from the conveniently located tiny fridge under the television stand. He sat and drank it all in long, greedy gulps, some of it escaping out the sides of his mouth and dropping onto his bare chest.

"God in heaven," he groaned, groping for her. "That was…a little scary."

"It was," she agreed, curling into his side. "And a whole lot incredible." She walked her fingertips over his chest. "I am sorry. About babies."

He sighed and kissed her hair, adoring the bare press of her skin against his and wishing this weekend would never end. He ran his hand along the firm thigh she had hiked up to his waist. "I just want us to enjoy each other. No more talk of babies. After your hearing, let's go away for a while, just us, somewhere quiet and private."

"Actually," she said, tweaking his nipple and making him flinch. "I'd like to go home for a while. To Germany."

"Oh?" He was surprised by this but sleep was rumbling toward him and his body and brain were headed into shutdown mode.

"Yes. I want you to meet my family, my brothers and their wives. And I want to go to Oktoberfest with you."

He chuckled. "Spoken like a true brewer," he said. "We'll do that, my love. Anything you want. Now, I must sleep or I may not be worth a tinker's damn for the rest of this weekend."

"I love you," she whispered, grazing his lips with hers before tucking her head into the hollow of his shoulder, right where she belonged.

* * * *

The rest of the weekend was pleasant, full of amazing meals, games, drinks and fun on the lake. He'd even managed to get Elisa out on a boat and into the water, which had indeed resulted in a harsh sunburn on her shoulders and face, despite the slathering of the strongest possible sunscreen.

If she wasn't in the kitchen, she was holding Rose, making her giggle with funny faces or even crawling around with her on the floor, playing with the metric ton of toys Evelyn and Austin had brought. After a Sunday morning spent playing on a blanket out on the grass in the weak sunshine, she handed the kid to Ross, saying that tonight's dinner was labor intensive and he was in charge of the *kinder* for rest of the day.

Ross held Rose close, wincing when she reached over to grab his nose with her usual shriek of "Da!"

"Why me? Where are—?"

"*Armleuchter*! Remember when you told me that children will mess up your sex life?"

He nodded, trying to keep the wiggling child from

climbing up onto his shoulders.

"Well, consider this a gift to your good friends." She nodded toward a couple walking downstairs, their arms around each other, a satisfied look on their faces.

"Ah, yes, of course." He turned to Austin and Evelyn. "Good morning, lovebirds. Just so you know, I have been given charge of the *kinder* and she and I will be very busy all day, doing…stuff…together. Consider yourself free of her for a while with my compliments."

"Ross," Evelyn said, yawning and stretching in a way that at one time would have made him miserable since he'd given her up for the greater good that was his friend, Austin. But he looked over at Elisa. She winked at him, waved, then ducked into the kitchen. "You don't have to do that," Evelyn continued, disentangling from Austin's arms.

"Oh, yes he does," Austin insisted, pulling her back and kissing her in such a way that made everyone in the room whistle with admiration. "Now, I say we go back upstairs. We have…some things to discuss." He grabbed her hand and pulled her toward the stairs. "Thanks, Ross."

"My pleasure, my friend," Ross said. He warmed a bottle from the fridge and plunked himself into the leather recliner and found a soccer game on the telly. Elisa brought him a bacon, lettuce and tomato sandwich on her homemade rye bread while the baby snoozed on his chest. He grabbed her hand and kissed it. "You make me a better person," he said.

She sat on the chair arm, kissed the sleeping baby's slightly sweaty head, then his lips. After drawing away she said, "I'm only doing for you what you do for me."

* * * *

They waved goodbye to the group at noon Monday and spent the rest of the day napping in the lounge chairs on the deck. Ross constructed a meal out of the pounds of leftovers in the tidy fridge, and brought it out, with a bottle of expensive Italian wine.

"Holding out on everyone else?" she asked, holding the wine glass to her nose and taking a long sniff. "Nice."

"Yeah, I was," he admitted, sipping, then cutting a bite of warmed prime rib and holding it to her lips. "Let me feed you."

She smiled, and let him do exactly that. They chatted about their trip to Germany, how they might split the time between Berlin and Munich, all the way through the dessert, a bit of leftover tiramisu that had sent their friends into paroxysms of joy but had been too rich to finish the night before.

"I think we should consider opening a restaurant," he said, as they enjoyed the last of the rich red wine, stretched out on the lounge chairs, their fingers entwined between the seats, watching the sun approach the horizon.

"I think that's the dumbest thing I've ever heard coming out of your mouth. And that's saying something."

"I'm serious, Elisa."

"I know you are. So am I. There is no way in hell I would ever do that."

Ross turned on his side to face her. She put her wine down and rolled so they were almost nose-to-nose. "You're certifiable," she said, running her fingers down his beard. "And you need to trim this up."

"We'd specialize in home-style meals — but home-style from around the world. I'll bet you make a mean schnitzel, no? And ratatouille? And meatloaf?"

"Please tell me you don't want to open a brewery at the same time?"

"No, no brewery. There are enough of those. I think Austin wants me to stick around, and since I'm sticking around anyway..." He tucked a ropy lock of her hair behind her ear. "We'd serve craft beers, of course, but have a full bar."

Elisa groaned and rolled onto her back. "You are a horrible, horrible man. Now I think I want that and it's complete insanity. There are too many restaurants, too."

"Yeah, but think about it. Trent can find us a good location.

You can run the kitchen. Melody might help us find kitchen staff. I think that Caroline chick works in marketing. Maybe she'd help —"

"Hoffman, stop." She snapped her fingers in front of his face, cutting him off mid-sentence. "You're delusional. And I don't want to discuss it anymore."

He grinned and pulled her up so she was standing on the chair, which put her on eye level with him. "A walk then, a sunset walk, on the beach?" He kissed her, feeling so at home here with her, he could weep, were he a weeper.

They headed down the long flight of steps to the grass then out onto the sand. Fingers locked, hands swinging, he regaled her with stories of his rich but lonely childhood, working his way right up to the bit about the woman who took his virginity and taught him most of the skills he now used to pleasure her.

"Wait," she said, stopping short and pulling him back. The sun was kissing the horizon now, and a thin scrim of pink, orange and lavender had formed, turning the beautiful view into something truly spectacular. "You said something about your mother's friend, a fellow teacher? You've mentioned her before…"

She let go of his hand and crossed her arms, glaring at him. He grinned and scooped her up, tossing her over his shoulder before running down the beach. The sand was warm on his bare feet, the breeze cooling and drying the sweat on his shoulders and face. Elisa was screeching and pounding on his back as he ran, so he stopped and let her tumble down onto the sand on her backside.

She glared up at him. "Nice deflection, *Herr* Stud Muffin."

He puffed up his chest and beat it with his fists. "I am your stud muffin and yours alone, *Fraulien* Bossy Pants."

She held out her hand. He took it, but at the last minute recalled her deceptive strength and found himself yanked forward until he landed on top of her, with a mouthful of sand. "If you wanted my body all you had to do was ask." He rubbed his beard along her cheek, making her squeal and pummel his shoulders.

"Get off me you great, mouth-breathing oaf."

He rose up, propping his hand on either side of her face. The heat of her skin through the thin batik fabric of the dress made his dick spring to life. She grinned. "You are an animal," she said before wrapping her arms around his neck and kissing him, sandy lips and all.

She dropped back onto the sand, her arms up over her head. The sun was more than halfway gone now, and he could hear laughter and kids' voices up and down the sand as families went inside for the evening. The setting sun lit up the right side of her face, making it glow crimson and gold. "I was born to love you, Elisa Henriette," he said, staring down at her.

She smiled and shifted her hips, drawing her knees up on either side of him. "You were, indeed, *Herr* Hoffman." She cupped his chin and slid a hand up under his T-shirt, making him shiver. "I never thought I'd find anyone like you. I honestly believed…him…when he told me I wasn't worth more than the effort it took to wipe shit off his shoes."

Ross frowned, and his jaw tightened at her words. "Don't ruin this," he warned.

She put a finger to his lips. "No, listen. I have to say it. You have to hear it. I would not be where I am now were it not for my time spent being broken by one man. And I love it that you are willing to bring me back, willing to put up with me and turn me back into the woman I was meant to be." A tear slipped down her cheek. Ross leaned down and licked it away.

"I am that man, Elisa. If you'll let me be. *Dein ist mein ganzes Herz.*"

"I will," she whispered. He rolled off her and sat, arms propped on his knees, staring at the gorgeous riot of color along the horizon. She got up and draped herself over his shoulders, kissing his neck and running her hands along his torso.

He sighed. "I never thought of myself as a nurturer. I

was spoiled as a kid. And treated women terribly as a young man." He pulled her hands to his lips and kissed her knuckles. "I was taught well." She stiffened. "Don't complain. You're the beneficiary of much of what I was taught by her — a long time ago. But I only felt any sort of emotion for one woman in my entire life — a woman I was not meant to have. Until I opened the door of the Fitzgerald Brewery and saw you, standing there in the steam, your wild hair in a riot, sweat-soaked, and screaming at the staff." He chuckled. "I was, as the English say, gobsmacked by you. And I haven't looked back."

He pulled the ring from his shorts pocket — the ring he'd had specially made for her the week before and had hidden the entire weekend — took her left hand, and slid it onto her finger, kissing her palm before letting her see it. She held it up, still laying across his shoulders.

"It's beautiful," she said. It was a round diamond, set in a thick band of platinum, with smaller, equally brilliant stones embedded into the precious metal on either side. "It's beautiful, Ross."

"I know," he said, pulling her arm so she was pressed against his back.

"How could you possibly afford it?"

"I've spent the better part of twenty years working without ever settling down or buying anything more expensive than decent wine or clothing. And I'm German. We are, as you well know, savers by nature. I may not be as rich as Croesus like Trent or a trust-fund kid like Austin, but I have enough. Enough to provide you with anything you might want or could ever need from me."

"I will work," she protested, pulling away. He grabbed her arm and dragged her around to his lip so he could kiss her. Ross thought he could kiss this woman morning, noon and night and never tire of it.

"I know that," he said, ending the kiss and touching his nose to hers. "But if we open this restaurant..."

She rolled her eyes. "Shut up and kiss me some more."

He did. And later, they made slow, silent love until long past midnight and they lay, spent, and happy in each other's arms.

Chapter Thirty-Two

Three weeks later

Elle sat on the hard, wooden bench in the courtroom, turning her engagement ring around and around. She'd not been able to eat much for the past week thanks to her anxiety about this hearing, so the ring was loose, as were most of her clothes. Ross sat next to her, dressed up for the occasion and looking incredible in a dark suit, white shirt and red tie. The place was filled with her friends from Fitzgerald Brewing, all there for moral support on this day when it would be decided if she had to stand trial for manslaughter.

After an hour, it seemed as though things would go her way. Austin's lawyer had spent the last week with her, going over her life in detail — as much as she would give — to establish that she was neither insane nor murderous. He'd called Evelyn to the stand, which was awful and made both Austin's and Ross' faces bright red when she told the story of how the asshole Tim attacked her in her office in front of the baby and was about to rape her when Elle had blown his useless brains out.

He'd interviewed Melody about that day as well, so she could testify regarding Tim's general demeanor and his past, inappropriate activities in the pub, hitting on women then getting angry when they rejected him. Bryan, fully recovered and content in his role as cellar man, told his story — how he'd tried to ask her out and had taken her rejection in stride but had noticed Tim being rude to her face, and talking about her behind her back.

By the end of the long day of testimony, a clear picture of

Tim as a sexist, predatory, angry man had been established, as well as Elle's as the innocent victim who only agreed to file the harassment report at Evelyn's insistence.

Elle spoke last. Melody and Evelyn had helped her buy a decent, navy blue suit for the event, with mid-high heels and a pair of pearl earrings so she felt physically ready for it. But inside she was a mess. Sweaty under the suit, breathless with terror, horrified that she'd even done it.

But the lawyer—Jack Galyan was his name—had prepared her well and she answered his questions calmly, in a clear voice. Yes, she was licensed to carry the gun. Her credentials were presented. No, she had never shot anyone or anything ever before. Her non-existent criminal record was shown. Yes, she suspected something when she'd pulled it out of her locker but she'd been convinced Tim would come for her on her way out of the brewery, which is why she'd been keeping the weapon at work.

No, she had no idea he'd go for Evelyn, but something had made her go back up the metal steps to the office overlooking the brewery that night. Partly intuition, but mostly the loud shout that only she had heard. And she'd seen them, Evelyn with her blouse ripped off, her skirt hiked up to her waist and that horrible man, fumbling with himself, while the child screamed from her the carrier on the table right next to her mother. She'd reacted on instinct. And now, he was dead and both Evelyn and the baby were safe.

"Thank you, Miss Nagel," Jack Galyan said, his dark brown eyes full of sympathy. "That's all, Your Honor," he said to the judge.

"You may step down, Miss Nagel," the judge said to her. She'd made her way across the expanse of marble floor and was almost back to Ross' side when the door at the back of the courtroom opened with a loud bang.

"May it please the court," a voice boomed into the high-ceilinged room. "I call a witness on behalf of the victim, Mr. Timothy Harris."

The judge frowned and banged his gavel to calm the crowd. Elle stood stock still, confused by the interruption. The strange man who'd walked in to declare the witness looked at her, then over his shoulder. That's when she saw him.

The Monster.

He was here, in the courtroom, standing tall and slim and smug, dressed in a coal-black suit, shiny black shoes and open collar shirt. His long nose, thin lips and slicked-back hair were all the same. His gaze darted around the room, seeking her, she knew.

Nolan Blanchard.

Her tormenter.

Memories flooded her brain, making her sway on her feet. Bile burned her throat. The myriad injuries he'd done to her body all flamed hot, most especially on her ass, where his initials were etched into her flesh. She put a hand to her throat. When their eyes met, his nostrils flared as if he smelled something rancid. She dropped her gaze to the floor and nearly fell to her knees in the sort of sick, Pavlovian way he'd trained into her. But Ross was there, holding her up and helping her back to her seat.

The crowd around and behind her, her friends, all muttered as one, "Is that him? Is that him? Is that Him?"

She pressed her face into Ross' shoulder, hearing the rumbling in his chest, indicating he was speaking. But she could no longer make out words. She kept her face averted the entire time the attorney argued with the judge and demanded that his witness be heard. It had direct bearing on the proceedings, he insisted.

Finally, the judge allowed it. She felt Ross stiffen beside her. Saw his right hand curl into a tight fist. She put her palm on it, but kept her gaze away from the front as Nolan Blanchard was called as witness for Timothy Harris, the deceased.

After being sworn in, he began to speak. His voice shot a spike of ice straight into her soul. It was thin, presumptive, bossy in the way only the French can be. He was leaning heavily on his accent, she could tell.

By the end of his testimony, the judge called both lawyers to the bench, then excused the witness. Nolan stood, shot his cuffs, sneered at the room in general, and made his slow way out of the witness box and across the floor. When he reached the bench where she sat with Ross on one side and Evelyn on the other, he stopped.

"I am disappointed in you, Elisa," he said in a low tone. "But I suppose you *think* you've landed well." He sniffed, indicating his general opinion of Ross. She gripped Ross' hands to keep him from reacting but he was pulling against her and she knew she wouldn't be able to hold him back for long.

"Move along," a voice said from the bench behind her. Brock, she thought. "If you know what's good for you."

Nolan buttoned his jacket and glared disparagingly at the gathered group. "We will meet again soon," he whispered to her. The sound of his voice curled up in her head, embedding in her brain, and bringing forth a scream from her throat before she could stop it.

"Go," she yelled, standing up and clambering over Ross' knees to get at him. "Get the fuck away from me, you god damned monster!"

Nolan stepped back, with a fake expression of fear on his face. He glanced at the judge, shrugged in a 'I told you she was a crazy bitch' way, then smiled at her. That tore it. Everything she'd been holding back for a decade — the memories, the humiliation, the filth, the pain and the final betrayal all rushed up from the soles of her feet, into her chest and burst across her brain like fireworks.

"You can't have me, Nolan," she said, moving close to him and shaking Ross' hand off her arm. She stood, glaring up at him, directly into the eyes she'd been trained defer to, to look away from out of 'respect' for his dominance over her. "You are not a real man. You only pretended to be. But I got away from you, in more ways than one. I'm free of you. And that's making you crazy, isn't it, you fucking asshole. I have a real man with me now." Her voice kept rising, clanging around in the cavernous space.

"Miss Nagel," the judge warned. "One more outburst and I'm holding you in contempt of court."

"I told you she was unstable, Your Honor," Nolan said in an apologetic tone.

"You can stop talking too, Mr. Blanchard." The judge glared at him. She hoped lawyer Jack had filled the good judge in on how, exactly, Mr. Blanchard knew her.

Nolan turned to her, his eyes snapping with fury. But for the first time since she'd met him and he'd seduced her so he could later hold her hostage in mind and body for his own sick pleasures, she didn't drop her gaze. "You have lost, Nolan," she said, keeping her voice light and conversational. "Now that you're here, I'm going to blow your little sick life right out of the water, do you understand me?"

In a flash, he grabbed her wrist, bruising her almost instantly and making her yelp in pain. "You always were a useless bitch," he hissed. She sensed the crowd around her rising, reaching for them.

In a slight trance, she raised her other hand and slapped him, hard, twice, then again for good measure. Before she could do anything else, Ross lunged past her, had Nolan pinned to the floor, and was pounding his face into a bloody pulp.

"Ross," she screeched, trying to pull him off. But arms were around her, pulling her back from the ugly scene.

The judge hammered on his desk so hard his gavel broke. Brock and Austin dragged Ross off the now inert form of Nolan Blanchard. The other lawyer was screaming about more lawsuits. The bailiff had her by her arms and wrestled her out of a door next to the judge's bench as she screamed Ross' name over and over again.

Chapter Thirty-Three

Ross sat in the holding cell, seething with rage, sick with worry but mostly satisfied that he'd had the singular pleasure of beating that bastard's face in. He stood when the officer appeared and called his name. Austin stood beside him, pinched-faced and pissed-off.

"Let's go, Hoffman. I posted bail."

He got up slowly, bruised and bloodied hands dangling at his sides and shuffled out of the piss-stinking jail. They walked out once Ross had collected his suit jacket, watch, phone and wallet. Austin stayed silent the whole drive to the brewery.

"Thanks," Ross said after they parked. He was at a loss and wondering where in the hell Elisa might be right now. She'd been so brave, slapping the guy, but Ross had not been about to let the opportunity pass without exacting some revenge on her behalf. No fucking way. He looked down at his raw knuckles. "Where is she?"

"They held her in contempt, like the judge said he would." Austin was gripping the steering wheel so tight Ross could see the bones of his fingers under the skin. "It's a God damned bigger mess and now the press is up my ass like a colonoscopy." He sighed and let his hands fall to his lap. "Let's just say that Elisa's outburst cost her, big time. They're holding her without bail for reasons no one can explain to me. The celebrity chef is recovering after the brutal attack by the brewer with the famous temper or some shit. Jesus, please us."

Ross sighed and put a hand on his friend's shoulder. Austin shook him off. "We have to meet with the lawyer in an hour. That asshole's attorney is threatening to sue you for assault, me for harboring you and her for all this time. He's out for blood and my company is gonna be the one that bleeds. I'm not in the mood for your shit." He climbed out of the car and stomped to the back door of the brewery without a backward glance.

Ross' heart pounded as he watched his friend wrench open the back door.

He'd done this. Or at least he was directly complicit and Austin, who'd never done a damn thing wrong, *was* going to pay the price. He got out and went to the rental that he'd left at the brewery, as they'd all ridden in Austin's giant SUV to the courtroom, in decent spirits, thinking all would be over and done with soon.

As he drove to his hotel, he self-justified his motivation for beating the guy bloody in the courtroom. His first call was to Jack Galyan's office, asking if Elisa could have a visitor. After being told that process, he got a quick shower, changed into jeans and a polo-style shirt, then drove to the county lock-up. But when he told the giant lady guard in charge he was there to see Elisa Nagel, he was told she didn't want any visitors.

Ross frowned. "Tell her it's her fiancé."

The woman rolled her eyes, wandered back to some mysterious place in the prison, then returned, her lips set in a firm line. "She don't want visitors. She knows who you are and says she especially don't want to see your…let's see how did she put it…your ugly, stupid face ever again."

Ross reeled backward until his legs made contact with a chair. He dropped into it, stunned into immobility for a few seconds. Finally, he got up and approached the wall of blue uniform. The woman lifted her face and scowled at him. "You again, blondie?"

"Listen, I know she's upset. But tell her I need to ask her something important. Something that will help her out…of this…mess."

The woman sighed, got up, lumbered through the door

that snicked shut behind her. For a hot second, Ross contemplated crashing through it, his need to lay eyes on Elisa and make sure she was all right was so strong.

But as before, the woman came, back, her face set in stone to inform him that if he didn't leave in the next five minutes, she'd have him removed.

Fury tickled his throat as he clamped down on the urge to bellow her name, to demand to see her, no matter what. She had some nerve, pushing him away now. He flopped down onto the front steps in the bright, hot sun trying to get himself back under control. Finally, he raked his fingers through his hair one last time, and headed for his car.

If she wouldn't see him, or talk to him anymore after he'd repeatedly told her how he felt, after they'd planned a trip home to meet her family, talked about names for their fantasy restaurant — then fuck her. A man could only do so much. This rejection, when he knew damn good and well she needed him too, was the final straw.

"Fuck her," he growled as he screeched out onto the road in front of the women's prison. He threw the SUV in park then ran up the steps to his stupid, ever-temporary living space. Ignoring the zillions of texts and missed calls from Austin, Evelyn and Trent, he scrolled through his contacts until he found the one he wanted.

He dropped onto the cheap hotel couch, opened a beer, drank half of it without tasting it, then hit Call.

"Hello? Ross? Is that you?" Holly's smooth, southern-inflected accent made him smile around the mouth of the bottle.

"Yeah, babe. It's me. You busy? I need someone to talk to." He closed his eyes, hating himself, but knowing this was the right move to make. He required action, and he was going to by God take some.

Chapter Thirty-Four

Five weeks later

Elle sat staring down at her hands as her second hearing got underway. Jack the lawyer was the only visitor she'd allowed herself for the past month, mostly as self-punishment. She knew she'd screwed everything up. If only she had kept her mouth shut, let Nolan spout his self-aggrandizing nonsense without reacting, she'd not be here, hungry, miserable, afraid to talk to anyone, much less make friends within the shocking array of humanity she'd encountered as a guest of the Kent County prison system.

She missed Ross so keenly it was a physical ache in her chest. It closed her throat when she tried to eat the random slop that passed for meals. It forced her eyes open through the long nights while women all around her snored, farted, sobbed, or had sex with each other for lack of anything better to do. It made her chew her fingernails until they were ragged and bloody. They'd taken all of her belongings, including her engagement ring, promising to keep it safe. But she figured she'd seen the last of it anyway, considering.

But still she refused to see him, or Austin, or Evelyn, or Melody. She only met with Jack, to try to salvage her future.

After stripping her of everything, including every item of jewelry she had on or in her body, they'd put her to work cleaning the infirmary, given her early training as a nursing assistant. She did her mopping and disinfecting, the emptying of bedpans and other disgusting jobs without comment. The horrific condition of the place flabbergasted her. She'd always held the common European misconception that American prisons must be pretty cushy, since people seemed to keep going back to them over and over again. But this place was god awful, understaffed, dirty and dangerous.

After a couple of weeks, she'd requested, politely, to change to kitchen duty and had spent her last few days helping make heads or tails of the god-awful, many times spoiled slop that passed for food.

But she had her nice suit on today, even though it hung off her frame as if she was playing dress up with her mama's clothes. The various holes in her skin remained that way, and they hurt more than anything. She sat at the front table this time, next to lawyer Jack, who, to his credit, never once blamed her for anything. Which was fine because she blamed herself plenty. And her punishment was even worse — cutting herself off from her beloved, her hero, her man, her Viking — Ross Hoffman.

She could hear the room filling behind her but she couldn't bring herself to turn around. She was more afraid she'd not see familiar faces — one in particular — than of seeing them. The commotion at the back of the room, accompanied by clicking cameras and yammering reporters, indicated that the famous, wounded, Nolan Blanchard had arrived. She sighed and tightened her fingers together.

If her life had been hell before, this had to be the seventh level of it. The final level, she hoped. She was so tired. She wished she could sleep — preferably curled up within the protective circle of Ross' arm. She blinked slowly, feeling drugged, and knowing she was killing herself slowly not eating, but unable to do anything about it.

The judge took a seat and gaveled the proceeding to order. Timothy Harris' so-called lawyer called his witness. Nolan took the stand, sneered at her for a half second, then told his false story again — the one where she had a wild, uncontrollable temper. That, during their two years together in Chicago, he feared for his very life at the end, as she was prone to threatening him with sharp knives and, the gun she'd supposedly obtained while living with him, the one she'd used to kill the poor, hapless Tim.

He was still bruised-looking and had his arm in sling, which was window-dressing. Jack the lawyer told her that Ross had broken Nolan's nose and his jaw but not his arm, for heaven's sake. She kept her gaze pinned to him, studying him, wondering how in the world she could have ever found him sexy or alluring or wonderful as she had those months spent in Paris as he taught her how to be his submissive. Or more precisely, as he programmed her to be his victim.

She didn't realize she was trembling until Jack put a warm hand on her clenched fists that were out on the table, encouraging her to put them in her lap. The next witness was Tim's weeping mother, who called him a 'good boy' who would 'never hurt anyone' much less his boss lady.

The final witness against her was one of Tim's friends who claimed that Elle had 'waggled her wares' whatever the hell that meant, in front of the whole staff. "She hardly ever wore a T-shirt that wasn't cut halfway to her navel," he claimed, fiddling with his necktie. "She was flat out slutty. I mean, she wanted it but when Tim offered it she called him names and made him feel bad."

When asked why Tim had tried to attack Mrs. Fitzgerald and not Miss Nagel, the rat-faced man had shrugged. "Guess he knew they were friends and figured he'd hurt her," he said, pointing to Elle, "by going after that—uh, after Mrs. Fitzgerald."

The crowd behind her murmured. Elle sucked in a breath. Jack patted her hands.

When it was his turn, Jack called the same witnesses— Evelyn, who had to tell the terrible story again. Bryan, who looked exhausted. Melody, who was positively green around the gills.

She's pregnant, Elle thought, with a brief thrill of happiness for her friend, followed by a poisonous cloud of despair. A tear dropped onto her hands. Melody walked past her and

254

patted her shoulder, then headed for her seat. Elle had not turned but she sensed him right behind her, staring at the back of her head.

Ross was here for her, but she couldn't let him know she cared. She had to let him go. It was only fair to him and to Austin and Evelyn whose business was getting dragged through this horror show, thanks to her. She closed her eyes against a bout of dizziness. Her stomach rumbled. She glanced over at Jack.

"My turn," she mouthed. He smiled and shook his head. Confused, as this was the order of things they'd practiced, she watched as he rose and addressed the judge.

"If it please the court, we would like to call the following character witnesses for the defendant, Elisa Henriette Nagel." She blinked up at him, still dizzy, but now anxious. What character witnesses? Why hadn't he told her?

"I'll allow it," the judge said. "Make it snappy, though, Galyan."

"Yes, ma'am." Jack turned and motioned behind him. Elle heard a loud rustling of clothes as what sounded like a huge crowd of people stood and made their way down the center aisle to the front. They filed into the empty jury box. Elle stared at them, her confusion lifting at the sight of familiar faces. So many familiar faces from so long ago.

When she spotted her brothers, a sob broke through before she could stop it. They both smiled at her, then checked with her lawyer for instruction. She saw her first professor from the nursing school in Berlin. And the owner of the first, second and third breweries she'd worked at—one of them was huge now, way bigger than Fitzgerald, so big they bought ads at things like football Super Bowls or FIFA World Cups. They all meet her gaze with huge, supportive smiles. The owner of the gigantic brewery winked at her.

She pressed her hands to the table and stared at Jack, questioning him without words. He jerked his chin behind her. She turned, hearing every creak and pop in the ligaments in her neck, and came face to face with Ross.

He was, indeed, sitting right behind her, next to the most stunningly beautiful woman Elle had ever seen. He smiled and blew her a kiss. She frowned but didn't have time to react as Jack began calling her friends to the stand to speak on her behalf.

The long line of people who either knew her well, or had worked with her in the past, all testified to her stability, her trustworthiness, her work ethic, and her general willingness to help anyone who needed it. The next-to-last witness was the original manager of the restaurant where she and Nolan had worked, first side-by-side as chef and sous then after he'd demoted her to pastries, then to dishwasher as part of his campaign to demoralize and degrade her in public.

At one point during the man's slow, careful description of Nolan's treatment of her, Nolan leaped to his feet. "Lies! This man is a liar! I demand another hearing!"

"Sit down, Mr. Blanchard," the judge bellowed. Elle looked around, surprised to see that the judge was an older woman, her long gray hair pulled up into a bun and reading glasses halfway down her nose. She'd been so out of it, she hadn't noticed that detail.

Mr. Blanchard sat down. The manager finished his litany of observations, including the ones about bruised wrists, bloody noses and black eyes. Then he stepped down. Jack sat, as if he were finished. A warm, familiar hand landed on her shoulder. She squeezed her eyes shut and put her palm over it. "Elle," Jack whispered. "I need you to know that the final witness is going to be hard for you. But it's necessary. It will free you and likely put Blanchard behind bars where he belongs. Okay?"

Elle nodded, keeping her hand on Ross'.

Jack stood again. "Your honor, the final character witness is Doctor Bernard Joseph."

Elle blinked, not recalling the name and wondering how in the world this would help her. An old man rose from the group in the jury box and limped slowly to the witness stand. He was sworn in, sat, then stared straight at her. She sucked in a breath, hand to her throat. Ross tightened his grip on her shoulder as if to hold her in place.

Once, a million years ago, when she'd been in labor and terrified at the pain and how long it was taking, faint from nonstop contractions and ready to give up, she'd seen this man's kind face over hers. He'd urged her to sit up, to push one more time, told her that her baby was ready to meet her and she could not stop trying. His eyes were hazel-colored, his already old face benign and non-judgmental. "Hold my hand, dear," he'd insisted. "I will help you."

She had latched on to his hand and pushed for another thirty, brutal minutes before her son had made it into the world.

"Dr. Joseph," Jack said. "How do you know the defendant?" It was the only question he asked of all the people in the jury box.

The man cleared his throat, straightened his glasses and said, "Eleven years ago this month, I helped deliver her baby. She was so small, her hips barely bigger than a pre-adolescent's. We were worried and ready to do an emergency C-section. But I didn't want to subject her to that, so I helped her, encouraged her and she delivered the child, a boy, naturally. Then he," the doctor raised a shaking finger and pointed it at Nolan. "He burst in and yanked the child off her chest as we were delivering the placenta and took him away. She cried and begged and pleaded, but that man only let the nurses have enough time to clear the child's airway and cut the umbilicus before he walked out of the delivery room, leaving us with the weeping girl. That girl," he said, pointing to Elle who was weeping again, although silently this time.

Ross leaned forward, both hands on her shoulders now. "It's all right, my love. I'm sorry but when we found him I knew he had to speak for you."

"*That* man," the doctor said, his long, bony finger pointed at Nolan. "Also tried to coerce me into sterilizing the poor, helpless girl." He smiled at Elle again, both hands on the edge of the witness box. "But I am not easily intimidated. I would never tie any adult woman's tubes without her express permission. This is not the dark ages. I let *him* think otherwise, of course."

Elle stared at the doctor, her pulse racing, as a wall of dizziness hit her again, making her sway in her seat. The warmth of Ross' palms permeated the fabric on her shoulders. She reached up and touched one of them for strength.

"Counsel, please approach the bench." The lady judge's voice was tight. Elle met her gaze, which was soft and sympathetic. The lawyers spent fifteen minutes that felt more like fifteen hours, talking in low voices. Elle was immobile, weak from shock and hunger. Ross' hands never left her shoulders.

Jack resumed his seat, patted her hands, then kept his face neutral as he made some fake notes on his pad, pretending to be busy when he was nervous — something he'd revealed to her during one of their prep sessions. Elle sat ramrod straight while the judge made some notes, consulted with the bailiff, then banged her gavel to stop all the muttering in the courtroom.

"It is the opinion of the court, that there is insufficient evidence to justify a manslaughter trial for Elisa Henriette Nagel."

The courtroom behind her broke into cheers. Cameras flashed. She closed her eyes and slumped down in her chair.

"Quiet! One more outburst and I clear the courtroom."

The crowd settled.

"Watch this," Ross whispered, making her eyes fly open.

"It is the further decision of the court that Mr. Nolan Blanchard should be taken into custody immediately and held without bail on the following charges — assault, domestic abuse, and the kidnapping of an underage child."

The crowd behind her went nuts but Elle barely heard it. She stared up at the judge who met her gaze with a wink before banging the gavel and telling the bailiff to take Mr.

Blanchard into custody.

"Your honor! I object!" Timothy Harris's lawyer squealed.

"Last I checked, you are *not* Mr. Blanchard's attorney of record. Unless, of course you are, in which case I will disbar you so fast your head will spin." She smiled serenely down at the spluttering man.

Elle sat, unable to move as the judge called the court back to order after Nolan had been taken away. "Miss Nagel," she said, staring over her granny glasses at Elle. "You have lived through more hells than any one person ever should. I wish you the very best in your future endeavors. This court is adjourned."

She rose as the judge exited, then watched as the jury box emptied and a crowd formed around her. It blocked her from seeing Ross, who was the only person she wanted at that moment.

When her brothers materialized in front of her, she fell into their arms. "I really could kill you for not telling us," Hans said in German, before peeling her off him and staring at her until she looked away. "Elisa, seriously. You should have told us. We would have handled that frog for you."

She shook her head, unable to speak. Her other brother hugged her again and whispered, "Your new man is wonderful. He found us, all of us. And put this whole thing together. Go home, eat some good food and be with him." He held her tighter. "And yes, I could kill you too, but please know we are here for you. And we always will be."

"Okay, thank you. I love you. I'm sorry."

"We will see you in September, Ross tells us."

She nodded, swiping at her streaming eyes and turning to greet her old teachers, employers, and friends. Finally, she made it over to Doctor Joseph. He was leaning on the witness stand, observing all the hullabaloo with a bemused smile on his face.

"Thank you, Doctor," she said, taking his hand and shaking it. "I can't thank you enough."

"Don't thank me, child. Thank him." He pointed his cane

to her left. "But you're welcome, anyway. I always knew that horrible man would be punished, or at least, I hoped he would. I'm so happy for you." He touched her cheek.

She turned. As she was opening her mouth to thank him, to beg him to take her home and hold her tight all night long, he smiled and stepped to one side, revealing a well-dressed couple with a young boy standing in front of them, looking nervous and antsy.

"Miss Nagel? Elisa?" The woman held out her hand. "I'm Allison Franklin. This is my husband Rick. And our son, Eric."

Elle stepped back, hand to her neck.

"We are…we adopted your baby, but we had no idea he'd been taken from you against your will." The pretty woman's eyes filled with tears. "We would never have… taken him from you like that, I swear it."

The man put an arm around his wife's shoulders. "Eric," he said, his low voice gravelly and calm. "This is your biological mother, Elisa."

"Pleased to meet you," the boy said, holding out his hand. His blue-gray eyes were wary but his smile was wide and genuine. His thick blond hair was cut close, like a little man's and he wore a small version of his father's suit, complete with tie and shiny dress shoes.

Elle dropped to one knee and took the boy's hand in wonder. "I am pleased to meet you too, Eric. I'm so glad you have a nice home and parents who love you."

He glanced up at his father, who nodded, then at his mother, who smiled at him and pushed him forward a little. The boy pulled something out of his pocket and held it out to her.

"What is this?" She took the small box from him.

"Ross says to ask you if you still want to marry him." The boy glanced at Ross who gave him a thumbs-up.

Elle took the box, opened it and found the dazzling ring she'd been so proud to wear a month ago. Her hands shook as she pulled it out and slipped it on her finger. She stood and turned to Ross.

"You did this. All of this," she stated, sweeping her arm around, indicating the room full of people who'd helped her, loved her, supported her.

"Well, he had some help." The scarily gorgeous woman who'd been sitting next to him appeared at his side, gave him a hip bump, then held out her hand. "I'm Holly Grant."

"Hello," Elle said, her jealous female hackles rising.

"Holly is a reporter. We met in Colorado. When I figured I needed help finding people, I called her. She did just as much of this as I did." Ross and Holly stood side by side. Elle swallowed the lump of anxiety and smiled.

"Thank you, Holly. I owe a lot to you."

"Don't mention it. I loved this guy for a hot second, once upon a time," she said, patting Ross on the head like a little kid. "I figure he deserves to be happy. And you make him happy. And I'm all about putting an asshole away, trust me." Her grin widened at something over Elle's shoulder.

Jack the lawyer stood next to Rick Franklin and his son — her son — Eric. Jack's eyes were fixed on Holly in a way that was so unlike his usual, super professional self, it made Elle giggle. Ross gave Holly a little shove, sending her over to Jack, who blushed, and looked at Elle. "Shall we celebrate? I know a place where the beer is great and the burgers even better," Jack declared.

"Hey, watch it, mouthpiece," Ross warned, as he pulled Elle close and put his arm around her. She slumped against him, exhausted, dizzy, and more than a little starving.

"We closed the place down so we could celebrate," Melody said as she approached Elle and gave her a tight hug.

"Congrats," Elle whispered. Melody pulled away and blushed.

"We haven't told the teenager yet. I'm leaving that to her father. The wedding's in three weeks so you're just in time to help me plan the menus."

"Let's get the hell out of here, I mean…sorry," Ross said,

glancing at Allison and Rick and the beaming little boy Eric.

"Can I ride with you?" Eric latched on to Ross' hand.

"Um, sure. If it's okay with your mom and dad."

The boy glanced at them. They nodded. Allison wiped her eyes. "We'll meet you there," she said, hooking her arm through her husband's.

Elle's ears were hot and buzzy. The room wavered in front of her. Voices seemed to boom then retreat like a wonky recording. She clutched Ross' arm.

"I'm not feeling very well."

His blue eyes were sharp with worry. Her knees buckled, but he caught her, as she knew he would, hollering for help as the room blipped to a pinpoint, then went out.

Chapter Thirty-Five

Three years later

"Are you sure?"

"Yes.

"A hundred percent?"

"A hundred and fifty."

"Last chance to back out…"

Evelyn stepped between them. "Would you *please* go away? I have bridal prep to do here." She shooed Ross from the room, breaking up the banter, then turned to Elle, who perched on a chair in front of the mirror, trying not to hyperventilate.

"Here, drink this." Evelyn put half a glass of stout beer in front of her. Elle picked it up, sipped then put it back down.

"I can't. I'm too nervous."

"It's pretty simple, really."

"I know. It's just… I want him to be certain, you know? He jokes with me all the time about letting me back out or whatever but I'm afraid he's the one who wants that."

Evelyn perched on the arm of the chair in the guest bedroom of Trent and Melody's lake house. Somewhere beyond the door a baby let out a squawk, then quieted. She took Elle's ice-cold hands in hers. "Elle, if Ross Hoffman were more in love with you I don't think he could get up every morning and function. He'd be laid out by it, crippled, and unable to move much less run that amazing restaurant with you."

"I know, I know." Elle patted her hair. She'd cut the dreadlocks shorter, but they still hung to her shoulders. For today, she them pinned up on her head, fixed in place with a comb that served as the bridal veil. "It's why I made him wait this long, you know. To actually get married. I needed proof, I guess."

"Well, now you have it. He worships the ground you walk on, woman. If I were the jealous type and not already blissfully in love with my husband, I'd be green with envy." She smiled and brushed Elle's forehead with her lips. "Now, let's do this thing, shall we?" Evelyn winced and put her hand to her back.

"Baby kicking?" Elle asked.

"Nonstop," Evelyn said with a smile. "Come on, before you change your mind."

Elle nodded, and rose. She had on cream colored, pure silk sheath, unadorned and simple, ideal for her figure and skin tone. For her flowers, she'd chosen a spray of edelweiss. Taylor was her maid of honor. Evelyn and Melody her attendants.

She paused at the top of the long flight of steps from the deck down to the grass where nearly two hundred people were standing and looking up at her. She scanned the crowd and saw familiar, smiling faces, including her brothers' wives and their kids, even old Doctor Joseph, who was waving at her. She smiled and waved back.

Her attendants took their places then Eric marched down the aisle in a pair of khakis and a crisp white shirt, open at the neck, with a red rosebud pinned to it, matching the men. He stood in front of Ross, their rings on a satin pillow held tight in his hands. Her brothers and Austin flanked Ross, who stood, his hands behind his back, his smile for her and her alone. He also wore khakis and a white shirt, but his boutonniere was a tiny clump of edelweiss, matching her bouquet.

The music, performed by a string quartet and harp, set up under a white tent near the temporary altar, changed. She took a breath, and started down the steps, gripping her bouquet in one hand to the strains of Pachelbel. When she reached the last step, something latched on to her legs. She reached down and picked up the girl, decked out in a fancy white dress that was already stained with something that looked like strawberry ice cream. "Mama, why cry?" The girl patted her cheeks, trying to wipe away the tears.

"Mama is happy," she whispered in German to the girl. "Liesl, why aren't you down there with Taylor, where you're supposed to be? Where is your flower basket?"

"I wanted to walk with you, to see Papa." The little girl's German was as flawless as her English. "Please, Mama. I don't like it down there without you."

"All right, my darling." She patted her back.

Taylor shrugged and mouthed, "Sorry."

Elisa smiled at her, then put Liesl on the ground and took her hand. The music was still playing, the song with the heart-beat like cadence that she had always loved.

"Walk with me, baby girl."

"Okay, Mama," the child said, beaming up at her with Ross' dark blue eyes, through a nearly uncontrollable mass of ash blonde curls. Elle brushed her hair out of her face, then straightened again and met Ross' eyes. His grin widened. If ever a man was more wrapped around a child's finger from the moment of her birth, she never knew one.

"Papa is waiting for us. He told me to tell you to hurry up!" Liesl whispered loud enough for the back rows to titter with amusement.

"Yes, my love, I know that. Just give Mama a moment to enjoy this."

"Oh. Okay." They waited. Ross frowned at her, then shrugged and pretended to walk away. Austin put a hand on his arm. She started walking toward him, never more conscious of the importance of this day, three years past her trial, two and a half years since the birth of their first child, two since opening the hottest new restaurant in the Midwest.

They'd chosen an old theater in the rapidly reviving Detroit to renovate. And now, thanks to Trent, Melody,

Caroline, and of course, her beloved, her hero, the man who drove her mad with frustration and equally mad with lust, they were, by any standards, a huge success. Elle had been adamant that she be allowed to hire women newly released from prison, and that program had also been so key to their success.

They lived within walking distance of their business, in a huge loft, overlooking the Detroit River, had two smelly dogs, who were currently splashing around in the lake behind the ceremony, and their Leisl—born a terrifying seven weeks too early but was now happy and healthy.

She stopped and let go of her daughter's hand. The girl ran to Taylor, as if conscious of the moment between her parents. Ross held out his arm. She took it and they faced the officiant. As the music faded, she leaned into him, going up on her tiptoes so she could whisper something in his ear.

"It's about time," he said in German. "We're never going to get to five Hoffmans if you don't pick up the pace a little." He put a hand on her slightly rounded stomach. "I knew it already. I could tell from your taste."

She smacked his arm. The crowd laughed. The officiant cleared his throat. "Shall we?"

"By all means, hurry up though, because I just found out my princess over there is getting a baby brother."

Liesl squealed and started jumping up and down. Elle sighed. "Sorry," she said to the man standing in front of them. "He's a real mouth-breathing idiot sometimes."

Ross turned her and kissed her hard, bending her back and making everyone clap and catcall. He let her go, smiling that smile that reminded her how lucky she was every single time she saw it.

"That was out of order," she insisted, straightening back up and handing her bouquet to Taylor who gave it to Leisl.

"I know. Just practicing."

"Get on with it, please." Elle focused her attention on the man in front of them, her natural nervousness about the extreme level of her current happiness fading, finally.

"Yeah, hurry up, Rev, before she changes her mind." His deep blue eyes shone as he gazed at her. *"Du bist die Liebe meines Lebens."*

Elisa nodded at him, her eyes swimming with tears. "I know," she said in English.

BREWING PASSION

TAPPED

A HOT HOOK-UP CHANGES EVERYTHING

LIZ CROWE

Tapped

Excerpt

Chapter One

The man must be out of his ever-loving mind.

Evelyn tried hard not to yell, or otherwise overreact, ever aware of her reputation as one of the sole females in this testosterone-soaked world of beer sales. But she simply could not stand for this sort of manipulation.

She rose to her feet. "I won't do it."

From his position behind the desk, her boss, Grant Taylor, president of Tri-City Distribution, tipped back in his chair and appraised her from head to toe. "He asked for you specifically. And I am certain I don't have to remind a professional such as yourself that Fitzgerald is our best craft beer brand—one of our *only* craft beer brands and the one I hope to use to build a better beer portfolio." He feigned a pitiful look.

"You look like a constipated crocodile when you do that."

Even as she accepted that her day had just grown that much worse, if it were cosmically possible, she slumped back into the chair on the other side of his desk.

"Evelyn, honey, it's not that bad. He's a good guy, really."

The foul liquid that passed for coffee at the Tri-City offices polluted her throat, giving her a few seconds to think. After only two years in the beer and wine sales business, she'd found her niche, and she even had an incentive trip to Barbados from the Corona guys nearly within her grasp. A day spent — more like wasted — trying to shove hipster beer down the throats of savvy buyers at her best stores would not get her any closer to that goal. Evelyn stared out of the window at the annoyingly perfect blue sky.

"Grant, you know I need a heads-up longer than an hour. Seriously, I have to shuffle the whole sales day. Jesus. I don't even know where —"

Grant held up a hand. "Spare me, please. I know you've already committed where Fitzgerald products are placed to that gorgeous, top-selling brain of yours. You sold more of their amber, IPA and Winter Spice bullshit than anybody. Don't kid a kidder." He grinned at her.

Stress bloomed in her chest and spread, bringing a familiar anxious mantra to the forefront of her mind.

This stupid job is the only thing between me and the homeless shelter.

Nothing would make her jeopardize what she'd built out of, essentially, nothing. A two-year associate's degree was all she'd been able to afford before she'd started working in a trendy downtown craft beer and cocktail bar. When a Tri-City sales rep had mentioned they were hiring and how much she could make in commission, she'd jumped at it.

Who knew she'd be a sales star?

"Fine. But if you think I'm gonna suck up to the Chosen Son of the Fitzgerald fortune, you are sadly mistaken. He can ride in my car and go on calls with me, but he'd better understand that I have a full day already set and I won't be giving him any special attention." She drained the last of the caffeine then set the mug down on Grant's desk with what she hoped sounded like a decisive bang. A sudden puff of air blew past her, ruffling the papers on Grant's desk.

Her boss's eyes widened. He pointed to something behind her and started to open his mouth.

"No," she cut him off. "Don't say another word. You know I'm right. Everybody knows he's just a trust-fund baby, opening a brewery with his daddy's money, then gallivanting around the world, getting his degree" – she hooked her fingers in the air around the word – "in brewing science. Jesus. Who needs a degree in that? He should just stick to improving his golf handicap and deflowering debutantes."

The petulant sound of her own voice annoyed her, but stories like Austin Fitzgerald's made her the maddest. She'd been raised by a single mother who'd waitressed by day and, she'd later learned, turned tricks at night while the young Evelyn had done homework and watched TV at her aunt's house. Her mother had died during Evelyn's second year of college, forcing her to quit after she'd figured out that the modest funeral would eat up every cent her mother had managed to save.

Grant cleared his throat and stood, buttoning his suit coat. She watched him, her brain still on fire with helpless frustration. Even if she'd agreed to haul Fitzgerald around, she had no plans to sell craft beer that day.

"I *need* to schmooze my wine buyers today, Grant. I can't be babysitting this guy." The back of her neck tingled when the ends of her hair fluttered in another sudden breeze. She frowned, observing her boss stick his hand out as if about to shake hers, a big smile pasted on his face.

"Well, if I weren't deathly allergic to both golf and debutantes, that might have been a career choice," came a low, raspy voice from right behind her.

Evelyn's entire body broke out in goosebumps.

"Grant, good to see you again," the voice continued.

She gritted her teeth and rose, giving Grant what she

hoped was a sufficiently withering look before turning around. Deep green eyes met hers. She was struck dumb by their depth and humorous sparkle. Dark jeans and a simple navy blue crew-neck — undoubtedly cashmere — sweater, brown box-toe loafers and a camel-colored dress jacket completed the look. He would have been at home on a GQ model as easily as he navigated a brewery floor. Close-cut dark-brown hair topped a clean-shaven, angular face.

A face that seemed pretty amused by her at that moment.

"And you must be Evelyn Benedict, saleswoman extraordinaire." His smile lit up the room, rendering Evelyn speechless. Grant nudged her arm until she stuck out her hand. Austin's warm, firm grip lingered long enough to make her uncomfortable.

"I see she's mesmerized by the size of my...trust fund already." He glanced over her shoulder at Grant then at her, pinning her in place again with that intense, still amused gaze. "Austin Fitzgerald, the albatross around your neck for the day." He gave her palm a friendly squeeze before letting go. "At your service."

Austin's gaze remained squarely on hers. She had on her best thrift store designer suit over a silk blouse open at the neck. Used to men eyeballing her from tip to toe, she found it refreshing for one not to automatically zero in on her cleavage.

"Never had such a lovely babysitter before, Grant. Thanks."

She swallowed when his eyes narrowed, then frowned as he gazed quickly up and down her front, lighting an unwanted and unexpected fire in her belly. Since when did she like it when some guy checked her out in such an obvious way?

He shrugged, sidestepping as if to get out of her way, the moment between them over. "Ready to go when you are. Rumor has it you have a big day ahead," he said, the expression on his handsome face suddenly neutral.

"Yes. I do." She strode past him, needing to regain her

composure. Loud, masculine laughter echoed in her ears all the way to the ladies' room. She splashed water on her face and stared in the mirror while her heart took up a loud drumbeat in her ears.

He is nothing but a spoiled-rotten trust-fund brat. No matter if he wears it like a stockbroker-slash-daytime drama hero. I do not need this distraction right now.

* * * *

Austin tried to focus on the guy behind the desk as they stood in the claustrophobic office. But his brain spun with a combination of fresh perfume and sudden, kneejerk lust for the woman who'd just stalked out of the room.

The day suddenly looked a lot better — less 'annoying ride-along crap' and more 'honest to God, get to know a beautiful woman.' He had countless headaches back at his brewery to deal with. Didn't need the time away any more than she seemed to want him around, but he grinned at the sight of her rich golden-blonde hair and deep blue eyes when she emerged from around the corner. Her expression was flat. He sensed her determination to resist whatever had occurred between them earlier.

Yeah. Not if I have anything to do with it.

"After you." He held out a hand and followed her down the narrow hall toward the parking lot door, adjusting himself behind the zipper of the stupid jeans he'd grabbed off the rack yesterday, desperate for something to wear that was suitable for selling and not brewing.

Good Lord, but she's hot.

Alarmed at his instant, adolescent response to her, he held the door open. She breezed past him. He had to shut his eyes against the quick breath of light, clean scent that invaded his nose again.

He helped put his sample bottles in the trunk of her one-step-from-the-graveyard car, then climbed into the immaculate interior, watching as Evelyn pulled out her itinerary for the day and studied it, a frown marring her perfect face.

"Okay, so I'm trashing this, I guess." She tossed the papers into her briefcase with a sigh. "Let's hit it, shall we? By the seat of our pants? Not the way I usually like to approach a work day."

"Yeah, good plan." Without even realizing he was doing it, he touched the hand she had resting on the gear shift between them. It was meant as a 'we're in this together' sort of gesture. Nothing more. She stared at it, then up at him. Utterly unprepared for the spark that leapt from her skin to his, he swallowed hard and jerked his arm back.

"Sorry," he muttered, grabbing his own thigh while she backed out of the parking space. Trying to quell the alarm rising in his chest, he risked a glance at her while they waited at a light. Her angry stare made him smile and hold up both hands. "Don't nail me for harassment, okay? My mommy and daddy won't bail me out anymore, or so they claim."

Her quick laughter was music to his ears.

"I'm sorry. I was just..." Her jaw clenched and he had to force away the urge to run his finger over it if only to get her to relax. Such a beautiful woman should not be so uptight. A surge of protectiveness nearly suffocated him.

Wow, Fitzgerald. Get a hold of yourself.

For a guy who'd never worried about where his next meal—or his next pair of designer sunglasses—would come from, Austin remained fairly introspective. He was well aware of his reputation, but hearing it tumble from Evelyn's mouth earlier had pissed him off, making him want to prove something to her.

The fact that he'd finally given in to his mother's harping on about marrying the Masterson girl had honestly slipped his mind since laying eyes on the gorgeous creature behind the wheel. He suppressed an inward groan at his dilemma. But couldn't resist encouraging the connection between them. He somehow sensed she'd love to play along. Some light flirting, nothing more or less. Harmless, really.

"It's okay. Really. Just an awkward moment we'll laugh about with our kids someday."

She snorted. "Sure we will. Just before you dump me and the brats for the trophy wife your mommy always wanted for you."

He narrowed his eyes, hoping she didn't realize how close to the truth she'd gotten about the mother-approved arrangements. When she grinned at him, two amazing dimples appeared on her cheeks, making him grateful he was sitting, since his knees had officially turned to jelly.

He looked away from her. Staring straight ahead, making a mental count to ten, he calmed his breathing, reminded himself he was there to work. Evelyn cleared her throat at that moment, effectively ending the internal break-up monologue he'd begun with his almost-fiancée.

Valerie, a girl who would have been a debutante—had such things existed in Grand Rapids, Michigan— as heir to the Masterson restaurant empire. She was an interior designer of some repute, pretty, bossy, and desperate for the Mrs. Fitzgerald designation. He liked her well enough and was so sick of the nagging about his continual reluctance to put a ring on her finger that he'd been ready to close the deal.

He put a hand over his eyes and muffled a groan at the mess he was about to make. All over this one, single, first impression.

But what *an impression.*

"All right, we'll swing north and hit the big chain stores first." She spoke as she drove, and Austin used every ounce of his willpower not to stare at the leg exposed by her short skirt, at the way her thigh muscle flexed when she worked the clutch, gunning the engine too high every time. "I'm close to getting the winter lager placement alongside your amber. Then I know the boys at Beer Baron and Hop Town would love to see your rock-star face, so we'll stop in there."

He glanced over to gauge her level of seriousness. The

tingling sensation in his scalp at her ironic smile alarmed him all over again. Every single memory and thought of the woman he'd been half-heartedly screwing for years had gone in the blink of Evelyn's amazing blue eyes. He swallowed hard and listened to her talk business.

"Also, I'd like to drop in on a couple of new boutique beer and wine stores that opened last month. Your esteemed presence gives me the excuse I need."

"Uh, okay. You're in charge. Just give me the high sign when I'm supposed to speak."

"Oh, don't worry, you'll figure it out. I'll have to do some inventory stuff at most of these places, so there will be time for you to bond with whatever management is on hand. A few of them are ladies — you'll make their day, I'm sure."

Unable to stop himself, he touched her again, this time letting himself own the heat that passed between them. "Don't be jealous, honey. I'd never cheat on you."

"Ha! I'll farm you out in a heartbeat, *sweetie.* You'll do whatever it takes to increase our bottom line. Hope you took your vitamins." She yanked her hand out from under his.

Smiling at her once more, he shifted in his seat to relieve the pressure building under his zipper.

He'd been damn close to asking Valerie to marry him, willing to leave her and her bitch of a mother to the wedding arrangements, ready to nod in agreement at what he hoped were the proper intervals. His mother had finally stopped haranguing him, left him to run his brewery in peace and he'd made a similar peace within himself, realizing the Faustian bargain he'd struck.

But now, as he sat in the passenger's seat of Evelyn's car staring out the windshield without seeing anything, a long-buried urge almost blinded him. And he knew Valerie was history.

More books from
Totally Bound Publishing

Book three in the Brewing Passion series

A chance meeting. An improbable connection. An exquisite attraction.

Surface Tension

The Face of Scandal

They say first love is forever...

Helena Maeve

Book three in the Surface Tension serial

*They say first love is forever. They don't say that
sometimes it's against your will.*

Book one in the Souls Entwined series

Savour the flavours, spicy and sweet…a taste of what's yet to come.

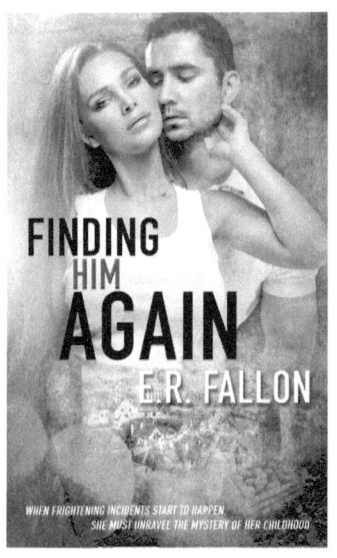

*She came home to find the one romance she always
regretted not having…*

About the Author

Liz Crowe

Amazon best-selling author, mom of three, Realtor, beer blogger, brewery marketing expert, and soccer fan, Liz Crowe is a Kentucky native and graduate of the University of Louisville currently living in Ann Arbor. She has decades of experience in sales and fund raising, plus an eight-year stint as a three-continent, ex-pat trailing spouse.

With stories set in the not-so-common worlds of breweries, on the soccer pitch, in successful real estate offices and at times in exotic locales like Istanbul, Turkey, her books are unique and told with a fresh voice. The Liz Crowe backlist has something for any reader seeking complex storylines with humor and complete casts of characters that will delight, frustrate and linger in the imagination long after the book is finished.

Don't ever ask her for anything "like a Budweiser" or risk bodily injury.

"Liz Crowe writes intense true-to-life stories that make you feel. Whether it's anxiety, love, fear, hate, bliss, or loss woven into her plot lines, you will feel it deep down to your very soul." ~ Audrey Carlan, #1 New York Times Bestselling Author

"Liz Crowe is one of those rare authors who knows how to take the emotions of her characters and make them real for her readers, binding you to the story." ~ International Best Selling Author Desiree Holt

Liz Crowe loves to hear from readers. You can find contact information, website details and an author profile page at https://www.totallybound.com/

www.ingramcontent.com/pod-product-compliance
Lightning Source LLC
Chambersburg PA
CBHW021515240626
47154CB00002B/642